T0274105

SAVAGE
BRED

Books by Victoria McCombs

The Storyteller's Series
The Storyteller's Daughter
Woods of Silver and Light
The Winter Charlatan
Heir of Roses

The Royal Rose Chronicles
Oathbound
Silver Bounty
Savage Bred

SAVAGE BRED

The Royal Rose Chronicles

Book Three

VICTORIA McCOMBS

To Remi
I hope the world offers you grand adventures,
and you always remember you have a safe harbor to return to.

1
EMME

There was no snow on the mountainside—only ice, stone, and the unmistakable feeling that I was making a grave mistake. I ran my numb fingers along the frozen wall and counted my steps. "One hundred and thirty-two. Turn."

I shifted. Behind me came the scrape of boots as Ontario and Clarice mimicked my steps, all of us attached by a rope at the waist to keep us bound together.

If one fell, the other two would save them. At least, that was the plan. None of us said it, but it was likely we'd all fall together. We each held a pickaxe to latch onto the stone walls for support if needed, but in this darkness, we'd be swinging blind. I swallowed, moving slowly through the pitch-black cave carved inside a mountain.

My counting reset to zero.

One. Two. Three.

Down. Down. Down.

It wasn't a cave that we were in. Not exactly, anyway. It started as a cave, then became a path—sometimes wide and other times no larger than the width of my shoulders and without a wall on either side. I held my breath during those times, the chilly air thick with our fear.

Twenty-one. Twenty-two. Twenty-three.

The rock face was wet beneath my leather boots, coated in a thin layer of frost that would catch the sunlight if there were any light to be found. Every so often, chips of the path crumbled beneath our feet and tumbled down into the cavern, knocking endlessly before finding the bottom, which was terrifyingly far away.

I kept my hand on the single jagged wall on my left as I counted my steps. There were many twists and turns here, tunnels that would lead to nowhere, and others that led to nowhere good. But one path, a path we'd paid heavily to get directions to, would lead to a cavern where rare minerals grew.

"Was this where a crew went missing?" Clarice asked. The jolt of someone else's voice almost wavered me. Her words bounced off the walls, sounding distant, though she couldn't be far if she was still attached to the rope.

"Some burned to fire, others drowned hundreds of feet above sea level," Ontario recited. "All still haunting these halls as ghosts today, luring others to their deaths to satisfy their hunger."

He needn't have said that in such a low, mystical tone. At that moment, wind snatched at my hair and I jumped.

"Three hundred sixty-two steps this way," I said to put myself back on track. "Keep your feet steady,"

"And your blade sharp," Clarice added. "I smell a fight coming."

I hoped not, but if it did, that's what Clarice was here for. She was our muscle. Ontario was the brains. And me?

I was the bait. First, we needed to reach those gems.

Forty-seven. Forty-eight. Forty-nine.

We continued in silence, holding our tongues and tightening our chests our nerves set on edge. It was strange, being in such a vast area and still struggling to find a deep breath. Without realizing it, I'd put my other hand on the hilt of my cutlass, and my teeth clenched together. I tried to relax, but the knots in my shoulders had no intention of leaving.

No one spoke again until I reached three hundred sixty-two in my mind.

"Turn," I said.

I stilled for a moment to clear my mind. The counting reset. Four hundred and two more steps, then we were to touch the wall and press where the rocks smoothed into a knob. I tried not to think of what would happen if we didn't find that knob, instead trusting that our information was sound. We'd survived so far.

One. Two. Three.

Three hundred steps in, and a distant explosion shook the ground. I crouched to my knees quickly, hand on the path to keep from falling. Behind me, Clarice cursed. The entire mountain trembled with vibrations that worked their way to our bones. A crack sounded, and my heart dropped.

Pebbles rained around us, clattering down the slope of the walls and into the dark abyss.

"What in the name of the dark seas was that?" Ontario asked.

"We have company," I whispered.

Then I sucked in my breath. It was as if the explosion had let loose something terrible in the heart of the mountain—something that should have remained asleep. But now it had awoken, a consciousness that slipped into my mind. It pulled at me, begging me to listen. And I wanted to. Everything inside me wanted to listen to that voice, to obey it, to please it. It asked me to move, and my feet inched away from the wall and dangerously close to the nearby plunge.

The ghosts of those lost here before us must be awake, and they were hungry.

Yet, *stars*, I had to obey. They tugged at me like nudges of wind, drawing me closer to them. Closer to the edge.

A war raged in my mind as I fought to expel the urges. Just

as I thought they'd gone silent, twenty more whispered my name in unison, in a voice so sweet that I had to see to whom it belonged.

My feet moved. Then a hand was at my waist.

"Emme," Ontario said in a demanding tone. With it, the other voices fled.

I blinked and straightened myself. "I'm okay."

"Which number were you on?"

For a frightening moment, I forgot my count. Then it came back. "Three hundred."

"Good."

The urge to jump remained like a prickle in the back of my mind, but Ontario didn't let his hand drop, and I focused intently on the practicality of that touch to keep from being lured to listen to anything else.

One hundred and two more steps. We were there.

We all let out a breath at the same time, though the struggle was not over. "There should be a smooth part here," I said. I touched the damp wall, very aware of how narrow a landing we stood on.

My hand worked over the wall, searching for something out of the ordinary. As I reached as high as my hand would go, my fingers slipped into a small cut. "There," I whispered. "I found writing here. Or . . . or a drawing."

"Can you open the door?" There was a slight edge to Clarice's voice that said what we were all feeling: this mountain wasn't safe.

I closed my eyes. We'd been confident going into today, when the three of us left the rest of the crew on the *Royal Rose* and trekked into the mountain while dawn was still knocking on the portholes. But the endless darkness had swallowed up our courage, and now I wished we'd found another way to lay this trap.

There wasn't any other way. We needed to get to the gems on the opposite side of this door.

A second explosion shook the ground, and we grabbed hold of each other.

"Hurry," Clarice pressed. The edge wasn't as hidden now.

I used both hands to trace the writing down to a rounded point, almost like a button someone had carved into the wall. It was tricky to fit my fingers around the edges of it, but I did, and I turned.

Stone grated together in an ear-shattering sound, and the mountain opened its mouth for us.

At last, we'd found light. A dim blue-green hue reflected from the walls of a gaping cave. We stumbled in.

"It's limestone," I observed, untying the rope that bound us as I took it in. Not gems like we'd been told, but still precious. A stream ran at our feet, and the limestones grew over top like giant fangs, stretching down to swallow us whole. The air was damp, humid, and unbelievably tight. "Will limestone work?"

"It'll work," Ontario said. He was already climbing to a higher point to drive his pickaxe into the minerals. Clarice followed suit. I was slower, my eyes scanning the cave to check for anyone else. There were too many dark corners, too many worries beating in my own chest.

Ontario's rough voice beckoned us. "Let's get to work. Our ship needs to leave port in three hours, and I don't care to be here any longer than we have to."

I lifted my pickaxe and swung.

We didn't cut in clean lines, but rather hacked at whatever we could reach until chips broke into our palms. We each had a bag, and we shoved the limestone into them.

It was tedious work, but I didn't mind that. A month ago, I wouldn't have been able to swing this pickaxe with precision, let alone an ounce of strength. But then, at the castle, Emric and I had met the Caster, and she'd given me back some control over my body. I no longer wobbled as I walked. I could write my name again. I could live.

Every swing was a reminder of the freedom I had now. It was much easier to focus on what I'd earned than what I'd lost. *Don't think of him. It will only distract you.*

The room exploded, and I flew backward.

My head collided with the opposite side of the cave. Debris billowed through the air, lodging itself in my throat as I fought to see through the dust. Somewhere, Ontario was shouting.

I worked my way to my feet and coughed until my throat cleared. My eyes flicked around the room, searching for my bag. It sat at the edge of the stream with limestone scattered around it. It was much easier to see than it used to be. There was more light.

Sunlight.

"Stars," I whispered. Someone had blown a hole through the cave wall.

The confident scrape of that someone's boots came from the hole. My mother appeared, standing over the wreckage.

I took in the sight of her. The last time I'd seen her, she was captured in the king's castle. Her vibrant red hair had been a tangled mess, her black dress torn along the hem, and her eyes blazing pits of anger. I'd been given a choice then, as Raven had already left with the hand of the king. I was told I could save my mother by taking her place as a prisoner, or I could go free and my mother would hang.

I'd chosen to go free. With it, I'd earned my mother's ire as well as the queen's, as she'd declared war on all pirates after that, using me as an example of how heartless pirates were.

If only she'd seen minutes prior to that moment, when my mother had turned her back on me. I was not the heartless one.

I'd returned later to leave a dagger in my mother's prison so she could rescue herself. Clearly, she had.

Standing before me now, she looked as she had in my

childhood, her hair in a tight knot on her head, leather bracers on her arms, and tight pants tucked into tall boots. She wore a deep velvet top and wry smile.

I straightened myself. I was different than the last time she'd seen me too. I no longer stood on death's door.

"You look well, my child," Arabella said. Her tone was taunting.

"We've no quarrel with you," Ontario shouted. He stood near the stream, his bag clenched tightly in his fingers. Clarice stood beside him, her cutlass already drawn.

Arabella's gaze swung to them. "I've learned that when you're a pirate, you have a quarrel with everyone."

At her words, pirates flanked her sides to storm the cave.

My cutlass was out in an instant. I rushed to meet them.

The clang of iron against iron reverberated through the enclosed space, making it sound as if a hundred men fought instead of three against ten. No, twenty. No . . . More and more came every moment, until there must have been a hundred at her side. This was not a fight we could win.

I bent my knees to drive my weight upward with my sword, pushing back against the man who fought me. He stumbled on the slick ground, and I advanced to drive the hilt of my blade against his temple. His eyes rolled back and he crumpled.

I took a heavy breath. "Who's next?"

The challenge was answered by two pirates, one an older gentleman with a stoic face and wicked swing of the blade, and the other a wispy girl with dark locks, who was all attack and no form. She was easily disarmed with a simple two-move block and hook, but the man was more calculated in his movements and lashed out when my blade stuck the girl's.

I blocked with the bracer on my arm. Sweat beaded my forehead. A healthy line was forming behind those two, each on their toes, waiting to see if they would be needed.

My weight shifted forward, and I drove the side of my

cutlass against the man to pin him against a wall. I jabbed one arm into his waist, holding down the hand that held his weapon, and with the other, I put my cutlass to his throat. His eyes thinned to slits. My attention dropped to his waist to check for more weapons hiding among his leather belt and poorly tucked tunic. I saw nothing.

From the corner of my eye, the girl I'd disarmed flew forward. A dagger was in her hand, and it aimed for my neck with no hesitancy. In one swift motion, she could kill me.

I jerked back. A sting spread over my skin, letting me know she hadn't missed entirely.

Ironically, both our next moves were to look at Arabella. The girl likely searching for approval, and me searching for allowance.

We both found it.

My mother remained as stone-faced as she always was while watching Emric and me train growing up. Her focus would be so into the movements that she'd forget we were fragile things that bled easily. She'd snap at us when we let up, then blink as if remembering we were four and five years old and not hardened pirates like her. Then she'd give us a rare smile and tell us how well we did, followed by a list of what we could do better.

She didn't blink this time. There was no moment of remembrance that I was her blood. Instead, she gave a small nod to the other girl.

My chest twisted. I lifted my cutlass over my face, blocking her image away.

From the other side of the small stream, Ontario was struggling to hold his ground. "We cannot win," Ontario shouted as he and Clarice faced an intimidating group of six. Already, five others advanced at me. I wavered at the sight.

"I will not relent to her," I shouted back.

"And I will not lose my First and my Second." Ontario

nodded to Clarice, then to me. "Blades down, now. That's an order."

I hesitated, then dropped my weapon. It clattered against the stone in the sound of defeat.

"*Tsk.*" Arabella clicked her tongue. "I had hoped for more of a fight. I'm disappointed, but not surprised."

She held out her hand. The pirate closest to Ontario reached for his bag. It had to be pried from Ontario's grip while he glared at the pirate as though he might change his mind about surrendering and run him through. But in the end, he gave it up. I hung my head as the bag was tossed to Arabella.

She opened it, and her eyes lit up. "Limestone, gypsum, and amethyst." Arabella pulled the strings to tie the sack together and flung it over her shoulder with a triumphant smile, coated in layers of mockery. "Thank you."

I wouldn't beg for it back. Instead, I kept my mouth shut as the men fled away, handing Arabella the packs from me and Clarice as they went. Arabella stood like a shadow in the entrance with her eyes locked onto mine.

Ontario and Clarice were scouring through the rubble for any lingering belongings, though they'd stolen our pickaxes as well. They muttered curses under their breath.

But I didn't move until the last pirate had left, and my mother tipped her trifold hat in my direction. "Welcome to the pirate life."

Still, I kept my mouth shut. She didn't wait for a reply anyway. She turned with fanfare, hollered like this was a great expedition they'd completed, and ran down the wreckage of the mountainside they'd just blasted.

Only when she was out of sight did I lift my fingers to my neck. They came back bloody.

"Are you okay?" Ontario asked.

I found my cutlass at my feet. "It isn't deep."

"Still, are you okay?"

He wasn't asking about the cut. There was pity in his tone that I didn't care for. I slid my blade into the sheath with a cold slice. "It's what we planned, right?" When I turned, the light must have caught on my neck, because Ontario was instantly at my side.

His hands went to my wound. "We hadn't planned for you to get injured."

Ontario was protective by nature. But to earn a pitied look from Clarice was rare.

I stepped away. "Arabella could have stopped it if she wanted." I climbed to the hole she'd created and watched as they all fled like spiders off the mountain and to the sea. Arabella's red hair stood out from the rest. She didn't turn back to look.

If she had, she would have seen my look of victory. *I knew she'd fall for it.*

I wiped the blood from my neck and started aiming for the other side of the mountain where our crew waited in the eastern harbor. "Let's tell the crew the trap is set."

2
EMME

I borrowed Ontario's quarters to do exercises in private. My muscles roared with each set I repeated, but I savored the feeling. That meant I was building muscle instead of losing it. That meant I was strong again.

I'd avoided these quarters at first, while nursing the broken heart that Arn left me with. These quarters were too . . . him. Arn had stayed here. Then I had stayed here. There was the table he'd leaned against as I'd nursed his wounds after the Nimnula attacked us—*stars,* that felt like forever ago. Here were the maps he'd pored over. There was the compass that had been seemingly always in his pocket.

He left you behind? I stroked the small compact. *Me too.*

But now, and for the same reason that I'd avoided this place before, I sought it out. The memories of him provided fantastic motivation to push myself to get stronger. And if I pushed hard enough, I'd forget him.

I did another rep.

It wasn't until I rolled onto my back to soak in deep breaths that the door opened.

Emric and Raven stood in the passageway, both their expressions crumpling into worry the moment they saw me limp on the floor.

"Are you okay?" Emric knelt at my side, his eyes roaming over me. When he saw my brow drenched in sweat, he relaxed. Then he frowned. "You push yourself too hard."

It was a challenge to catch my breath enough to say, "I'm fine."

They exchanged glances. Emric and Raven had both seen me at my worst with Paslkapi, and Emric had never stopped looking at me like I was one day away from death. I wiped my brow. "I push myself just as hard as you do."

"How was seeing Arabella?" Emric's mouth twisted as though her name was poison. He hadn't told me yet what he'd gone through on the island with Mother, but the experience had taken his love for her and drained it dry.

"It was cold," I recounted. "Short." I sat up with my hands on my knees. "Exactly like we thought it would be."

We'd suspected Arabella would come after us. I'd secretly hoped she wouldn't. But we had let news spread that we were after whatever this cave held, then given her time to seek us out. Arabella's determination to find us assured that we'd always be able to find her.

We had prepared with fake minerals in that bag that hid a tracking device. Now, wherever she went, we'd know.

There was pain in knowing she could have gotten the limestone anyway, without me there first. And, even then, if she'd really wanted it, she would have held us at sword point as she mined the rest of it.

But she didn't care about taking limestone. She cared about taking it from me.

She could have killed me in that cave. But I knew she wouldn't do that either. She wanted me to live, watching her rule the seas again, knowing I could have been at her side through it all. Stealing the limestone, letting me live, it was all part of her plan.

But it was also part of mine, and she didn't see me twisting the strings behind it all.

"At least we will be warned if she tries to come after us again," I said. Arabella's pride had to be wounded after I went free from the castle and she didn't. It would have been wounded further when she needed to use my dagger to free herself. That damaged pride would not go unanswered, and we preferred to control how she took revenge.

Raven hovered behind Emric like a stoic shadow, clad in black leather and kohl. She jutted her chin toward me. "You're cut. Did she do that?"

I swallowed. "I'm fine." I moved away.

Outside, the clocktower in town chimed five o'clock, and already the skies were darkening. We'd be leaving port soon. Usually, a captain would be with their ship, preparing it for the next journey, but Ontario had been gone since we'd returned from the caves. He hadn't even stepped foot on deck before claiming of matters to attend to and disappearing into the narrow streets of town.

The port was alive with the snap of ropes tightening, as crates were lifted, and the knock of pullies hitting the deck. A few other ships were docked like ours, all sailing under merchant flags. We'd change ours soon after leaving so the bleeding rose hung again.

Snow coated the town, collecting on eaves and under sills. A lick of wind bit through the porthole, and I drew my cloak closer. "Did you do as I asked?"

Emric was always filled with life, like the energy of his early years had never died out. But since he'd almost drowned in the sea a few months ago, he'd come back different. He was somber now and wore his shoulders like they carried a great weight. He gave a curt nod. "You were right, Em. Ontario is not who we think he is."

I shut my eyes for a moment. This hurt worse.

I knew Arabella would disappoint me. I knew she would be true to her name—Ruthless. She couldn't let me down if I had no hope in her.

But I hadn't expected Ontario to betray us.

Arn, my mother, now Ontario. My trust in people was wearing thin.

I lowered myself into a chair by the desk to think. Ontario had been different ever since becoming captain, but I'd been too focused on surviving Paslkapi to give it much thought. But now that I was his Second, I saw clearer that something was amiss. It was the moments when he thought no one was watching, when he'd draw his fingers down the bridge of his nose and stare at his papers, how his eyes would flick over his shoulder like he always thought someone was watching. How he'd flinch when people came near. How he skirted around the deck like a man who couldn't sit still.

It was more than the heavier responsibility of captaining. A desperation had turned his eyes wild.

I'd seen many desperate men call upon my mother over the years. Men looking to save themselves or to find themselves, seeking Arabella to give them what they wanted.

"Did he go to her?" I asked, almost in a whisper.

Ontario saw the emotional scars my mother had left me with, before we knew she was alive. Him going to her now— beseeching her help to establish himself as someone to be respected on these seas—was a personal betrayal.

Emric nodded grimly. "He met with Arabella by the cove. They shook hands." His words carried a chill to them that sent gooseflesh down my arms. "A deal was made on the beach tonight, and it wouldn't surprise me if it was our necks that were wagered."

3

ONTARIO

We sailed from port, traveling north through icy seas. It wasn't until the sails were steady and wind consistent that I left the helm and went into my cabin. Across the deck, Raven and Emric played dice while keeping an eye on the ship as others drifted to sleep.

I peeled my heavy cloak from my shoulders, then rolled up my sleeve, where a long cut ran down my forearm.

"My trust is bonded in blood," Arabella had said.

"Let me guess, only mine? Or are you to bleed to?"

She'd laughed at that, but even her laugh was calculating. *"You called upon me."*

I'd held out my arm, and she'd solidified our plan with a dagger. She'd claimed it was so I had an easy reminder of what I'd promised her, but I suspected her intentions were more conniving that that. It was so I knew what to expect if I went back on my word.

Before I'd left, she'd stood in front of me. *"Are you certain you can do this?"*

"Without hesitation."

Those words ran through my mind now. Over and over, hoping that if I heard them enough, they'd start to sound like me instead of my father.

Without hesitation.

All she'd asked was that I would turn her children over to her that they might be a family again. I'd warned her that they'd likely jump from her ship rather than sail with her, but her demand was clear. She wanted her own blood relations at her side, and she was willing to be my ally if I brought Emme and Emric to her.

And I'd said yes—without hesitation. There were many things my father did without hesitation, things I swore I never would. This would have been one of them.

Light from the half-moon slipped through the porthole as the coldest parts of winter clung to the sills, leaving webs of frost. I pulled my sleeve down and sat at the desk.

I chided myself. It was only a matter of time before Arabella ruled the seas again, and aligning with her was the smartest move I could make as a young captain with few allies. I needed her resources, her numbers, and her unsavory reputation on my side.

Especially now.

I cast my gaze outside. Most wouldn't notice, and so far, none aboard had. But the stars had changed color. Their usual white tint was dulled as hues of green took over the sky, so subtle that it'd taken me several nights to be sure of what I was seeing.

The night was changing. The prophecy was coming to pass.

I thumbed through my father's books. Admiral Bones had seen this coming, and he'd been prepared for it. Obsessed with it. Now I could build on what he'd left. *"Great wealth is to be made here,"* he'd said since I was a boy. This prophecy had gripped him.

In a way, he'd sculpted me to be prepared. And I was ready.

I found the prophecy scribbled in the back of his journal. The lines were so familiar to me, that I mouthed along.

Under emerald stars, the prodigal child will rise.
And under that child, comes the greatest power
ever known to the seas.

But which child?

It could easily be me, the son of the greatest merchant in fifty years to hold trade routes on the high seas. Or it could be Emric, the confident child of Arabella. When I'd met him, I'd been certain it spoke of him, as he was clearly made for the seas. He had the makings of a captain and the true hand of a leader. Our crew had willingly followed him after only knowing him for a month.

Then Emme regained her strength and found her passion for the sea, and now I suspected the prophecy meant her.

Or.

I slid the folded paper out from the back pocket of the notebook and peeked inside again.

Or it could be the little stowaway on board. Calypso. The daughter of King Isaac.

Four of us, all aboard this ship, all fitting the child of the prophecy.

One of us would rule before the emerald stars faded.

4

ARN

The first punch was merciless. It rattled my teeth and blurred my vision until the fighter before me was hazy colors of maroon and green. I almost couldn't see the ring of the crew watching the fight around us, including Landon, arms crossed and weight shifted to his left foot as he nursed the injury in his right one. Fragments of light came from wavering lanterns set on barrels on the main deck as our anchors were dropped for the night, and the crew was hungry for a brawl.

Crew wasn't the right word. They were born on Az Elo, and that made them giant men with beastly instincts.

The second punch came, and I couldn't see anything at all.

"Fight better than that, Arn!" Landon shouted from the side. I couldn't tell if he wanted me to fight because he cared about me or because he knew that if I couldn't fight, the Az Eloians we sailed with would have no one to beat on but him. I'd wager money on the second.

This was their way of training us to be fighters like themselves. Over the past few months, we'd trained more than we had our entire time preparing for the king's navy. Still, they weren't impressed.

I strengthened my stance and swung, hoping to make contact.

My fist met a shoulder as my vision crept back just in time to save me. I ducked as my opponent, Jakob, took another swing.

Jakob's eyes flared as he missed. I lurched forward, barreling him to the ground. I regretted it as soon as his full weight crushed upon my arms.

Jakob grunted. That small noise was as close as I'd ever get to approval. If you hurt Jakob enough to make him grunt, it might as well be a win.

Then he shoved me to the side and brought his fist down over my head. I quickly rolled away, slamming into the corner of a wooden crate as pain splintered through my side. One of the narrow planks cracked loose.

Landon was beside me now, shaking his head. "You're sloppy."

"I'm hungry," I croaked back, jumping again to get away from Jakob's advances.

It'd been two months since King Isaac appointed Landon and me as co-captains of this vast vessel, the *Commander*, with instruction to find his daughter. Calypso had been missing for years, but Landon and I had seen her a few months ago with my crew. We now sailed to bring her home.

King Isaac had promised Calypso's hand in marriage to whoever returned her, which gave me a clue as to why she'd run away. We only met the king briefly, but if he was anything like the crew here, he was a brutal man.

I knew the promise of kinghood tempted Landon. My thoughts latched solely onto Emme.

The last time I saw her, she was weak and wanting to get to the countryside before she died. But Ontario sold me and Landon to King Isaac, and I couldn't even say goodbye.

If I didn't find Emme alive, it would be Ontario's price to pay.

But first, Landon and I had to survive the trip back to Julinbor.

Even though we were supposedly the captains, our crew of brutal Az Eloians had no love for us and barely respected our orders. Most of their obeyed commands came from Jakob, their original captain.

I ducked as Jakob came at me again. He'd certainly found his way to get revenge on us for taking over his ship.

There were only so many times I could dodge his attacks. This time, as he advanced, I summoned every sliver of strength I had to grab the crate I'd knocked into and rip the loose plank free. Jakob's eyes widened just before I swung it, connecting to his side with a crack.

He held like stone, then punched me in the gut.

Mercifully, I still stood. I used the remaining fragments of wood like a shield to block his next punch, and drove my weight against him, hooking the nub of my left arm across his cheek.

He staggered back and wiped his mouth clean.

"Good," he said. Jakob resembled the mountains where he was born—giant, cold, and expressionless. His voice was a deep rumble and his face always clean-shaven, blue eyes seemingly always fixed on Landon and me. They slid over the both of us now. "You stood up better. You may eat."

Beside me, Landon exhaled. He grabbed a small crate from beside Jakob, where our food had waited like some treasure we had to earn, and he marched into the captain's quarters.

I started after him, but Jakob pounded his fist against the crate I'd broken. I flinched. "You need to fix this," he growled.

I'd heard his growl enough that it didn't strike the same fear into me as it used to. I kept a calm face and brushed past him. "That's not my job as captain," I said. "Ask the boatswain."

Jakob gave me a withering look, but I wouldn't take orders from him. The moment I did, any authority I had left on this ship would be gone, and it would risk the crew altering their path from Julinbor where Emme was. Though we had seen Calypso there two months ago, the crew wasn't eager to go to the country of their old enemies and argued that she'd likely moved on. I happened to know she had indeed moved on, as they were departing at the same time that Ontario had kidnapped Landon and me, but the crew needn't know that. Emme was on Julinbor, so that's where our sails pointed.

I slipped into the safety of the captain's quarters where Landon already sat hunched over the food, prying fish meat from bones with his teeth.

"I thought he'd take you down," Landon said between bites.

"It feels like he did." I closed the door behind me, thankful for the barrier between us and the rest of the crew.

There was once a time where I was grateful for distance between me and Landon, but the trials of the past few months had forged an uneasy tie between us, like fragile threads holding us together by nothing more than desperation for someone who wasn't our enemy.

Landon tossed the fish bones on the ground and wiped his mouth. "Have you noticed that they're pushing us harder the past few weeks?"

I took a loaf of bread before he could eat it all, even though it was now cold and hard. "I've noticed. Jakob always looks one breath away from fighting for the helm back. I think he's trying to break us until we beg for relief."

I eased myself into a seat with a groan. My body ached everywhere from relentless months of training, and a headache was forming at the back of my skull.

"They'll have to try a lot harder than that to break us," Landon said. But there was a weariness to his tone that belied he couldn't take much more either.

These were a different group of people than I was used to sailing with. I wasn't convinced they were entirely human.

Az Eloians needed to be strong to work the mines of the mountains and to survive the harsh winters that lasted months longer than nature ought to allow. All things soft had iced over long ago, leaving only brittle people with stubborn minds that never forgave us for their princess going missing years ago. The war was over, but no friendship would be melded here. Trying was like throwing seeds over rocks and hoping for something to blossom.

To them, we were weak and foreign. Something unappealing. But their king had put us on their ship, and they did the only thing that they knew how to do. Day by day, fight by fight, they worked us. Molded us. Broke us.

Aside from the bread lay the green capsule of vitamins they'd been feeding us every day for two months. I wouldn't have taken them if I hadn't seen Jakob and the rest of the crew do so willingly and regularly.

I didn't know what was in them, but I'd never been physically stronger. Still, it was only a fraction of the strength the Az Eloian's had, but I suspected these vitamins had a large part to do with that.

I swallowed mine, then bit into the bread. They went down dryly.

"I'd give anything for one day without a fight," Landon said. He'd slowed eating enough to sit back lazily in his chair with one foot up on the table as if he were home. He covered his discomfort better than I, but it still showed. One of his eyes was black, and his shoulder weak from being pulled out of place so many times, and he limped as he walked. He covered it with a swagger, but it didn't fool anyone.

They didn't fight like respectable pirates here, more like savages with their fists. It was a style that was taking a while to get used to.

The first week aboard the *Commander* was the hardest, when they'd make us fight late into the night until our legs shook and our chests rattled.

"There is no war, what do they fight for?" Landon had asked.

"I think it's like breathing to them. They just do it."

We learned quickly the rules of the ship—we stood at the helm, but we were not in charge.

That was fine. I didn't need this crew. I needed Emme.

"Are we still on course?" I faced the steel-lined porthole. Outside, endless dark waves met a black sky.

"On course."

"How many more days?"

"Thirteen."

I could survive thirteen more days here. I hoped.

Just then, a rap came at the door before it swung open. Jakob's frame filled the doorway, a parchment in his hand.

My heart sank. I knew what that parchment meant. It meant King Isaac had a side task for Landon and me. It seemed that while finding his daughter was his first priority, it wasn't his only one, and he had a lot of enemies to settle scores with along his way to retrieve Calypso.

It was always dirty work, and it delayed us further.

Jakob dropped the parchment at his feet. He despised us so much that he wouldn't pass anything directly—like he had to have a wall between us. "Your next order," he said. Then his other hand brought out a sack, and he flung it to the table. I hungrily took in the sight of the dried meat, fish, and cooked eggs that spilled out. We never got extra portions.

Then I realized why he was feeding us double. We needed our strength for whatever assignment this held.

"Eat up," he said. "Then raise anchor. We make for port in an hour."

5

ARN

The coast rose along the horizon like a splinter of light against the night, with us crawling on its doorstep before the sun could rise. Landon and I stood at the helm to guide the *Commander* into the mossy berths. The town was still. Winter bit at our necks, where our wool cloaks were tied, and threatened to seep through our fingertips as we pulled the wet ropes up to tie us down.

The gangplank was lowered to knock against the pier. I shoved the assignment papers into my pocket, tightened my leather glove, and crossed the plank. Landon was on my heels. The rest of the crew kept their distance.

Clouds of pink fragmented the sky. Morning was coming. The food we'd been given hours ago was wearing off, and weariness tugged at my steps, threatening to trip me over uneven boards.

"Business?" A scratchy voice demanded. It was not all still, after all.

"Farming," I replied curtly. "Here to study."

The town of Ver Vallum was familiar to me, with its flat plains, low hills, and miles of farmland. It rested across the sea off the northern tip of Julinbor, keeping a tight alliance with its neighboring country, fueled by trade. Ver Vallum had no king, just a few wealthy merchants overlooking a small town and stretch of farms.

I didn't grow up here, but my father had several fields in these parts, so we came by sometimes.

These docks were the last place I'd seen him—when he waved me and Landon off as we joined the king's navy.

"Go make me proud." I shoved the memory away.

The town must have grown if they had a post at the berths now. The official stood before us, alert even at the wee hours of the morning, staring down his narrow nose with a sneer like we were hardened criminals trying to stir up trouble in his peaceful town.

How right he was.

I put on a placid smile and went to stride past him. Behind me, Landon moved as well.

The man widened his stance. "New trainees in the dead of winter? Not much to learn right now."

If we'd known we'd be questioned, we'd have come up with a better answer. I looked along the fields behind the town, all cut down and frosted over. "Farmer said now is the best time to learn. Something about being prepared so we can do it right the first time."

His brows lowered until his eyes were almost black pits that stared at us. I was very aware of my pistol at my hip and Landon's hand inching toward his own. But then it stopped.

"Mr. Mangelo's fields are growing, and he wants to make a big profit this year," Landon added.

I blanched. Landon could've named a dozen other farmers in this town instead.

The man's eyes widened. "You didn't say you were with Mr. Mangelo. He's a kind fellow. I didn't know he was looking for hired hands."

"Sure is. After his only son died in the king's navy, he's been hurting for help. His wife is dead, too, you know. Poor luck. But we are here to help. You'll let us through to help him, right?"

The official gave us a look, then one at the *Commander* behind us. "Quite a large ship carrying two recruits."

"It's on its way to fight for the queen's army," I said. "We paid fare for a ride."

I took a step past him now, hoping he was done with his list of good questions. My cloak brushed the top of his feet as I went by, and I felt his eyes on me until I was strolling down the pier, pretending to take in the town for the first time.

"It'll be harder to leave than it was to arrive," Landon muttered beside me.

"We'll think of something."

"Hold up." The official's sharp voice stopped us in our tracks. His heel scraped the dock as he strode our way. "Mr. Mangelo doesn't take his winters in these parts."

This man won the award for the most thorough berth official I'd ever met. I turned slowly. "We are staying with Mr. Scheve first."

Landon shot me a withering look. If he could bring my father into this, I could bring up his.

The official reached a hand to his hip. "Mr. Scheve is dead."

Landon stilled. I could practically taste my heart in my throat. What an awful way to find out your father was gone—with a man reaching for his gun so we could join the count of the dead. But it forced us to swallow the shock. The official's intent was clear—no one would get past him. The official whipped out his pistol, aiming it directly at me. But my hand was quicker, and before his barrel was steadied, I pulled my trigger.

He fell.

Jakob watched from the helm of the *Commander*. He had his own gun drawn. Our eyes met.

Now that the official had fallen, Jakob's gun pointed at me.

It would be a good time to shoot me. He could claim to King Isaac that trouble in town had killed us, and Jakob would have control of his ship back. I couldn't reload my pistol faster than he could fire his, and Landon was too dazed to even see Jakob.

He'd spent months breaking us down. Now he could finish it.

My weight shifted to the balls of my feet, prepared to knock both me and Landon down if Jakob's finger twitched on the trigger.

We held gazes for a moment, before Jakob's gun lowered. His eyes flicked to the dead man at our feet, then back to me. Ever so slightly, he nodded.

It felt like approval.

I gave a rather shaky nod back, then grabbed Landon's arm and yanked him after me.

"Are you alright?" I asked amidst the town's sea-soaked shops. The scent of salt came strong here, barnacles clung to the stone walls of homes, and the whisper of the tide flittered like music that played at our backs. As wind rattled through boarded-up windows, it brought a chill that prickled my skin.

It wasn't colder than Landon's eyes, though. Those were hardened ice.

"I'd rather not speak about it." Landon set his jaw.

I studied him. If I'd just found out my father had died, I didn't know how I would react. I might not weep. But there would be a pit inside me that hurt from being ripped open so quickly, and I couldn't fathom how to close that up again.

I wouldn't want to speak about it, though. I'd want to do something to forget.

"Okay then." My hand went to my pocket, and I handed him the assignment. "We have work to do."

He snatched the paper and read it. "A brothel? Since when does Ver Vallum have a brothel?"

"They don't. It's actually a smuggling business," I said. "Headed by the queen. She gets crops at a fraction of the cost, then provides a generous donation to them that they don't have to pay taxes to their benefactors for."

Landon found that information at the bottom of the paper and let out a whistle. "And in return, they use their surplus of money to shop at markets on her land. The money goes back to Julinbor, and the queen keeps Ver Vallum from getting rich enough to become a true country."

"It must be profitable enough that King Isaac wants us to shut it down."

Landon flipped his hood up. "I can do that."

I drew my own hood over my head as a shop door opened from down the cobblestone street—the first sign that the town was waking. We stepped into an alley, then headed inland, where the shops were built smaller and closer together, their paint fading, and half the lampposts were broken beyond repair. I tried to recognize anything from when I was a boy, but it had changed enough that everything appeared foreign, especially these forgotten-looking streets with crooked signs.

I wondered if I'd be the same way if my father saw me again. Changed enough that he couldn't recognize his own son.

I gave Landon a glance. He'd never get a chance at reconciliation.

As if reading my thoughts, he sent me a look. "No."

"I wasn't going to say anything." Then I hesitated. "Do you think your mother is alright?"

"Arn. I'm not talking about it."

There was a crack in him that I didn't usually see. Landon didn't show emotion, and I thought any left had been calloused over. But the shaky way he now breathed warm air into his cold fists and skirted his eyes around showed that he was more upset than he'd admit.

"You should reach out to her."

His eyes darted to me. "The moment you write to your father, I'll write to my mother."

"Maybe I will."

He laughed and broke away. "Not a chance. The next letter either of us writes will be to King Isaac, telling him we found his daughter. Now if you're done fussing over me," he took out his small pack of gunpowder, "we have a fire to make. That's the place, right?"

I followed his point to a large, single-story home, built of driftwood and straw. There was nothing ordinary about it. But a closer look brought out the iron posts around the door and in the corners, fortifying it. And the windows were boarded up twice, so no one could see through. While the other doors had thrown a hinge, this one stood straight with a solid lock.

Shops in this town didn't need a lock like that.

Even without those clues, there was a design burned into the wood beside the door indicating three stalks of corn. It matched the design on the paper. "That's the place."

We kept low at first, skirting the perimeter with steady steps and frequently glancing at the abandoned-looking shops nearby, careful that no one saw as we poured the black powder into sections on the sills. As the sun rose, we moved with more urgency.

"Is it ready?" Landon tucked his empty pouch away and took out his loaded pistol.

I backed up. "Ready."

When Landon was a good distance away, he took aim and fired. The bullet collided with the gunpowder, and it lit up. Flames sparked quickly, soaking up the dry wood with hungry licks, and sending heat far enough that I felt it.

Others would see this soon.

Silently, Landon and I treaded for the sea.

We got no more than twenty paces before a second explosion echoed through the town, followed by another wave of heat. We swung our heads to look. Black smoke billowed in the air above the remains of the shop, surrounded by the destruction of all the nearby establishments. The flame was still spreading.

"Grain shouldn't explode like that," Landon observed with a frown.

"It wasn't grain the queen was buying from them," I realized. "It was gunpowder. King Isaac just took out one of her military bases."

Shouts came, first from behind, then from all around, as the flames woke the town.

"Run!" I urged. "Now."

We weren't the only ones running. As farmers and shop owners stumbled into the streets, chaos emerged. Luckily, it was so disorganized that no one questioned the direction we were headed. And no one noticed the official sprawled out on the pier.

We moved around him to climb aboard the *Commander*.

Jakob waited on deck, looking at the fire with a satisfied smile on his lips.

I threw down the hood of my cloak. "Your king is using us to fuel a war."

"War is already here. King Isaac is assuring that the fight does not last long enough to reach us." He gestured with his chin to the helm. "Steer us out of here. I don't want to be close when reinforcements arrive." He called orders for the sails to be raised, the oars to move, and our navigator to come above deck.

Landon obeyed with no questions. As he took the wheel, I watched the town drift further away. Thanks to whatever gunpowder that establishment held, the flame was burning bright and had reached so far in such a short amount of time that they had little hope of stopping it without extensive damage. Shops would be ruined. Fields would burn. People might die. My eyes went to the docks. Someone already had.

Even if I got to Emme in time, she might not forgive me for what I had to do to reach her.

I might not forgive myself.

6
EMME

I'd seen Raven as a stoic shadow over my brother's shoulder. I'd seen her as a driving force that led us out of the king's castle in the middle of the night. I'd seen her callous as she tucked a head into a bag and slung it over her shoulder.

But I hadn't seen her cry before.

She was hunched in the crew's cabin, clothed in leathers with a black ribbon holding back her pale blonde hair, and sobbing into her hands. Crying was rare on board, and the noise cracked my heart.

I went to her and put an arm around her shoulders.

She looked up. "These are happy tears," she eventually said with a choke. She held out a folded letter. "The children are okay."

I blinked at the parchment. Raven had left her life of royalty behind to sail the seas with a band of orphans, recruiting those with no other options and giving them a life on the seas. Her eyes would light up as she talked about them, and I knew it agonized her to be away so long. They'd gotten separated as she went on a mission to get the head of King Unid in return for a favor from Sea King Valian—a favor that she'd given up for me. Without it, I couldn't have removed the oathbinding on my foot.

Now I was free, but Raven had spent the past few months sending out letters, hoping that the messenger hawks found her ship. And according to this letter, they had.

"That's incredible. And they are all safe?"

She nodded through a sniffle. "Perfectly safe and waiting on standby for me to join them."

I searched for a handkerchief to give her. It was wrinkled and weathered, but she blew into it all the same. I waited until she'd dried her cheeks. "How soon will you join them?"

From how fondly she spoke of the children, I thought she'd be jumping at the chance to reunite with them, and I'd find her untying the rowboat in the next few minutes and wishing us well. But from the weariness in her eyes, it seemed it wasn't that easy. She ran her hand down her face. "I'd like to go now, but the seas aren't safe. And seeing as I played a big part in putting them in their situation," she gave me a knowing look, as I was right by her side when we'd faced the queen, who later declared war on all pirates, "I'd like to fix that before I return to them."

I passed the letter back and searched for the right words.

The truth was, she was right, the seas were dangerous. Now more than ever.

Arabella's return sent unease through every ship on the high seas. Ontario had already drafted letters to the other pirates to forge tedious friendships. Many had not replied, likely keeping an eye on how things would fall before they picked sides.

But everyone's eye was on Julinbor now, as the queen stretched her fingers well beyond her lands to declare that any form of piracy would not be tolerated. Even if it meant severing alliances with other countries who didn't join her in the fight. She was looking for a war to start her rule with, hoping a victory would guarantee her respect throughout the rest of the years.

She'd easily killed her husband and many others. It wasn't hard to picture how far that coldheartedness would go.

We could hardly keep our own selves safe during these times. I couldn't imagine having an entire crew full of children to worry over. "No one would fault you for going to the children and sailing far away."

Raven's eyes went to the porthole. In them I saw all of her emotion—the relief that the children were safe along with the heavy concern for their continued well-being. And, most of all, longing to be there with them. It was the look of a mother, and for a brief moment, I felt jealousy that I never had someone looking out for me that way.

I did, I reminded myself. I had Bart and Emric. It was incredible those children had Raven.

"I think about it sometimes," she admitted slowly. "I'd steal a rowboat and sail to them." She held the note close to her chest. "But it never would feel right to leave this ship with a battle still to be won. Besides, we need a co-captain." Her eyes lifted. "I'm not leaving without you."

I hugged her shoulders. Raven was the embodiment of strength mixed with kindness, and she had been a joy to sail with during these past few weeks. When all this was over, I planned to co-captain alongside her and give those children a good life and education.

The ship's course changed. It was a subtle shift, the turning harsher than usual. The rocking grew less, even as we came near a shore. From above, the mulled voices roughened into barking orders. Then came the splash of oars guiding us to the right berth.

Raven dried her cheeks for a final time. When her hand moved away, her expression was back to what I was used to seeing—the stoic girl clad in black. As the heir of Az Elo, she likely had many more faces I'd yet to know, but this one served her well on deck.

"We are docking?" she asked.

"Simple supply run," I said. Then lowered my voice some. "Ontario wants to make sure that if a fight comes, we have enough gunpowder to survive it."

7

EMME

Our ritual was so consistent, that we didn't even discuss it beforehand. Emric, Raven, me, and most of the crew would stumble into the nearest tavern, ready to order enough refreshment that the tavern-owner would be so grateful for the sudden influx of coin, his jaw would unhinge. We'd gather as much information out of him as we could about the passings of others through these parts—be it pirates or merchants—while Ontario would be next door with Bishop and Clarice, requesting new inventory. By midday we would be loading crates onto the *Royal Rose*, bellies full, and be on our way. It had become routine.

It didn't go that way today.

Today, we barely got a boot inside the dimly lit tavern before the owner came rushing from behind the counter to shake his linen apron at us.

"Out, out, out!" He gestured.

Emric stalled, keeping the rest of us from coming in after him.

"Out," the owner repeated with more insistence. He bumped into a hanging oil lamp in his hurry but continued with his sole focus on getting us out of his tavern.

Emric kept his voice cool, but I saw how his brow ticked

with worry. He gestured us back out into the chilly morning. "You heard the man." We crowded outside the tavern, staring in at the warmth.

Ontario sighted us before going into the shop next door, and frowned. "Allistar, what's this?" he called out.

Allistar poked his head outside. He sighed when he saw Ontario. "You know I like you, boy. I always have."

"And that I've never given you trouble," Ontario reminded him. He strode over, his cloak flapping at his feet, and his expression darkening. The tension in the air sharpened with each step. When he wanted, Ontario could look like an incoming storm, built with shades of shadows laid over a strong frame, and it contrasted well next to Emric's warmer colors as they stood together—our two strong men. Most would tremble beneath the gaze of one of them, much less both, but Allistar stood his ground.

"That's true," Allistar admitted. "Never any trouble from you." He stepped from the shop with reluctant movements and wrung his hat in his hands. "You know this pains me."

"What's going on?" Emric demanded.

"I can't serve you."

"What?" Ontario's tone sliced through the air.

"I can't serve you," Allistar repeated. To his credit, he held his conviction, even as one clearly unarmed in the presence of a band of fully armed pirates. "The queen would know."

Ontario and Emric folded their arms in unison, forming a strong wall before the man and forcing him to look up at the two of them.

"The Queen of Challace?" Ontario asked.

Now Allistar glowered. "You know of whom I speak."

"The Queen of Myue?" Ontario exchanged a questioning glance with Emric and shrugged as if it were a puzzle. "It certainly can't be the queen of Julinbor, whose territory you don't belong to. Who, I remember you saying, is like an old rosebush with only the thorns and is a shriveled-up beauty."

Allistar's eyes flicked down the streets, wary someone might have heard. "Now listen. I'm a self-built man. This tavern is my pride. But I can't be seen serving your kind anymore."

"Allistar—"

The man held up a hand. He didn't have Emric's size or Ontario's tattoos, but he did have an array of scars that suggested he could combat at least three of us if he felt challenged, and by the quickness of his words, he was losing patience—and eager to not be seen with us. "The queen will hear of it if I let you in, and I'll lose everything."

That stilled us. We weren't even in her territory, yet her influence was so great that this man wouldn't let us in for a meal.

No, not influence. From the tremor in his eye, this was backed by fear.

I looked through the tavern windows. It was too late for fishermen to be here and too early for midday visitors. If Allistar was worried about someone reporting our presence to the queen, the odds were low.

Allistar shifted to fill the doorway. "Besides, an entire town was just burned down at the hand of pirates. I want no part in whatever is going on here."

That stole the breath from our throats. Even Tess, who'd been prone to hanging back recently, shifted closer.

"A town burned?" Ontario pressed.

Allistar was already retreating back inside. "The entire thing. Two cloaked figures moved through the town, setting fire to it. By the time they left, there was nothing to salvage. Ver Vallum burned to the ground."

Two cloaked figures. We'd heard of these men before. The stories started a month ago, then spread like the fire he spoke of, overtaking the seas with allegations of the ruins they left in their wake. People missing. Ships destroyed in their harbors. Businesses unraveled. Bodies found. Homes had been burned before, but never a whole town.

We had enough enemies right now to worry about, but I shifted these up in my mind to mull over later.

Allistar moved to close the door, but Ontario stuck his foot in the way. "Allistar, please. One meal."

His eyes softened, but then hardened just as quickly. "I'm sorry, Ontario. You can try down the street, but you'll get the same answer." He hesitated like the next words pained him. "You aren't welcome here anymore."

The door shut, and the lock clicked.

It was just for dramatics, being as he had a customer he was locking *inside,* but we got the message. We had to leave.

Thick silence clouded our walk back to the ship.

Ontario's voice broke it first. "Drop the sails. To the oars. Boatswain, check how long we can go without stopping for inventory. Tess, to the crow's nest. Watch the town, though, not the seas."

Tess scaled the mast with ease.

"Watch for what?" I asked.

"For Allistar to be that frightened, the queen must have officials there."

"Where to?" Clarice asked, already behind at the helm.

"Due west. As far away from here as you can get."

She didn't ask for more clarification.

"I'd like to see Arabella go up against the queen," Emric said to me. "That'd be a fight to see."

I let out a puff of breath. "The queen would like that too. She's likely not happy that Mother escaped."

Now that Ontario's orders were given, he came over to us and lowered his voice. "We cannot take on a war against the queen. She has a fleet, and we have one ship."

His words dropped like a rock in my gut. "Where could we go?"

"Not too far west," Emric said. "Az Elo would be no more pleasant to deal with. North has the untamed high seas, but those have little nourishment to support us. And no merchants to plunder." He let out a slow breath as he thought. "Of course, we could go south and build a farm. Leave the ship behind." There was mockery to his tone at that last part, but also a hint of defeat. Julinbor was one of the most prominent countries in the world, and if we wanted to get away from their reach, it might mean a totally different life.

Raven had joined us. "These seas are our home. We should fight for them."

"How?" Ontario pressed. "Are you trained in battle strategy?"

As heir to a kingdom, it was quite likely that she was. She didn't offer such information. "I'm only saying that if we are so easily pushed back by the queen, other countries will be drawn to join her, and the time of piracy will be over."

"We could see if Sea King Valian would fight with us," I said.

Emric chucked. "Not like you to believe in bedtime stories."

I swung my gaze to him. When we were younger, we'd debated whether we believed the tales Mother brought back about mermaids, but that time was long gone. Now, Emric and I had met them. Emric had more than met them, he'd fallen in love with one.

Now that I thought about it, he hadn't mentioned Coral once since I'd been healed. If she still visited him, he didn't say.

My brother wasn't one to bare his soul to me. He wasn't one to even share a morsel of it, instead keeping his thoughts tucked away behind a smile or a sword. I looked over him now, wondering if he'd been hurting and I'd missed it.

"I agree that we should fight if we can, but the way to do so isn't clear," Ontario said.

"There's no chance that Arabella will run," Emric said. "So

we can bet that she's planning an attack on the queen of some sort. I hate to suggest . . ."

He didn't need to finish.

"No," I said. "I'm not working with my mother," I said.

He gave me a look that reminded me he wouldn't like that any more than I would, but we were limited right now. "It's an option that's on the table," he pointed out.

"I'm taking it off the table. I'm *throwing* it off the table," I said. "I'm chucking the option into the sea and drowning it."

"We get it."

"I don't think you do. She can't be trusted." I deliberately avoided Ontario's eyes. He would have to learn on his own that she couldn't be trusted. But I would not be going near her if we could avoid it. And thanks to the gems planted to track her, we could.

"Then running is the only option we have right now."

I shook my head. "That's not an option either." I had just recently realized what I wanted from life—to be here on the seas. I wasn't ready to lose that.

Emric gave an exasperated sigh. "You aren't being very helpful here."

I raised an invisible flask. "Thank you. I wanted to see if you had any good ideas before suggesting my own."

"You have an idea?" Ontario asked.

"I do. At least, I have parts of a plan, but it might work."

"*Parts* of a plan. *Might* work," Emric said with sarcastic scrutiny. "I suggest we leave my options on the table."

Our captain was serious as he looked at me. "Tell me why I shouldn't be running to Arabella right now."

"I think we should go to her," I said in a hurry, trying to piece together parts of a plan that took root weeks ago. It was still just the roots though, no branches and nothing blooming—only a fragile idea that I didn't love. It was more malicious than I could usually stomach, and that, above all else, kept it in my head instead of on my tongue. But we needed ideas now, and it could work.

"I want to ambush Arabella and turn her over to Queen Isla in exchange for our pardons."

The words hung in the air between us, thickening it until I could feel Emric's shock like a shroud. He crossed his arms over his chest and stared at me with a look of worry. I thought he was going to say no—it was cruel and unlike us—but when he opened his mouth, he surprised me by saying, "She's clever, though. We'd need to be smart about it."

I breathed a sigh of relief that he was considering it instead of looking at me like I was broken for thinking such a thing.

"We will be. But Queen Isla hates her most of all, and she might accept Mother as the price for the end to this war."

Ontario's eyes were slits, and I could see the wheels turning in his mind. Raven was the only one whose expression, as always, hadn't changed. Emric looked at her now. "What do you think?"

While I didn't know the story between her and her father, I knew Raven was familiar with estranged parents. It was no surprise to me when she answered in an even tone, "It's smart. You have an enemy. You defeat her."

"How?" Ontario inquired. "How do we trap her?"

"Use your tracking tablet," I said. "Check where the gems are."

Ontario looked to the captain's cabin on deck. "I'll go get it."

When he'd gone, Emric took me by the shoulders. "Are you certain you'd want to turn Mother over? You just saved her from the queen a few months ago."

"That was the wrong call," I said, trying to keep from thinking about it too much. If I got to thinking, I'd forget the times that I waited for her to come home but she never did. I'd forget how she missed every moment that mattered in my life. I'd forget how she walked away when I was in the cell. If I only remembered the bare hints of affection she gave, my vulnerable heart could latch onto those to taunt me into believing I was the evil one who turned on my own mother. That was what Queen Isla had thought when she'd offered me the chance to take my mother's place as her prisoner.

A monster who chooses itself over its own mother.

But Arabella had been given enough mercy. Now she would get retribution.

Raven's voice bit through my thoughts. "It was a noble call. As is the one you make now."

Emric dusted himself off like he was removing the accountability of this plan from himself. Whether we brought Mother down or this went south—either way it would not be on him.

But if this worked, if Queen Isla accepted this one prisoner in exchange for the other pirates going free, we would be saving many, many lives.

Ontario emerged from the captain's cabin with the tablet in hand. It was an odd device, which we had no idea how he had acquired, and he never let us see too closely.

"Where is she?" Emric asked him.

He let us see it now.

"She's in Ver Vallum," he said abruptly. "She's in the town that just burned." He jammed the tablet into the folds of his cloak and climbed up the helm. "Clarice, turn us northbound. Emric, train the crew in combat." Despite the cold, a bead of sweat formed on his brow. "We are about to get daringly close to Julinbor."

8

ARN

There was one word that we'd picked up from the Az Eloian's, simply because of how often they said it. Especially Jakob—usually while throwing a polearm at us. That was how it came this time. I didn't want to catch the weapon, but the other option was letting it knock me upside the head, so I did.

I pulled myself to my feet and rubbed the sleep from my eyes as silvery light from the moon crept through the porthole, keeping dawn at bay. We'd gotten maybe four hours of sleep, if that.

"*Hnoll*," Jakob said. "We fight."

"I don't want to *hnoll*," Landon replied, rolling from his hammock. "I want to *sleep*."

Jakob threw a second polearm at him. It did hit his head. "Hnoll."

Landon glared like a man who didn't fear for his life. I had more tact. "Food first, then hnoll."

Jakob looked between us. He stood outside the door again, not coming close enough to enter, twirling a dagger between his fingers. Since he didn't plan to fight us polearm against dagger, I knew it was only theatrics, but it didn't stop him from appearing menacing.

"Hnoll first, then I give you double portions." His dagger tip pointed to me. "You're too skinny."

Compared to the giants of Az Elo, we were all too skinny.

Landon and I shared glances. "Hnoll," we agreed. We'd take the double portions. Anything to fill the empty ache in our bellies.

Jakob frowned like he was disappointed we didn't object further and turned on his heel to lead us through the narrow passageway to the deck of the ship.

Half the crew was awake. Those who weren't tending the ship were strung along the main deck in two lines, blunt polearms in hands, feet spaced, and shoulders squared as they ran through drills.

Before I could thank the stars that it looked like I would spar against Landon, Jakob shoved me opposite a burly man by the name of Koa.

Koa was around our age, though his thick beard made him appear older. His ashy skin and chilly eyes paired with dark lips that curved upward as I faced him. He was a quiet fellow, more prone to watching those around him than saying words, but when he did speak, he didn't have anything useful to say. It was his skilled hands that kept him on deck, both as a warrior and as a carpenter.

He was still finding his place among the crew. Unfortunately, he earned respect by expressing his dislike of us. He was someone I might have been friends with once upon a time. But not now. "We are running the *Beggar*." Koa announced the drill, a ruthless one designed to attack your opponent until they begged for mercy.

He looked at my hands . . . or rather, my *hand*. He dropped one arm. "To make it fair." That was all the warning he gave before he attacked.

His polearm came down, and I held mine tight to absorb the blow.

In less than a breath, Koa jerked his polearm back up and struck again. Somehow, I managed to hold fast. Just barely. My grip fumbled, and he saw it. This time his weapon connected with mine, and he thrust his weight forward to push it into my stomach.

I doubled over.

Even as my vision blurred, I kept my weapon in front of me to block whatever came next. I tried to guess his moves, but that was the point of the *Beggar*—there were no specific moves. No identifiable twist or maneuver to disarm your opponent. The only agenda was relentless attack.

He undercut. The polearm smashed against my jaw.

It hurt *richly*.

He swung again. I blocked better this time, then shoved with enough force to send him back a step. His next swing was harder, and I struggled to stand beneath it. At least beads of sweat were forming on his brow.

I glanced quickly at Landon, training beside us. I couldn't guess Kao's moves. But I could guess Landon's. We'd been fighting together since we were little.

When Landon shifted his hold down on the polearm, I took the opportunity.

I slammed my polearm sideways at Kao, then drew back to repeat the action, giving him enough time to sidestep. He did.

But he failed to see Landon.

While Landon swung at his opponent—who ducked because Landon always aimed too high—his polearm whacked Kao's head. He crumpled to a knee.

Kao took a shaky breath before glaring up at me. "That's not a win for you."

"It's certainly not one for you."

I offered my hand, which he swatted away. "You always let other people fight your battles?"

"It doesn't matter who hits the hardest. All that matters is that the enemy goes down."

Jakob stood watching us. The fur of his wool cloak bristled under the grays of his beard. His eyes fixated on mine, but they weren't as hard as before. Usually when he looked at me, all I saw was a man calculating how soon he could get me off his ship, but now they'd shifted, as if interested to see what else I could do.

It was the same look I'd seen from him after I'd killed that man on the docks. A tedious respect.

He glanced at Landon. Since missing his opponent and hitting mine instead, Landon had lost the upper hand and was in a string of defensive moves that earned him no ground. With a quick motion, his opponent fixed his polearm on the opposite end of Landon's and ripped it away from him. He twisted his grip and raised the weapon.

Jakob flinched.

I stilled, uncertain I'd seen it right. But Landon's opponent saw Jakob's hesitation too, and he stalled.

Landon used that moment to try to tackle the man, but it broke him from the trance. Before Landon could recover his weapon, his opponent had brought the polearm down on his head. Landon slumped to the deck.

Jakob looked away with a grimace and something else.

That was not the same look he'd given me. That was not one of a respecting soldier. That was a look of concern.

If he did hold concern for Landon, there was no further note of it. As soon as Landon regained his composure, Jakob was back to pushing us through relentless drills until our hands had blisters and our legs wobbled. The sun was well above the horizon before Jakob lifted his hand.

"Enough for today. Switch shifts."

The crew shift that got a full night's rest—the one we were supposed to be on—was awake and coming to take their positions along the deck, checking the nets we'd cast during the night, cleaning the fish, going through the ropes, and routinely running the lines. I was so exhausted that I wasn't certain I could captain now. Every part of me wanted to grumble at Jakob that if he wanted his ship back, he could take it for the next shift. Instead, I dragged myself past Landon, who looked worse than me.

"You rest," I told him. "I'll take first shift."

Soon, food was brought to the helm, and I devoured the double portions.

My eye often went to Jakob, mulling over that moment in my head.

He flinched. I'm certain of it.

He never flinched when I got hit. But now I was going through every moment he'd fought us himself and wondering if he'd been pulling his punches with Landon or if he treated us both the same.

By the time the navigator climbed to the helm, I was thoroughly curious. "Tell me, what's Jakob's story?"

The navigator was an old man and not prone to gossip. But he was very loyal to Jakob, and I suspected there to be a reason for that. He looked down to where Jakob stood on deck, his eye on the water and jaw set firm.

"He joined King Innoc's navy when he was young and has been a part of it ever since," came the reply. He unrolled maps and looked over them like that brief comment was the entire story. Jakob's entire life summed up in one line.

"No family?"

"He has a wife back home," the navigator replied dryly. "She used to sail with us a long time ago." Something in his expression changed, and I knew where to push.

"What happened to make her stop?"

He lowered the maps. At first, I thought he wasn't going to say anything. But as his eye took in Jakob, again it softened, and his tone dipped. "Their son died, taken down at sea in the war against your king."

The accusation in his voice was clear enough that I might as well have put the cutlass through his son myself. The navigator had likely known Jakob's boy.

Sympathy swelled in my chest. It was the first time I'd felt that emotion for Jakob. I swallowed the pit in my throat. "Which battle?"

The navigator had to think for a moment before replying. "Witherstons."

I blanched. I truly might have put the cutlass through his son.

When we were in the king's navy, our mission had been to bring the Princess of Julinbor to Az Elo, where we were told she would marry their prince. Instead, she was meant as a sacrifice. She never made it there. Our captain killed her in his cabin, and Landon and I freed the pirates, who were prisoners on our ship, to begin our path to piracy.

Three weeks later, we came across a ship from Az Elo. It wasn't large, not meant for war, but it had soldiers and supplies, and that was enough for us.

"Ready to see what it's really like to be a pirate?" Our pirate captain had asked us.

We were. We'd stared wide-eyed and gripped our new cutlasses as the other ship came nearer, drawing out their cannons. But our shots were truer and much quicker. In a matter of an hour, the other ship went down. There were no survivors.

It all took place off the coast of a town called Witherstons. I'd bet silver that Jakob's son died on that ship, and Jakob didn't know it had been pirates to bring him down, not Julinbor.

Jakob hated Julinbor for the loss of his son, but he should hate pirates more. Either way, his hatred in me was properly placed.

The navigator tucked the maps into the folds of his cloak

and gave a curt nod. "Turn two degrees to the south," he ordered. "Then steady on."

9
ARN

Since Landon slept through the morning, he wasn't offered food until well past midday.

"I deserve three by now," Landon grumbled as he tore apart a sliver of dried meat.

Jakob let out a boisterous laugh, though the joy didn't touch his eyes. "For what, napping all morning, then holding a wheel? Eat your meal and be grateful. When you first came on my ship, you were tiny things with no meat on you. Look at you now. You're becoming men."

Phrases like that that concerned me. *My ship.* I knew how it must feel to have someone else steering your ship—I'd felt it when Ontario had seized control of the *Royal Rose.* The agony of watching someone else command the helm had carved into me, deeper and deeper every day, until I'd devoted everything to regaining control. No doubt, Jakob felt that too. He'd likely run through every way to kill us, every rope he could use to bind our wrists and throw us overboard, every hook sharp enough to tear our skin, and every cutlass he could drive us through with.

It was because he could do those things to us that Landon and I let it slide when he said *my ship.*

I thought of it as strategically ignoring his undermining so I wasn't ripped in half.

But when he threw a parchment down, I frowned.

"Another assignment," he said in that low voice of his, cutting the ends of his words short so there wasn't room to argue. He backed up as soon as the parchment left his hand.

"Hold on," I shot. I swiped the letter up. "What is this?"

"Another assignment," he repeated through his teeth, daring me to argue.

"King Isaac gave us one task and seemed urgent about it. We are to find his daughter. Last we saw her was in Julinbor, but she'll move on soon if she hasn't already, giving us little time to doddle on frivolous missions meant to stir up the war between Julinbor and pirates. This"—I waved the parchment—"can't be more important to him than Calypso."

"Calypso has already moved on from Julinbor," Jakob fired back. My body chilled. He couldn't know that. If he knew where she was, we wouldn't be here. But my sureness in that was undercut by the confident way he delivered the news. But then he shrugged. "She never stays in one place for long." My shoulders relaxed until he growled. "Going to Julinbor is a waste of time and will yield nothing but false leads that will take months to follow."

He said it like a threat. Like if we continued on our course, Landon and I wouldn't be alive to see the shore.

I pulled every ounce of authority into my tone. "We continue to Julinbor without delay."

Landon kept quiet by the wheel, still eating, while Jakob marched to the top of the helm and spread his stance wide. If he hoped to intimidate me, he'd have to do a lot more than be big.

Before he could say anything, I reminded him whose orders we were both under. "King Isaac put me and Landon in charge. We are going to Julinbor."

"I know His Majesty's orders. It is only because the king thinks you are worth something that you are still alive. But these," his eyes dipped to the parchment, "are also your orders. *From him.* You will follow them, or I will run you through for insubordination."

He had nerve to talk about insubordination. It was only because I knew exactly how he felt that I didn't serve that punishment to him.

I glanced over the assignment. Another port out of our way and another man to kill. I stashed the paper away.

Jakob nodded like the conversation was resolved, then started down the stairs.

I called after him. "We are a long way away from King Isaac right now. A long way. It would take a messenger hawk days to find us. At least."

He looked over his shoulder. "What are you getting at, boy?"

I opened my mouth, then halted my tongue. "Merely impressed at the skill of your messenger hawks to find us. That's all."

He stood a moment, searching my expression, but I'd turned to take the wheel from Landon and heard his departing footsteps. When Jakob was out of earshot, Landon looked at me.

"What are you thinking, Arn?"

I passed him the assignment. "I don't think these are coming from King Isaac. I think they are coming from Jakob."

He read it over twice. "What good would this do him?"

"Perhaps we are taking care of his personal business. But I suspect there is more to it than that. He doesn't want us to find Calypso."

"I repeat my question. What good would that do for him?"

"I don't know." My mind was half lost in thoughts, going through our assignments and our time on this ship. King Isaac had sent many others out looking for Calypso, but Jakob could be what was keeping them from finding her. It certainly seemed like he was deterring us by these pointless missions, giving Calypso enough time to run from wherever we'd seen her last so we couldn't find her again.

Frankly, I didn't care if he didn't want us to find Calypso. But he was keeping me from finding Emme.

"This is the last assignment we do for him," I stated. "And the next time he gives me an order, I'm making sure he knows who is captain here."

Landon grinned. "It's about time. Things have gotten boring around here."

10

EMME

Arn's note was already faded. The edges were yellowed, the writing blurred, the parchment sea-damaged, and the side cracked where it had been folded too many times. Still, I opened it again to devour every word.

The day was unusually warm for winter, and I'd taken advantage of the opportunity to climb along the bowsprit that extended forward from the ship's bow, holding onto the forestays for balance as I breathed in the fresh sea mist and held the note close. The bowsprit and the crow's nest were the only two places on the ship which provided privacy, and Tess was always in the crow's nest. She even slept up there.

But I loved the bowsprit for another reason—I could climb all the way out here. A few months ago, I couldn't. I'd fall, and Arn wasn't here to fish me out of the water anymore. But now, I could sit here without fear.

Only with a heavy heart. I'd traded one burden for another.

I knew the words in this letter so well that I had to force my eyes to slow to actually read them.

My dearest Emme. I love you, but I'm not ready to leave the seas. I'm sorry. Yours forever, Arn.

It was barely a note. I could recite it in under three seconds, and it'd long lost all meaning for me. I'd searched for answers.

I'd searched for emotion. I'd searched for a clue that Arn wasn't like my mother every time she'd left my father and me wondering why we weren't good enough to make her stay.

I replaced the note in my pocket before I could take that train of thought too far.

"He is not the man you thought he was," I reminded myself aloud. "And you can't blame yourself for that."

"Who are we blaming?" Raven had crawled behind me along the bowsprit, keeping her balance like an acrobat, and showing no remorse when I startled and nearly tipped into the sea.

"You," I said, finding my footing again. "For almost drowning me."

She wrapped her legs around the spar. "I'd have caught you."

Raven wore her hair loose today—a change from her usual tight braid—and it made her appear softer than usual. That, and her tight clothes had been exchanged for a more flowing, white tunic and calfskin pants. She wore brown leather bracers with silver buckles that matched the color of the necklace she always wore.

She eyed my pocket. "Thinking of Arn again?"

"Well . . . now that you mention it, he's a passing thought." She raised a brow, and I let the humor drop. "It hurts more today, but I don't know why."

Raven reached out and squeezed my hand.

I was unused to touch, and it was impossible to receive it now without my traitorous mind latching back onto Arn. I put up iron bars in my mind to keep him from coming in further. Instead, I moved my thoughts to Raven.

Her company felt natural. It took me a while to pinpoint why. Somehow, I'd gone nineteen years without having a female friend to rely on, and I hadn't realized how much my soul craved the connection. From what Raven had shared about growing up, she hadn't gotten this either. But now she was here, daring the bowsprit with me, and it made me feel less alone.

"Do you want to talk about Arn, or do you want a distraction?" she asked.

"Distraction," I promptly replied. "Definitely distraction."

Raven scooted closer. "Distraction it is." From the dip in her voice, she sounded like she was about to tell me a secret, but what came out was a story. "Long ago, fortune tellers ruled the world. They served at the right hand of kings, but their fortunes shifted the tides of fate, and what started out as predicting futures became manipulating them, until every thread of time was but a plaything for their own whims. Kingdoms fell at their commands. Seas rose, farms grew, and riches changed hands all to their liking. It was a power none had seen before."

I had experience with fortune tellers. Someone who claimed to see the future had predicted I'd bring death, and captaining a black ship, she'd hunted the *Royal Rose* down and tried to kill me to prevent my future from coming to pass. If the fortune tellers of old times were anything like her, I shivered at the thought of them ruling the world.

I had an additional encounter with a fortune teller a few months ago, back when my disease controlled every part of my life and when Arn was still with me. That fortune teller had told me the same thing: I'd be a catalyst for death.

Now here we stood, staring at the threat of war. If we didn't stop the war, the fortune would be right.

Raven went on. "Soon the kings of the world feared the fortune tellers more than they relied on them, and they banded together to be rid of them. It was the first time all the kings worked in unison, and the last. They overthrew the fortune tellers and banned them from the lands. It took hundreds of years for them to seep back in, but they never regained the power they used to have."

"My mother always hated them," I commented when she

stopped. I remembered how she told us to stay away from them, and for a mother who wanted us to live on the dangerous seas with her, her warnings carried weights. "She didn't trust them."

The power to predict fate was strong enough. The power to manipulate it could be detrimental in the wrong hands.

"There's more to the story," Raven said. By now, she'd leaned even closer. "Before the fortune tellers were cast out, they gave a final prophecy. They warned that one day, a power would rise again that would hold command over the whole world. A power in the hands of a prodigal child."

"A prodigal child?"

Raven looked at me with interest. "I think it speaks of you."

"I thought this was a story," I complained.

I could fit that description. A wayward child of prodigy. But so could many others, and I'd had enough predictions of my future. "It could be you."

"I used to think so," she admitted, also letting me know it was far more than a story. "But now that I know you, I think you are the child it spoke of." Her eyes danced with the intrigue of it all. "Aren't you going to ask me when you'll rule the world?"

I humored her. "When?"

"The prophecy was said to pass when the stars turned emerald."

"Emerald stars?"

Her head tipped upward. "Haven't you noticed?" she asked. "The stars are changing color. Your time is coming."

From behind her, Emric was shouting to get our attention, pausing his work as he trained the crew, but my mind was too latched onto the prophecy she'd just unfolded. Ruling the world. "I wouldn't want to rule the world." My mother had wanted that, and the drive for conquering had destroyed her. No one could handle such responsibility without it eating away at their morality. Even Arn, who was good at his heart, had been blinded by his drive to regain his control over the *Royal Rose*. That was only a ship. I couldn't imagine what controlling the world could do to a person.

Raven was already moving to return to deck. "People aren't usually given what they want. Nor are they given what they can handle. They are simply *given*, and it's up to them what they make of it."

She hopped from the bowsprit as Emric came up to us. He reached into a barrel to pull out a dulled cutlass. The edge of it gleamed with sunlight. "If you've nothing else to do, I could use help training the crew. Tess hasn't trained for weeks, and she's always preferred your teaching."

I eased myself back to deck. "I'll train them, but Tess won't join us if I'm there."

"Nonsense." Emric waved off my words and called up to Tess, "Come train with us."

She shook her head.

"See? She won't come down."

But Emric frowned. "What did you do to her?" he asked before raising his voice. "Come fight, Tess, so you don't die in the next attack."

Raven leaned back to whisper to me. "He has such a way with young ones."

"Well, he had such a wonderful mother as an example."

"I'll train later," came Tess's response.

"She's avoiding me," I told Emric as I took the cutlass from him. I held the weight better than I used to, and by now it felt familiar in my hand, almost like an extension of me. It hadn't felt like that since I was young, when Mother would spend all day working with me and Emric on drills. "And before you ask, I don't know why."

Emric thought. "She's been odd since we left Julinbor. Was she close with Landon or Manty?"

"Who are they?" Raven asked.

"Manty was a crewmate who likely left with Landon," Emric explained. "Landon is the one I don't care to speak of." He twirled a blade once before handing it to her.

She took it with a nod. "That's right. I remember now."

They moved away to start training, but I stayed where I was.

According to Ontario, Landon and Arn had sailed away on the *Dancer*, and I'd assumed Manty had left with them. I hadn't given him another thought. But perhaps I should have. My hand went inside my pocket to the corners of the note.

"Are you coming?" Raven looked back at me.

By now, I knew hope could be a powerful thing, but it could also be a dangerous thing. Either way, I was helpless against letting it take root.

"Manty," I breathed. I took out the note and read it again, this time not seeing the words as much as how the words were written. "Manty was a forger."

11

ONTARIO

When the jewels were split, I didn't tell anyone. But I tracked them as one half was taken south and the other stayed in Ver Vallum, leaving me to guess where Arabella was. Best guess: she'd pawned some here and taken the rest south. We likely came to an empty city.

From the deck, I viewed the land before us.

It was burnt, empty remains.

A fire had raged recently, and its destruction was massive. Even the distant farmlands had been touched. Streets were littered with piles of ash as if someone had tried to sweep before abandoning it completely. A quick scope of the hills showed that Arabella wasn't here, but I brought the *Royal Rose* to the berth anyway.

Emric came beside me. "Are the jewels here?"

"According to the tracking, they are."

Even if it wasn't Arabella who had these jewels, someone did. The tracking device confirmed that. The jewels hid among the wreckage.

Some homes partially stood, wind rattling through shards of windows and kicking up smoke from tiny fires that kept sparking. I admired their tenacity to burn after all this time.

"Tie here," I instructed. "She's close."

Emric lowered the gangplank, and Emme crossed the deck to tie the ship down.

The crew moved onto land, grouped together as I looked over the tablet. "The tracking indicates the spot is three blocks this way—" I pointed east. "Emric, lead a third of the crew through these streets and approach from behind. Clarice, you will lead a second group through that way," I pointed again, "to come from the south. I will lead the third group from the north. Wait until I advance, then at my sound, attack. We can't know how many men are here, but you have permission to kill on sight. Arabella is to be left alive."

We split in three groups. Our steps were quiet, but in this ghost town, I could hear the other two groups as they moved. If Arabella really was present, we would have no chance of ambushing her. As it was, some jewel trader was about to get an unpleasant surprise.

Smoke hung in the air like a thick cloud, lodging itself in our throats as we tried to stifle coughs. Charred, black trees lined the streets, looking over the destruction. It was impossible to walk through the town and not think of what it should have looked like: snow falling over the fields, windows fogged up as little faces pressed against them to watch the frost come in, their cheeks warm from the cocoa. Farmers would already be scoping their fields and testing the soil by now, and merchants would be counting their books, figuring how to make a bigger profit next year.

Instead, it was prime for looting and a playground for criminals.

Emme chose to be in my group, and I turned control over to her. "Keep everyone as quiet as you can," I instructed. "I want to sneak ahead to know what we are dealing with."

She took hold of my arm before I could start off. "I should go. I could talk to her."

"Emme, the last time you saw her, she was willing to let you die. You are beyond talking."

"I meant I could talk to her as a distraction for you to ambush her." There was a crack in her expression, something in the way the corner of her mouth tugged inward, like she was trying not to let this bother her. But the weight of what she was offering wasn't lost on me. Emme, the girl who'd cried the first time she'd heard the mermaids sing, who'd treated every customer with respect at the tavern, even pirates like me, and who'd gone back to save her mother after being abandoned, would now turn Arabella over to the queen.

I half expected her to stop us before we got too far and insist there must be some other way, not to offer to single-handedly face her mother so we could trap her.

Emme lowered her head. "Don't look at me like that. I know the seas have changed me."

"They've strengthened you," I told her. "You've nothing to be ashamed of. Still, it's best if I scout it out first. Stay with the others."

She nodded rather reluctantly and I ran ahead.

I gave little care to what noise I was making, more concerned with arriving before anyone else, so I could verify that Arabella was not here. If by some chance, Arabella was actually in Ver Vallum, I needed to call the ambush off. If the crew threatened her, she'd unveil my involvement with her, and I'd be ruined.

I halted, looked down at the tracking device, then up again. It'd led me to . . . nothing.

There might have been a home here once, but now there was nothing but brushed-over piles of planks, the remains of furnishing, and what used to be a rocking horse. One wall stood miraculously untouched, but the other three were skeletal remains. I stepped over to go through the mess.

I checked the device again. "The dot is right here," I muttered to myself. "Where are the jewels?"

Ash coated my pants as I dropped to my knees to dig through it. Slowly at first, then sporadically, searching for anything that wasn't burnt. It was useless. Arabella must have traded the gems away before the fire, and not after. No one is here," I said, defeated. "Not even a jewel trader."

I looked down and squinted. Everything was blackened from the fire, but beneath this board lay something green that had been untouched by flames or smoke.

Was that my bag? I pulled planks away. Sure enough, my old satchel, the one that held the jewels we'd pretended to lose to Arabella, lay in the wreckage.

I tore it open. Inside was only half of the fake gems, along with a crinkled note.

I read it.

I do not take kindly to those I'm in business with betraying me. Next time, if you want to know where I am, ask.

Blood drained from my face.

"Ontario?"

I jumped. Emme came into the charred ruins, looking around. "Where is she?"

I slid the note into my pocket. "Turns out, your mother is no stranger to being tracked," I held up the bag, "She left the fake gems here."

Emme's face fell. "It didn't work. All that work to plant the fake gems and get her to steal them from us, and she didn't fall for it."

I slung the bag over my shoulder and stepped out of the former house. "It didn't work this time. We will still catch her. But we better do it soon, because I reckon her anger at us is growing."

12

ONTARIO

I turned the *Royal Rose* westward, keeping to myself that we still followed Arabella. It could be another trap, or we'd gotten lucky, and she'd only discovered half of the fake gems and thought the rest were real. Either way, we had a lead, and we'd follow it quietly.

The crew was in low spirits, so I let them throw a party on deck that night to cheer them up. As they drank, I went belowdecks into the captain's cabin and closed the door.

I took a swig from my flask as I read through the note again. Father would be angry with me for working with Arabella. *"There are people even I wouldn't get into business with,"* he'd said.

But Father was greedy and only saw money, and he knew Arabella was the same. Two sides of the same coin couldn't work in tandem. I was getting nothing financial out of this. I did it for my crew. *I'm doing what it takes to get Arabella away from them.*

The rum went down hard, and I put it away. I listened to the songs of the crew from above as they'd finally cast aside their worries for the night and lightened into the crew they should be. The desire to give them that was wound so tightly in my gut that I could hardly think of anything else. I wanted to be a captain they trusted to protect them. One who gave them a safe home here. Someone people knew and respected and feared.

Loved, I corrected myself. Knew, respected, and loved.

So far, I hadn't had the chance to give them that. My few months as captain were stained by countless struggles that would drive any weak heart in the crew away. It was a wonder they remained, but I knew I couldn't keep them here forever if things didn't turn around soon.

A noise close by took me from my thoughts. My hawk at the porthole, holding a small sack in his talons.

"If these are threats from Arabella, you can drop them in the ocean," I grumbled. He landed at the sill and held out his foot.

There was no seal. No symbol to identify the sender. That was never a good sign. I untied the package, reached inside, and drew out a round thing like a compass, but the top was flat and nothing opened. It looked like a glorified coin, but the gold was clearly fake, and the design of it not intricate enough to keep as a trinket. I shook it and it rattled softly. Who was sending us things?

I checked the fabric it came in, but there were no markings.

I dropped it on a table and didn't bother to pick it up when it rolled to the ground. Instead I turned back to the porthole.

The hawk dipped his head at me, then took flight again, winging back to my father's place of business—where the other managers still worked. Likely, this token was from them. I'd get a letter soon with an explanation.

As I thought on it, a voice came from behind me.

"Are you worried about Arabella?"

It was not a voice I knew.

Within a heartbeat, I'd whirled around and drawn my cutlass in one swift motion to hold it beneath a man's throat. He was an older gentleman, around my late father's age, with sun-tinted skin, a slender face, and pale-blue eyes. He didn't waver at my weapon.

The door was still shut, and I hadn't heard it open. Whoever he was, he must have been inside my cabin this whole time. The thought gave me chills.

"I don't host stowaways," I growled. "State your business or walk the plank."

His grin was lopsided. "My business is you. Tell me, are you worried about Arabella?"

"Your name, sir." I hissed the last word through my teeth so he knew my forced hospitality would only go so far.

"No." He spoke with an air of authority. "I want to hear your answer, first."

My blade pressed against his neck. "You come onto my ship and demand answers from me?"

"I do whatever I want."

His hand touched the hilt of his pistol. I tensed. He smiled, but the worst was the gleam in his eye, as if there was nothing I could do to stop him from doing anything.

He was a mad man. Or a dangerous one. Either way, I wouldn't let him put a bullet through me.

I drew back my cutlass and swung.

It passed through his body.

I blinked. He still stood, unharmed. Unmoved. He watched me with amusement.

"What magic is this?" Stilling the trembling of my hand, I moved the cutlass again, slower this time, and watched as it went through his figure as if he were a ghost. But that couldn't be. He was *here*. His image was so clear.

Some other creature then. But this was not a normal man.

"Now that I have your attention, I'd like to start again. Answer my question, and I will give my name." He dipped his head to look at me better, one silver hair dropping out of place over his forehead. "Are you afraid of Arabella?"

I was in too much wonder to come up with a false answer. "Of course," I replied. "Any man in his right mind would be."

From the glint in his eye, that was what he wanted to hear. "Your father would have answered differently." He leaned forward to utter words that rattled like dry branches in winter. "Your father was a fool. I want to make you a proposition."

I drew nearer and circled him. "How are you doing this? Are you here?" My hand swept through his image. It passed cleanly.

"Not in person, no." His own hand lifted, showing a device like the one I'd just received in the package. The color was different, as the sun didn't catch on this one, seeping through instead, but it was the same. My eyes flicked down to where I'd dropped mine. This man's image appeared directly over it, hovering a few inches up.

He set the object to the side, and it disappeared from my view. "I transport my image through this. That's how you see me."

"You're somewhere else," I mused. "But your image is here." This was astounding.

"Precisely. We call it a communication pod."

I knelt, running my fingers along the brassy edge of the communication pod, feeling the warm hum of it like a greeting. When I pushed it, the man's image shifted likewise, sliding into the edge of the table unproblematically.

He didn't even give the sharp corner jutting into his side a passing glance.

I have more silvers than I could need, and jewels so precious that men were still searching for where my father hid them. But this small device just became one of the most valuable things I owned.

To be able to transport your image elsewhere . . . the possibilities were endless. Communication would be changed. I could meet with business partners through this rather than relying on messenger hawks. I could captain one ship while on another. I could be all places at all times.

Gifts like this didn't come freely.

"What's your price?"

"Business relationship. With you, preferably."

I stood to my full height, conversations like this were best when eye level. For the first time, I took in his attire: Everything showed he spared no expense. From his pointy, leather shoes to his golden cuff links to the padded doublet and red peasant paltock lined with silver stitching—he had so much money he could line his clothes with it.

Merchants didn't dress so boldly.

"Who is *we*?"

A brow lifted.

"You said: 'we call it a communication pod.' Who is we?"

"My patrons."

I narrowed my eyes. "Who are the patrons?"

He tilted his head, and it was the first time he didn't have the answer right away. It was the briefest hesitation, but I caught it. He wet his lips before replying, "They prefer to remain anonymous."

Warning bells rang loudly in my head. "I'm out." I straightened a stack of papers on the desk before dropping them into a pile. The papers had absolutely nothing to do with the man—who still hadn't given me a name—but it mimicked an action I'd seen my father use many times when he wasn't signing a new deal, and it gave me a sense of power. "I don't go into business with men who aren't forthright."

"That's rich, coming from the son of Admiral Bones."

"You came to me because I'm different from my father." My glare was sharp. "Don't fool yourself into thinking words like that will wound me."

He hesitated again. "I'll give you a full list within a week.

I think you'll find the patrons irrelevant when you hear the business proposal."

"I've already said no."

He grated his jaw. "Every businessman wants to hear new proposals. If I go away now, you'll never know how that device works, nor what else I can offer, and that will drive you mad until you desperately seek me out. I guarantee you, my offer will be less generous the second time."

I did want to hear his proposal. And I knew that I'd hear it anyway, no matter what I said. What I wanted to know was how badly he wanted to be in business with me, and from how his body had tensed, I'd guess it was a lot.

He needed me for something. That meant I could get a lot out of him in exchange.

I pretended to mull over his words before settling into a chair, throwing my feet on the stack of papers on the desk, and leaning back. "What sort of business?"

There was a quiver there, right by his lips. Something that said he didn't favor coming to me in the first place—a boy a third of his age. But he pulled himself together, that devilish gleam back in his eye, and spoke. "I'm in technology. And what you see here is only a fraction of it. I've been growing my business silently for years under the patronage of nobility from Julinbor, the Southern Isles, Az Elo, and all the small islands in between, and now I'm ready to launch it into the world." From the way his lips twisted, I could tell this next part pleased him to say. "The world you see now will look very different in a year, and you can be at the front of it."

It was a fine pitch, with absolutely no details on what it was or how it would succeed.

"Is this your first business?" I asked.

"No. I was in oil first and manufacturing before that."

"And what made you leave?"

"I found a way to change the world." His answers were

fast. Rehearsed. I wondered how many patrons he'd secured by this point, without them asking for the specifics.

I threw my feet down and put my elbows on my knees. "That's some big talk. The world is a vast place."

He spread out his arms. "I'm doing it already. And you," he pointed to me, "are already hooked. You were ready to say yes the moment my image appeared over the communication pod."

"I was ready to kill you," I corrected. Yet, one minute later, *yes*, he'd hooked me. But there was one important part he was leaving out. "If you're so confident, you shouldn't need me. I'm no engineer; I'm a sailor."

"Your inherited merchant routes are unrivaled. With your routes and vessels, my technology can move twice as fast as it otherwise could."

"So I'm to be a patron?"

"No." The power in his tone surged forth. "You are no puppet, patron, or tool. You are far more valuable to me. If you join me, you are to be my right-hand man, and when people hear of this new technology, they will think of you."

The words latched onto me, luring me in with promises of power that my father could only dream of.

The offer was looking more and more tempting.

"You never gave me a name."

"Jackson."

I'd never heard of it. But his name didn't matter, and he knew that. He didn't need a legacy to stand on, like I did, when he had this technology. The world would want it, and they'd pay a high price for it.

He was right; the world was about to change.

But I would not be a part of it. "My answer is still no."

His face fell. "I'm offering you twenty percent on all profits."

"No."

He was looking at me like he didn't understand, though the word was quite simple. "You know the technology is excellent, and you'd still pass by the opportunity? What sort of business are you running?"

"I'll buy the product," I admitted. "Because I trust the product is good. But I don't trust you, and I don't tie myself in business to men I cannot trust."

Emotions passed his face. Surprise melted into understanding, then exhaustion. He sat down, and the image of a chair appeared beneath him. His voice changed, altering from its sales pitch tone. "I have no sons, Ontario. No one who shares my love of technology or business. No one to pass this on to. I'm looking for more than a partner, I'm looking for a son, and something tells me you've been looking for family too." Jackson sighed. "Tell me what you need from me to earn my trust."

I told myself that I didn't need family. The word had gone bitter on my tongue over the years. But when he spoke it, a hollowness in me wanted to absorb it.

But at this point in my career, I could not afford to fail, and *I didn't trust him.*

"I'm sorry. I'm not the man you want."

At that moment, his head turned. "Come in."

I automatically checked my own door, before realizing he meant someone on his end. A hand came into view on his shoulder, followed by the appearance of a young woman. "Your next meeting is about to start."

He nodded, but made no move to stand. She didn't leave, but instead faced me. I was struck by how beautiful she was. Warm tones, dark hair, thick lashes, and brilliant blue eyes that gave away her relation to Jackson. I guessed it before he said it.

"Ontario, meet my daughter, Zara. She helps with the business, though she has no desire to take over after me."

"Business is no fun," Zara said with a daring look in her eye.

"It seems Ontario agrees with you," Jackson told her. "He said no."

Her brow raised, and she looked at me with new interest. "Pity," she said. Her fingers went to her collarbone to twist an emerald necklace across the band. At the color, I remembered the prophecy.

Under emerald stars, the prodigal child will rise.

And under that child, comes the greatest power ever known to the seas.

My mind jolted. Here was a man, offering that to me. If this was the power that was foretold, it was knocking at my door. If the prophecy was to be trusted, then . . .

Suddenly, I knew. Satisfaction flooded my chest. I was the child it spoke of.

Zara's eyes locked onto mine. "My father is a good man. Not many pass up the chance to work with him."

I quickly lifted a hand. "I've changed my mind. I'd be honored to partner with you."

13

ARN

Hnoll.

Day after day, as cold wind bit the air or snow fell over the deck, whether sunup or lanterns lit—we fought. We trained. We grew.

One evening, hours after the sun went down, when the oil lamps wavered in their glass cages and their light crawled lazily across the deck to the rails of the helm, Jakob came up the steps. The jagged light made his features sharper than usual and set his grimace deeper into his cheeks. He carried two plates, both overflowing.

"You know what that means," Landon groaned. He'd taken the first shift for the night, so I was settling in with my thick cloak draped over my shoulders to find some rest.

"Nothing but trouble." I eyed the food warily, but Jakob set it down without sign of an envelope.

"No assignment. You both need protein to keep up with our training," he said. "You've been slacking."

I pressed my lips into a thin line. We fought for most of the day every day. It was a wonder that our weary limbs still supported us.

Jakob surveyed the seas. "Are we en route?"

"Yes," I lied. "The navigator was just here to confirm."

Another lie. We were going to Julinbor, and no assignment or mandate of any other kind would deter us.

Landon reached for his plate. "You know, no matter how much food you give us, we'll never be as big as your men." He bit off a piece of dried meat. "We will always look small to you."

Jakob stayed a few feet back as usual and looked at Landon with an unreadable expression. His eyes slid to me. "I know. But this will help you fight."

He reached into his cloak to draw out a metal hook that glistened in the night.

Landon and I flew back.

Jakob startled, then he laughed. Landon and I gripped the taffrails, wary of his hold on a hook that could slice through our skin with ease. Jakob's chuckle turned into a roaring laugh.

The sound would have been nice, if it weren't over the glint of that steel. With the hook in hand, he looked menacing. "Fools. This is not to hurt you."

I eyed him suspiciously. "What's it for?"

"You." He flipped it in the air to catch it by the hook and hold it out to me, showing the back with a black casing and a cupped end. "To cover that gnarly thing."

My gaze dropped to my hand, or rather, where my hand should have been, had Landon not cut it off months ago. I usually kept a scarf tied around it, but hadn't yet learned how to leverage it in a fight. More often than not, it held me back, as I would forget and try to use my hand only to find it missing.

Landon had stepped away. Maybe it was disinterest, but I could swear there was something else. Perhaps a tinge of regret for what he'd done.

He wasn't alone. I'd hurt him in that battle, too, in emotional ways that I couldn't know the depths of.

I tentatively took the hook from Jakob.

The cup fit up my forearm with laces to strap it in place, and the hook stuck out well past where my hand would be.

The hook unscrewed, which was good, or else I'd likely slash myself in my sleep. But when in battle, this would be quite the weapon.

Jakob gave a short nod. "Now you look like a fighter." Then his eyes pierced mine. "Use that on my men, and I'll butcher you." He went back down the stairs.

When he was gone, Landon put his back against the wheel and gave a low whistle. "He's right. You look like a proper pirate."

I chuckled. "The tattoos and missing hand didn't give that away?"

"It's not the same. You look like a warrior now, and it's not just the hook. Whatever they've been feeding us here has grown you into a man, complete with facial hair, which I'm sure you've noticed."

I had. My beard had taken its time to come in, but now the roots of it were here, and I was so happy to have one that I might never shave it. The food wasn't as plentiful as I'd have liked, but I'd also never worked this hard, and that inflated my appetite.

"Stroke your beard with your hook and tell me you don't feel like a vicious pirate," Landon challenged.

I did, and he was right.

"Now tell me you haven't already pictured taking down Jakob with that thing." He made the motion of slashing his arm, then put his hands on his hips. "Well, I feel a lot less guilty about injuring you now that you've got that."

"You shouldn't," I said dryly. "And have I plotted Jakob's demise seconds after he gave me this and walked away? No."

"I'd have thought of seven ways by now."

He would have. And a week ago, I would have too. Now that he'd mentioned it, it was impossible not to picture usurping Jakob and captaining this ship without him for the crew to look to.

But after hearing about his son—call it Emme's influence over me—I felt something.

I never was a true cold-hearted pirate. I really had no chance.

"I don't mind putting up with Jakob for a while."

Landon turned back to the wheel. "I do," he grouched. I hadn't told Landon about Jakob's son, and most likely, I never would. With this gift from Jakob, I hoped his ire against us was fading.

I inspected the steel of the hook. Landon said I looked like a warrior, but I looked like more than a warrior. I looked like a killer. Like the assassin for King Isaac that I was.

For months I'd been worried that I was too far changed for Emme to recognize me if I ever saw her again. Now I was.

I unscrewed it and dropped the weight into my pocket, almost wishing Jakob had given us a letter instead, though both meant the same. We were his king's fighters, and we did what he asked us to do.

14

EMME

My knock rattled against the door to the captain's cabin as I went over the words in my head. A beat later, Ontario swung the door open. His hair fell over his eyes, the edges still shaved but the top hanging loose and untamed. He wore a long-sleeve linen shirt, and it looked like a second beneath that one. It might have kept his body warm, but the chilly night still left its marks on his cheeks with hints of pink crawling up his skin.

"You're awake?" he said with surprise.

"I'm on the night shift."

"In that case," he opened the door wider, "care for a drink? I've got coffee." He held up a mug as I stepped into the room.

The cabin was messier than I'd ever seen it, scattered papers on the desk, jackets hanging from chairs, and wax spilled in various locations along the wooden floor. The bed wasn't made, maps stuck out from cabinets, and shoes were thrown in a heap in the corner.

Arn would hate this.

Ontario handed me a mug, keeping his eyes on mine like he was trying to see into my thoughts. Ironic, because I was here to get his. "You still think of him?" he asked.

So, he *could* see into my thoughts.

I shrugged. "Not if I can help it." I took a sip of coffee, then gagged. "Ontario, this tastes alarmingly like medicinal syrup."

He laughed and took a long drink of his to show me up. "We didn't all have mothers who stole southern coffee for us to drink."

I couldn't combat that. Mother had indeed stolen coffee, and it had been glorious.

He spoke softly, as if debating the words even as they came out. "You say you don't think about him. Is that true? Have you really put Arn behind you?"

"I don't know about that; it's more that I'm just living onward." I shook my head. "That sounded better in my mind. I don't know how to explain it." I set the drink down and wrapped my arms around me. It was warmer in this room, thanks to the ludicrous number of candles he'd lit that made it difficult to believe it was the middle of the night and not day. They gave off the acrid odor of tallow.

"No. It makes sense." Ontario was quick to assure. He motioned for me to take a seat, then took a chair himself. "What do you see next for you? Will you stay, or are you leaving with Raven?" He moved aside some papers from the desk to set down his horrid coffee, and it was impossible not to see Arn there, brushing papers into piles and putting everything in its place, obsessing over his maps and the routes. Later obsessing over me.

I dropped my gaze to the floorboards where there were no memories to haunt me. "I think it's best if I join Raven. There's too much here."

Ontario's cup scraped against the table as he drew it close. "You'll teach her kids?" There was a hint of mediocracy to his tone that I didn't care for, making me look up.

"It's an honest life."

"But you could do more." It was almost a protest. He leaned forward to hold the metallic mug in hands. "Emme, you are the daughter of Arabella the Ruthless. Rumors are already spreading that you killed the king. You are feared by some and loved by others. Do you realize what career you've set up for yourself on the seas? People would line up to join your crew for less pay than others, and merchants could raise their fees if their merchandise traveled on your ship. You can take control of the seas if you desire."

My heart stirred at the words, the same way it had stirred many times over the past several months. But the sensation was usually clouded by confusion, and this time it was only a dull desire. I knew what I wanted now, and I wanted to be a part of the good Raven was doing: rescuing children and giving them a home.

"I don't want to control the seas," I told Ontario. "Just to sail them. I never wanted the pirate life, and that's not going to change."

He shook his head as he took another drink.

I studied him. It wasn't the first time he'd made a remark about using my position as the daughter of Arabella to further myself. To him, I was wasting it. But if I followed even one inch in her footsteps, it would lead me to ruin.

From the look in Ontario's eye, he'd take ruin.

I set down my cup, "You'd do differently if you were me, and I know that. You'd go after the power that comes with being an offspring of a powerful parent, but chasing that won't lead anywhere good."

He grinned devilishly, tipping his mug at me. "You don't know that for sure."

"I do know. I watched it in my mother. Power is the quickest way to corrupt a human."

It may have corrupted him already.

I steeled myself with every ounce of courage I could gather. "Ontario, what deal did you make with my mother?"

The silence that followed was endless. His body went rigid, fingers frozen on the mug.

He didn't bother denying it. That much was good, for I held no proof other than the word of Emric and Raven. But despite that, I held onto a slight hope that everything was easily cleared up and that I could still trust my captain.

His first movement was to bring a hand up to stroke his beard. Then he spoke slowly. "You saw us on the beach?"

I nodded.

He gave a slight nod back. Strain built up in the room until it crowded into every nook.

I'd had enough of lies this year, and if Ontario had turned to Mother, I couldn't stay here. "Were the gems we planted real?"

"The point of those were to be fake."

"Don't do that," I said sharply. "You know what I meant."

After a moment, his posture drooped a little. "I apologize." There was a sincerity in his tone, and it sucked some of the tension from around us. "Yes, the tracking was real. I don't know how she found out they were there. And yes, I did meet with Arabella, but I'm not working with her. I'm trying to keep her away from us."

"At what cost?"

Ontario was handsome, but that wouldn't tempt Mother, although the age of a man didn't matter to her. He was rich—richer than any of us knew—and that was possibly what she was after, but I feared it was something more. When he looked at me, I knew. She didn't want him.

"She wants me."

"And Emric. Alive, if that's any consolation."

My next breath was shaky, rattling in a chest that was already too tight. "It is not. Did she say what for?"

"To sail with her."

My brows scrunched. "Why does she think *you* can get her that?"

He cleared his throat. "She wanted me to break you down until you wanted to leave, then I was to capture you, and she'd rescue you."

"My mother," I said the words slowly, but was hardly surprised, "wanted you to break us down and imprison us, so she could fake deliver us?"

"Would now be a good time to offer apologies for who your mother is?"

I looked him square in the face. "It would be a good time to tell me when you planned to break me."

"I didn't." He stood and crossed the room, daringly close to me. I held my hand out to keep him at a distance. His voice lowered. "Emme, I promise. Look, it's been a week, and I haven't done a thing."

"That's not enough time to convince me. You should have told me."

"I was trying to deal with it."

"You deal with it by telling me. Right away."

The tension was back again, and this time, it clouded my throat.

"Ontario, I have had a lifetime of lies. From my mother, from Arn, and some from you. I've lost almost everyone I love, and I almost lost myself. Trust me when I say, I am beyond allowing people to lie to me now. Do not do it again."

He dipped his head. "You have my word."

"I should have more than your word, I should take your cabin." I went to the porthole, feeling a little pleased that his eyes flared in worry. "But we both know I'm not going to do that."

I looked out. Frost webbed along the glass, and gray clouds gathered overhead. Everything about my mother was twisted. I thought she wanted me dead, but instead she wanted to manipulate situations to get me and Emric by her side again, in her warped version of caring. But her desire for me and Emric was rooted in vanity.

Her logic was flawed. No matter what happened to us, we never would want to sail with her again. Ontario could have broken us a million ways, but she'd broken us worse of all.

"Do I have your trust?" Ontario asked. He tried again when I gave no answer. "Emme?"

"I am your second. You have my loyalty. But it's as shaky as sand right now."

He stepped beside me to gaze outside. "Thank you." He hesitated. "Now that you know, I can let you in on my next plan."

I shifted to him. "You have too many of those for your own good."

He flashed a smile. "This one is foolproof to catch your mother. One month, and she's gone for good."

"You have my attention."

15

ONTARIO

I locked the door when Emme left. The sky was already brightening, and my eyelids were heavy after we'd stayed up all night going over details. I ought to have shared the plan with Emme sooner, for she had many excellent ideas to improve it. In the end, we both agreed we had something that would work.

It was ironic, because it was almost the same plan Arabella had.

Arabella believed if she was trapped again, Emme would rescue her. From there, she believed she could convince her daughter to join her crew.

"She won't." I warned Arabella.

Arabella's tone was confident. "I'll give her reason to."

Knowing this, our plan came easier. She'd play naive as we entrapped her mother, but instead of Arabella swaying Emme, we'd bring her straight to the queen.

"Why does she think I'd join her?" Emme asked.

"I don't know. But it doesn't matter. She'll be walking into the cell and locking it herself."

"Then why are we still chasing her?"

"Emric would never speak with her on his own accord. If she

walked aboard, he'd turn away. But if we chase her, and if she's captured, and if you ask Emric to help free her . . ."

"He would do it for me,"

"She'd get you both."

My coffee mug was dry, and my body ached, but there was a final step to assure this plan went smoothly, and that was to communicate with the queen. To get her to listen, I had one piece of leverage that I needed Emme to not see. Now alone, I penned the letter. The offer was clear.

> *Your Majesty,*
>
> *You do not know me, but I am the son of Admiral Bones, heir to his legacy. I've already met with all his advisors and have their trust, should I ever need to call upon them. I know many of your merchants use my routes as well, and for a good price. I thank you for your business and hope to keep working with you.*
>
> *I am also the captain of the* Royal Rose.
>
> *And I happen to know you killed your husband.*
>
> *That knowledge could topple you from your throne, and I have the power to do it. But I don't want that. In fact, I want what you want. To see Arabella the Ruthless gone.*
>
> *I propose a deal: I will deliver her to you, alive, for you to do with as you wish. You show the kingdom that you brought down the fearsome pirate, you call the end to the war. You are now a hero among your people, and the seas are safe for me and my crew again.*
>
> *Refuse me, and I will turn the Bones Legacy against you.*
>
> *I hope we can come to an understanding,*
> *Captain Ontario*

I folded the letter and marked it with my seal.

Before I could do more, the communication pod beeped.

I straightened my jacket and turned the device on. Jackson's form came into view, his face lit like sunlight hit it, suggesting he lived further east than me. Julinbor, maybe?

"Ontario, you look well. Have things been good?"

"They've been fine. You?"

"Good, good. Listen, I'm continuing to hear stories of Arabella, and each is more concerning that the last. I've asked once but I want to be certain: should I be worried about her?"

I stilled. Arabella was causing a string of problems for me, and I couldn't eliminate the threat fast enough. I glanced to the letter I was about to send. "I'm taking care of it."

"And her children? They sail as well, do they not? If the mother is gone, two more will simply rise in her place."

Unsure how much he knew, I said, "I'm taking care of them as well."

He was looking at me but clearly lost in thought. "Maybe I should reach out to them also," he mused. "Expand my empire over the seas."

My blood chilled.

If his offer was extended to Emme and Emric, either could easily become the child of the prophecy. They'd no doubt discover I was the son of Admiral Bones from someone in Jackson's network. More than that, as Arabella's children, they had an influence over others simply through the correlation. They would fall into power without wanting it—without reaching for it—and leave me with only scraps at best.

"I don't think that's wise," I said as evenly as I could manage. "I've not found them to be ambitious in the way a business partner ought to be."

Jackson raised a brow. "Not ambitious, or not power-hungry? For I have found there is a difference, and one is more preferable."

I thought about it. Emric had more ambition to him, but I wasn't going to let him know that. "I firmly doubt either would handle a business partnership," I said. "They don't have it in them."

"That what do you suggest we do with them?"

"Frankly, nothing. We get Arabella off the seas, and the Ruthless name will fade away."

He swirled a cup of whisky. "I find it hard to believe that Arabella bred anything other than savages."

"These two are anything but savage." My confidence in those words wasn't faked. "They will not affect this company one way or the other."

Despite my words, and despite how many times I had to say them, he still set down his cup and looked me in the eye. "Are you certain?"

The words prickled me. It was the same feeling that I'd felt in the presence of my father as I constantly strove to gain his approval while he questioned every move I made. In the end, I always felt worthless. No one would make me feel like that again.

At that moment, Zara stepped into view, inspecting me with the same look as her father—trying to figure out what I was made of.

"I know what I'm doing," I told them both.

If he was anything like my father, Jackson would demand to know how. He'd want to know my plan and then my backup plan in case things went wrong because *they always do with you.* But Jackson only nodded. "Okay. I trust that you will."

He folded his sleeves and pinned on a cuff link. "If you'll excuse me, I have a meeting to attend to."

He disappeared from my view, and I was left with Zara.

She didn't turn off the communication pod. Instead, her eyes trailed what I assumed to be her father as he left, then she faced me. "Thank you for joining with us."

"Of course. Your father has good technology."

Her lips twitched. "The design for the communication pod was mine, actually."

I was floored. "You created this?"

"I did." She was more relaxed now that her father had left, and her smile less rigid. She leaned back in his chair to untie the twine around her braid and slowly unravel it.

She was so much more than I thought her to be. "In that case, thank *you* for working with us."

Zara laughed, then her eyes darted in the direction her father has gone. "You know, my father doesn't always express what he is thinking, but he's quite glad to have found you. I've seen him excited about business partners before, but it's different this time."

Her hair was down now, and she stood. "I'm grateful as well," Zara said. Then she stepped out of sight.

I sighed when she left. There was a flicker here, the sparks of something that I didn't want to lose. This wasn't anything like I foolishly once thought I felt about Emme. And it was unbelievably nice to have something not tainted by the past few months at sea, and someone who looked at me the way she did—like I was someone who could mean something. I'd wanted many things, but right now I found I wanted to be worthy of meaning something to her.

If this partnership with Jackson went well, and if this relationship with Zara went even better, I could be set up for a great life.

Security hadn't been available to me before. My father had offered me a future I didn't want. Instead, I'd turned to piracy, only to quickly became a slave. That was where I'd met Arn and again got cast in the shadows as the light of honor shone on someone else. I'd been the son of a rich man, the slave of a pirate, the First of a captain. But if I played my cards right, I wouldn't be second to anyone. I'd be a revered and respected man of business with connections all over the world.

Emme was wrong. Power wasn't the quickest way to corrupt a man. It was the surest way to establish one.

At the thought of Emme, my mood darkened.

She and Emric could take this away. With the influence they had as Arabella's descendants, they could turn other captains against me and control the seas themselves, even weakening my trading routes.

They had to be taken care of. Sentiment had no use here.

The perfect way to guarantee that I became the prodigal child from the prophecy was to kill the other three possibilities.

And it was the only way to guarantee I didn't lose this future.

Within an hour, at my summoning, Tess was in my cabin. She wore a capped-sleeve tunic with bare arms as if proving her seaworthiness by not wearing a coat. She'd chopped bangs for herself recently, and she looked through them at me. But the childish freckles adorning her nose still reminded me of her age.

"Clarice said you asked for me."

I pushed aside my breakfast plate and stood. "I did. I have a job for you."

Tess had been useful before. She'd spied on Arn and Landon for me, and all for a low price—even when she was working for Arn and Landon both. Then when I went behind her back to hand Landon and Arn over to the king of Az Elo, she'd been quick to readjust any loyalties to Landon and pledge her loyalty to me. She had a grit about her that I admired, and I could count on her silence.

But she hesitated in the doorway now. Before, she would have done whatever I'd asked merely because I was captain and she wanted to fit in on deck so desperately. But I sensed now, after all she'd been through, she'd need a little extra motivation. The girl Tess used to be was changing.

I fished into my pockets. "I'll give you ten silvers."

I had her. Hungry eyes traced the movement of my pouch. "Twenty," she countered.

My hand wavered. I almost felt guilt. Tess was maybe fourteen, and she used to be so lively. After only a few months she'd hardened. But it was not my job to preserve her youth. Tess chose her path, same as us all, and if she stayed close to me, she could share in the power I acquired.

No use beating around it. "I need you to kill someone for me."

A normal young girl would shrivel away at that, or run. At the very least, I expected her to bat an eye. Stars, even I would bat an eye. But Tess wandered into the room, pretending to be very interested in the wick of a candle.

"For that, I charge fifty."

Charge. As if she was a hired mercenary who'd done this before.

"Does that largess cover the fee for your silence as well?"

"You already have that." When she looked at me, I saw all the secrets between us she'd kept quiet about when we worked together to betray Landon and Arn and send them off to Az Elo. I could trust her about this.

"Fifty silvers." I stuck out my hand. She wouldn't know I'd been prepared to pay two hundred. "Deal."

16

ARN

Training the next morning was different. I didn't hold my hook up for people to see, stroking it with my finger and exaggerating the sharp tip—but they saw it anyway and a shadow would cross their eyes. They weren't lining up to fight me first. Even Koa held himself at bay, sitting atop a barrel and sharpening his knife while giving my hook a wary glance.

I could get used to this.

"I'd let you cut off my hand, too, if people looked this fearful every time I appeared," Landon said aside to me.

"Careful," I warned. "I might do it."

Jakob was the first to ruin the morning when he twisted a wad of hard wax over the tip of the hook. "Can't have you taking out someone's eye."

"Ahh, then where's the fun?" I quipped. His hard gaze met mine to remind me that fun was not had around him, and I dropped my smile. "That sounds fair."

"Glad we agree." His voice then lifted so the others could hear, but it was different today. Harder. "We are going over defense positions today in the event we should ever get attacked. Not one pirate steps foot on these decks, you hear me?"

"What about the two we already got?" Koa smirked. A few around him chuckled as he kept sharpening his blade well beyond necessity, looking at me the entire time so I knew exactly what he intended that blade for.

"These two won't be on deck for long," Jakob muttered under his breath.

The temperature plummeted. Maybe that was just me. But beside me, Landon blanched, and I knew he felt the chill too.

Jakob raised his voice again. "You're right, there are two pirates on deck." He stroked the dull edge of his blade against his beard, then swung it to point at Koa.

"New training. Pick four men. The five of you will defend the ship against these two. Arn and Landon, you are playing the part of enemies who have snuck aboard the ship. Your job is to reach the helm before Koa and his four take you down."

Koa hopped off the barrel. "With pleasure."

"You two start at the bow," Jakob ordered. "Koa at the helm. Everyone else to the sides."

"We can take five men," Landon said to me as we took our places and held our training cutlasses.

"When we do, he will just order ten more to stand next time."

Jakob *was* different today than he was last night. When he'd given me the hook, I'd thought his distaste for us was simmering. Overnight, it seemed to have boiled over. A harsh winter wind blew by, but I doubted he felt it as he crossed his arms to watch.

"Begin," he barked, and five men were advancing upon us.

Landon and I both had the same idea: the further we got before they reached us, the less time we needed to breach the helm. We didn't need to defeat them, only to touch the wheel.

The *Commander* was twice as large as the *Royal Rose*, which gave far more room to run between lines and masts, but the layout was similar. We could either go up the stairs or swing from a line and drop to the helm. Koa stood at the stairs, waiting for us to approach, so I'd have to go the other way but—

No, I could. I could climb now.

I gave the hook a glance. *Let's hope the straps hold.*

As Landon went forward, I grabbed the pegs of a mast with one hand, secured my hook over another, and climbed. I felt the strap tighten around my forearm, but the hook held steady.

Two men climbing after me spurred my movement.

If I'd had one more moment to plan my attack, I'd have chosen a better suited mast to climb, but as it was, I'd need to risk a lofty jump to grab a line that could swing me to the helm. I sucked in a breath of courage as I climbed higher, keeping out of reach from the two who followed. Their bigger size didn't allow them to scale quickly, and while I wasn't as limber as Tess, I could climb faster than these two. With a few days to practice with the hook, I'd be even faster.

Below, Landon was halfway to Koa. The opponent's focus remained there, so I'd have a clean shot to the helm.

My moment of triumph was short-lived. From the ground, one of the men threw a polearm like a spear and the blunt end hit my side. My hook slipped, and I almost fell.

I cursed. He might have broken a bone.

I flung my hook back around the peg and stepped up again, only to have someone grab my ankle. Once caught, they threw me down.

I couldn't keep my grip this time, and I fell the distance back to the deck with a sickening crack.

The two men jumped down to look over me as I fought to find air.

The moment I did, one of them showed his teeth.

"Better?" he asked. And before I could mistake it for kindness, he drove the hilt of his blade into my gut.

"That would have been my sword," he announced to Jakob. "This one is down."

I was very down. I didn't want anything more than to stay down for a long time. I only managed to look up when another sickening crack came, and saw Landon against the stairs, his head at an abnormal angle.

"This one is down," Koa declared.

The deck cheered.

We slowly dragged ourselves to our knees, each groaning with our own pain. But I quieted when Jakob jutted his chin toward the bow. "Again."

I looked at him in disbelief. "Again? With other trainers?"

Jakob frowned. "You. Again."

Now I was thinking about all the ways I could kill him with my hook.

Landon and I regrouped at the bow, pretending we could stand. "We should have fought together," he said.

"I think my ribs are bruised."

"That's because you didn't fight with me."

I glared.

"Don't look at me like that; I made it all the way to the stairs. If you'd been there—"

"I had three on me," I pointed out.

"Go," Jakob shouted.

Landon took off, noticeably slower. "Together," he threw back over his shoulder.

So we fought together. Poorly, but at least when we went down, it was at the same time. We weren't anywhere near the stairs.

"I'm going to try the mast thing again." I grunted, holding my waist as I rolled over.

Landon was breathing heavily, a red lump forming over his brow. He wiped his mouth. "Maybe Jakob's had his fun."

But Jakob hadn't. "Again," he said.

I didn't try the mast. I didn't have time to reach it. But Landon and I did take down two men before the other three brought us to our knees. Koa was done waiting at the stairs for us when we weren't close to reaching them.

Jakob flicked a finger at the ones we'd defeated. "Two others take their place. Run it again."

I held my hand to my stomach, using every ounce of willpower to find any strength. My insides were bruised, my head roaring, and every movement burned. "Jakob, others need to stand in for us."

"No. You will do it again."

This was ridiculous. "If you want this to be an effective drill, you need to run it with men who aren't worn out."

"Az Eloians do not get worn out." I raised an eyebrow and gestured to the two he'd just swapped out, but his gaze only hardened. "You will run it again."

I didn't know what this was about, but it wasn't about making the drill effective. His hatred for us burned, and I doubted even a letter from his king would be enough to make him play nice.

Perhaps this was why he'd given me the hook. Not to give me any power or advantage, but to prove that even with this, I could never be strong enough against someone like him.

"Go." Jakob barked, then the drill began again.

The two who'd stepped in were eager to fight but less skilled than the others, so we got past them easily. Koa came at us next, driving his blunt cutlass against my own with a strength that almost ripped it away. I planted my feet into the deck and pushed back.

When he relented, I kept the momentum to slice the cutlass at him. He jumped back.

"What's wrong?" he taunted between breaths. "Don't want to use your pretty new hook?"

"I know when I don't need to," I said.

And I wouldn't have. I could have bested him. But it wasn't a fair fight, and while my attention was on Koa, one of the other four used the hilt of their cutlass to crash it into my temple, and I crumpled.

Landon went down next.

"Get up." Jakob was merciless. "Run it through again."

From behind Jakob, looking out the window inside the cabin, the navigator watched. His lips were drawn in thin lines, his eyes downcast, like he pitied us. No, not us. He pitied Jakob.

When he caught me looking, he shook his head and turned away.

He knew why Jakob's mood soured. And that could mean one of two things, but I guessed which one it was.

"I'd rather jump in the sea than get beat up again." Landon panted as he brushed his fingers along the busted curve of his lip.

"Jakob would fish us out and make us fight again."

Landon dragged his feet to reset at the prow, and I savored the moment of rest. When he reached my side, he pretended to stretch his back. "What did you do to him?"

I tried to look busy prepping myself as well to buy us more time. "It's something we both did."

Jakob's voice split the chilly air. "Again!"

I sensed this wouldn't end until we got to the helm. Maybe not even then. But this time, I dragged every bit of remaining strength from inside to attack each man who came at me. I didn't focus on the helm, but rather on each strike and each step.

And this time, I used my hook.

The first man reached me, and our cutlasses met in the air. As they carved downward, I brought my other arm up to whack the curve of my hook against his head.

He fell unconscious.

The next man hesitated in his step, and Landon took the opportunity to attack.

Another man taken down, and another. Only Koa stood in our way.

"Last one," I said grimly. Koa should be tired by now, too, and the odds of two against one were better than we'd had so far.

But he wasn't as tired as we were. He'd kept to the back during each fight while we'd taken hit after hit, and his first swing tore the cutlass away from Landon. Landon should have put up his hands in defeat, but he didn't. Instead he charged Koa. Their bodies slammed against each other, rolling to the ground.

I couldn't put my cutlass between them. I dropped it and swung my fist. It connected with Koa's cheek, but the large man hardly grimaced before driving his elbow against Landon's chest to shove him away, kicking at me, then raising the hilt of his blade.

I was glad it was the hilt. I was equally glad that he chose to swing it against Landon and not me.

Koa crashed the hilt against the top of Landon's head, and he melted to the ground.

I took the advantage to slip past Koa unchallenged and reached the helm.

"It's done," I shouted. "I've done it."

Jakob whistled for five new men. "Again."

The other crew shifted amongst themselves. Usually they were eager to fight, especially us, but now they lingered at the sides looking between Jakob and us.

Landon struggled to pull himself to his feet. A trickle of blood ran down his head. His eyes were pits of fire that bore into Jakob. "What are you doing? What are you trying to prove? We've done nothing but obey your king."

"I said, again!" Jakob roared.

Landon steadied himself with a hand on the main mast. "No. Tell us why."

I tried to grab his jacket to pull him back when Jakob spoke through his teeth, "The battle of Witherstons."

"Witherstons?" Landon lowered his voice and glanced to me. "Does he know we weren't in the navy long?"

I managed to take hold of his sleeve and yank him after me to hiss under my breath. "He's not talking about our time serving King Unid. He's talking about our first battle as pirates when we sunk a ship that his son was on."

"Jakob's son? At Witherstons?" His eyes went wide. "We killed him?"

I nodded.

Landon paused, then swung his head to look at Jakob. He stood still, but his eyes gave away the pit of sorrow within him, a deep well that nothing could fill.

"How did he know we were on the pirate ship?" Landon hissed.

"I spoke with the navigator and must have given it away."

I couldn't guess what was going through Landon's mind, but he pulled himself together for another fight. Landon and I couldn't know about losing a child, but he'd just lost his father, and while he didn't show it, I knew it hurt.

We understood Jakob's anger now. His pain somehow made him more human.

"Again." His voice cracked. Men rushed at us.

I didn't try to run this time. I braced myself on the prow and held my cutlass up.

But Landon threw himself across the deck faster than I thought him able to move right now and hauled himself partway up the mast. There, he hooked himself on and leaned out to shout at Jakob.

"The battle of Witherstons began before the sun was up," he shouted. "When the mist was heavy on the sea and all else was calm. Our captain's horn cut through the silence to warn us of an incoming ship, and the battle was unavoidable. We had to fight. We had to *hnoll*."

Jakob flinched, then froze. I couldn't read his expression, but the angle of his head hinted that he was listening to Landon.

Soaking in every word. He was getting the tale that he'd likely wondered about for days on end, and one that most men would never get.

Landon couldn't bring back his son, but he could take away the questions.

The entire deck quieted as Landon continued to shout. "The Az Eloians came swiftly upon us without the slightest trace of fear. Their first cannon tore through our mast, but ours hit their hull."

"Our captain didn't like to take prisoners or leave anyone alive, so every hit was meant to bring the ship down. Our next cannon struck closer to the prow, and water filled the hole. The men fought anyway by using grappling hooks to hold us and climb aboard. We had to fight."

As he spoke, my mind filled in the details I'd long forgotten.

"Those men fought honorably, every single one. But our crew was more numerous, and because of our size and location, they likely mistook us for a merchant's trading ship rather than pirates. It was too late to pull away when their ship began to sink. Captain Nathaniel sent fire arrows to your ship to burn it down, trapping the remaining men with us. Your men didn't show any fear as they fought, even after each man fell. They went to death with dignity, every single one of them."

Landon's voice was getting hoarse. "Your son fought like a true warrior. After his death, we loaded the bodies onto their row ships and let them burn. It took us six months to recoup enough to have a full crew after that, and the crew never stopped talking about the bravery those men showed that day."

My eyes went to Jakob.

He brushed a hand over his eyes. "We are done for today." He barely got the words out.

"They killed your son," Koa said, standing in his way. "We should get our justice."

"I said we are done." He growled, pushing past him. "Leave me be." He marched into the cabin and slammed the door.

Koa stayed put, adjusting his grip on the hilt and watching to see what we'd do. If we fought now, he'd for sure kill us. I dropped my weapon. After a long moment, he scowled and went belowdecks.

The crew drifted apart, and Landon dropped down to his knees, exhausted, and closed his eyes.

I rested my head against the mast and breathed out. I'd be feeling the pain from today's wounds for a while. "That was a worthy thing you did there."

Landon opened an eye to look at me. "Don't go spreading that around."

"If we ever see our crew again, I'll be sure to tell them how dreadful you still are."

"Appreciated."

He was still so long that I thought he'd fallen asleep right there in the middle of the deck. Then he mumbled, "It's all from you, you know. Anything good in me. It's all from you."

This was turning out to be a surprising day. I knew he didn't expect—or want—a reply.

In part, he was the reason why I'd turned out halfway decent—because I didn't want to be like him. But those feelings were long gone; the resentment, anger, and betrayal all drowned one by one as trust had built back up on a sturdier foundation than shifting sands. Now, he'd become somewhat like a brother to me again, and it felt like he was the only family I had right now. There was a time I never would have imagined it, but I was grateful for Landon's presence.

I thought of Jakob. Maybe the beating my body had taken had a greater purpose.

17

ONTARIO

These days it seemed we were waking to dock at another port just as often as we were waking to enjoy a morning on the open sea. All the more reason to get rid of Arabella and this whole mess, so I could savor my time on the water.

Today would not be that day.

"Remind me why we are here?" Clarice stood at my side, overlooking the city as we came upon it.

"Supplies," I said. It was honest enough, as we did need supplies. But if Clarice, loyal Clarice, was asking, it meant others were wondering too. It was an unnecessary stop and close to a county that would like to see us hang. The entire crew had lined up to load their pistols and fill their pouches with gunpowder this morning, and the sound of scaling fish was often broken up by the *zing* of sharpening cutlasses.

They wanted a better answer.

I'd give it to Clarice to pass along. "I've good reason to believe Arabella came this way," I said. "I want to search the city."

It wasn't a full answer, either, but she accepted it.

I could say I still traced half the gems, but after last time, I didn't want to be humiliated when Arabella was not at the other end of them.

We docked along a long string of other ships and, one by one, crossed the gangplank.

Emme walked beside me, where I suspected she'd stay for the day. "Have you been here before?" She wore her hair loose, save for a thin braid on each side of her face. Leather bracers adorned her wrists, and a golden-colored cloak lined with sheepskin kept her warm.

I handed the parchment with needed supplies to Bishop and sent him on his way. "Once," I replied, looking over the town. It was one of the largest I'd been to, almost as big as the capital, and known to be so busy during holidays that the crowds pressed against the sea. I had business here I'd gladly attend to, but having Emme as a shadow would make it difficult.

Her brother and Raven veered off to the right, while Emme confirmed my suspicion that she wasn't going to leave me alone. At least she had the decency to follow me outright this time instead of sneaking behind me.

"I'm headed to a shop," I said before she could ask, "where some of the gems I was tracking ended up."

She frowned. "I thought Arabella hid all those in the burned-down city?"

"Evidently not. It could be a trap, or she might not have identified them all as false."

"We should bring others then." She looked down the streets, but they were split in every direction and busy enough that our crew was lost among them.

"If we find your mother, we'll come up with a plan from there. But I didn't see her ship in port, so I'm uncertain what we'll find." I pulled the tracking device from my pocket. The gems led us higher through the town, over a short bridge, and to the foot of a polished shop.

The windows, doors, and sills all shone with the sign of a tender hand, though the doorstep had numerous muddy footprints from coming and going. It was a busy place, then. A black-and-ivory flag hung above with the picture of a quail stitched into the fabric, and through the frosted window, I spotted a man standing behind a counter.

We stepped inside. The man had short white hair, with hints of brown, full brows, and the corner of one eye pressed in like he was permanently inspecting those around him. He wore a velvet suit with a perfect cut and seemed obsessed over cleaning the counter in front of him.

A quick sweep of the shop told me why the gems were here.

"She pawned them off," I whispered to Emme. "This is a pawn shop."

She sagged. "That's done, then. Maybe she's still in town."

"She chose this pawn shop for a reason, and I want to know why. Take these coins and buy something while I look around."

"I don't want anything."

I encouraged her anyway. "The owner will be more likely to talk if we purchase something."

She nodded, but not before checking out the windows, as if Arabella might be around the corner. Then, she covered part of her face with her dark hair—the one attribute she got from her father—and approached the counter.

Meanwhile, I wanted to know why Arabella came here out of all the seaside towns and out of all the places here. Something about this pawn shop interested her.

Emme was asking for henna from the man who happily passed over a pouch of leaves. She probably overpaid for them, but I didn't want any argument over prices before I asked him for information. I heard the clatter of three coins. Definitely overpaid.

The shop wasn't special from what I could see. No aged artifacts, no small doors that led to secret meeting rooms, no great treasures to boast about. The gems, wherever they were, would be the nicest thing in this shop if they weren't fake.

"How much for those?"

I turned at the deep voice. A man, dressed in business attire, stood beside Emme and pointed behind the counter. My eye trailed his finger.

The gems.

The owner smiled with his teeth. "Those are something, are they not? Dragged up from a sunken ship. Just cleaned them myself."

He said it so smoothly, it was almost believable.

"How much, Connor." It was more statement than question and held a threatening edge.

Connor took his time bringing the gems out, a few jasper and sapphire, plus a couple amethyst. The last of the fake gems. He set them down before the man while Emme stayed close. "Eighty silver."

The man shrugged. "Deal."

The shop owner's eyes bulged. The man hadn't thought twice about dropping that much money on the counter. He would have gotten the gems easily, had he not turned to wink at Emme.

I recognized him. He used to be in business with my father.

"I'll pay ninety."

Connor was just reaching for the man's payment when he stopped. "Ninety silvers?"

I approached the counter, hoping my facial hair did as good of a job covering my face as Emme's hair did for her. The man hadn't seen me since I was a young boy, and even then, he hadn't given me more than a passing glance. "You heard me. Ninety silvers."

The man, Mr. Miskowi, I recalled his name, studied me far longer than I cared for. Meanwhile, Emme was frowning.

I couldn't explain now; all I could do was pat my pocket as if I carried that much coin and see what he did.

"One hundred," Mr. Miskowi said.

"We don't need to get these," Emme said in a sweet voice as she put her hand on my arm and tugged in a not-so-sweet way.

I pulled away from her as subtly as I could manage. "Oh, but I know how much you like special things. One hundred and twenty."

Jumping up so high caused both Emme and Connor to flinch, but Mr. Miskowi countered without hesitation. "One hundred fifty."

I kept my face impassive as I pretended to mull it over. Finally, I clicked my tongue. "Let's skip all this, shall we? I'll go as high as one ninety-five. And you?"

Now he flinched. He eyed the gems, then thankfully, he shook his head. I beamed. "Very well then. I shall buy them."

He tapped on the counter a few times before exiting the shop.

Connor was in bliss. "You won't be disappointed," he said, happily bundling them up. "A fantastic purchase."

"I won't be purchasing them."

He stilled. "Sorry?"

I looked him in the eye. "They are fakes. You knew that, and had you sold to Mr. Miskowi, he would have recognized it too. Before dinner, I'm sure. Then you would have had a legal issue on your hands, and your shop would have gone under. I just saved you."

He didn't look grateful. He looked mad. "I had a solid offer on the table, and you drove him away without planning to buy anything? I should charge you half anyway."

"You should thank me. And while Mr. Miskowi would have realized they were fakes rather quickly, the next man won't. You'll still sell them before the week is up."

It was the truth and he knew it. "Just get out of my shop."

"In a moment." I leaned toward him. "The woman who gave those to you, what did she buy?"

"Who said she bought anything?"

"I've very little time for games. I'll give you five coins if you describe everything she purchased and show the receipts."

"Ten."

My patience wore thin. I was so close to getting everything I'd dreamed of. My favorable temperament for people, especially people standing in my way, dwindled. I drew my pistol, ignoring Emme's quick intake of breath. "Or I could shoot you, report it as witnessing a brawl over fake gems, which they will find, and leave with the receipts myself."

The owner gulped. "Six sounds fair."

I had to admire that he had courage to continue to barter with a gun pointed at him. I lowered it. "Six will do. What did she buy?"

He dug under the counter for a tin box, which he flipped open to pull out a single receipt. "Just one thing: a net."

Emme and I exchanged glances. "A net?"

"Not just any net." He flipped the paper so I could see it. "One for a very big fish."

18
EMME

We gathered the supplies we needed, which included an unsettling amount of gunpowder, all the while wondering what Arabella needed a large net for.

"We should ask the others what they might guess," I said to Ontario as we watched the crew load the last of the supplies on deck.

He stood with arms crossed and brow low, with lines in his forehead that only seemed to grow deeper with each passing minute. "Tell them Arabella was here, but now she's not, and she bought a net, but we don't know what for? It would be pointless."

"It would be honest." I persisted.

"Captains don't have the privilege of honesty, Emme." Ontario stepped onto the gangplank. "Besides, it's likely for her ship."

I followed him on deck to help raise the plank as he started barking orders. "Navigator, to the helm. Others, raise the sails and angle us northwest."

Afterward, I went belowdecks to stash away the henna leaves, the question of why Arabella needed that net bothering me. She had to know we'd follow those gems and discover what she'd purchased. So was it a threat? Something about how she's reeling us in? A symbol of how we will never be free from the tangle of her desires? Or was this something else altogether?

I could come up with a hundred little threats based on one net alone, but until she showed her hand, we'd never know for sure.

A scrape came from behind the bunks, and I peeked around to see my brother standing near the porthole with Raven tucked in his arms and his head mighty close to hers. I had to blink a few times to be sure I knew what I was seeing.

I would have been a fool not to have seen the chemistry between Emric and Raven, but it was still a surprise to see how far it had come. Arn and I had known each other for years before he'd finally kissed me.

No. Stop thinking of him.

And also stop looking at them.

I pulled away too sharply, and my elbow jabbed into the bunks. Emric and Raven flew apart.

I cleared my throat in the most awkward, uncomfortable way as heat rose to my cheeks. Raven skirted her eyes away, but Emric stood as calm as ever. "You were not supposed to see that."

"I'm very happy to pretend I didn't."

"Good. Pretend you don't see this too." Emric gave Raven a quick, final kiss, then brushed by me, whistling, to go above deck.

Raven lingered. "I should have told you."

I held up my hands. "Truly, I don't need to know."

"I understand. Well," she said with more confidence, "if you'll excuse me."

As she walked past, I cleared my throat. "Does he know who you are?"

From the way she looked in alarm at the door, I'd guess the answer was no.

"You can tell him," I said. "He's trustworthy."

"I know." She gnawed on her lip a few times while staring after where Emric had gone. "It's just that when we met, he was pretending to be a fancy lord, and I was a lady. We laughed about how that life wasn't for us, how those people weren't for us, and it was the first thing that bonded us."

"You met him before joining our crew?"

She smiled warmly. "I met him before I ever met you. It was you he was looking for that night. Emme, my upbringing isn't something I'm keeping from him, it's more something I'd rather wait to share." When my brow wrinkled, she clarified. "Do you feel like someone can't know who you are unless they know who your mother is? Are you rushing to tell people that? Or do you want them to know you, for yourself?"

"I don't tell people who my mother is because she's sadistic."

She shot me a look. "You get my point. My family background is not who I am. This," she spread her arms wide, "is who I am, and that is who Emric knows."

She walked by, but I added one last thing. "He'd want to know all of you. Your real name, for example."

Raven paused, then sighed. "I know. And he will."

That was enough for me. And truthfully, I liked the two of them together, once I had the chance to get over the initial shock of how close they'd become. She had strength and kindness that understood him in a way most never could.

But I didn't get a chance to tell her that, because Ontario was shouting above deck. He wasn't giving orders anymore; something had angered him.

We raced from the bunks to climb the ladder.

Ontario was storming down the stairs from the helm with a parchment crunched in his fist. He held that fist up. "Who was manning the ship?" He took slow steps around the crew, who'd paused from tending the lines to shrivel back. Emric didn't, however, but Ontario knew he wasn't the one in charge of watching the ship as we docked, so he ignored him.

"Who," he repeated, "was watching the ship? It wasn't my first, and it wasn't my second, so tell me who I need to throw overboard."

That would get them to speak.

When no one spoke up, Ontario made a big show of opening the note. "This was left at the helm, where someone walked up the gangplank, across the deck, and up the stairs to the *very hidden* helm, where they left us a note. Not just anyone. Arabella the Ruthless was on our ship, and apparently, *she's invisible now.*"

He glared at the crew. "According to this polite note," his tone suggested that Arabella's tone was anything but polite, "we are to go to these coordinates. It is only because we seek Arabella ourselves that I am going to look into this. But it would have been *so much easier* had we captured her while she was on our ship." Ontario threw the note on the ground, where it rolled near Emric's feet. We all stared at it, as Ontario marched back up the stairs to grab hold of the wheel.

A storm raged behind him, making him appear even more frightening. A shiver trailed its way across my skin.

Emric now held the note, scanning quickly. He looked up as he tucked it away. "Be ready, mates. Something is about to go down."

19

EMME

It went down in two hours, when we'd ventured further into the sea to follow the direction of the coordinates. We watched meticulously for another ship, preparing the cannons and filling our pistols with gunpowder, but it wasn't a ship that we found.

"Are those rocks?" I squinted over the side of the *Royal Rose* at the looming silhouettes jutting out from the sea.

"They look like caves, sitting in the middle," Raven said. She was fidgeting with her necklace relentlessly, and her neck had a red streak because of it.

As we sailed closer, the formations grew bigger, until it was apparent we could sail through them. It was like a maze of rocks on a bed of water, some sprouting straight upward, and others forming archways or short tunnels we could sail through.

"Do you think your mother is hiding in the rocks?" Raven asked.

"Maybe." It was a frightening picture, my mother braced against the rockface, waiting for us to sail past so she could hop on board and ambush us. Then she'd steal me and Emric away, and we'd be trapped with her.

I shuddered.

The evening was too quiet. The sea too still. We could hear the water lapping on the hull and tapping against the stones, and every flap of wind in our sails. It beat on and on and on. We moved slower. Tension clouded the air. Raven dragged her locket across its chain, over and over, back and forth, never stopping.

I stepped away from the rails and took a deep breath.

"Ontario," I shouted up to him. "I don't think we should get closer to the rocks." We were close enough already, and some of the passageways were narrow enough that we might scrape our hull on the sharp sides. I didn't fancy being shipwrecked here, especially knowing Arabella was nearby.

"We won't," he replied. His eye was trained ahead, scouring through the rocks for anything that moved. Ready to react at the first sound. I could only guess if he would run toward it or away. I was grateful when he said, "Let's sail around."

My gratefulness was short-lived. At that moment, a sharp scream pierced the air.

Everyone on deck jumped. Someone's pistol went off. My bet was on Bo, but right now, we were all searching for the source of the screams as they echoed off the sea, crashing against the rocks and howling in our ears.

Ontario was already turning us around.

That's not Arabella," I yelled.

"Doesn't matter. Something is afoot."

I ran up to the helm. "We knew something was afoot; that's why we came." It was hard to hear over the screaming that wasn't stopping. "Someone needs help."

"That does not mean we must go to the rescue."

Clarice tucked her gun away and stood below the helm. "I say we help," she said. I gave her a thankful look.

"Nothing good will come from this." Ontario stilled the wheel from turning us further. "It will leave us shipwrecked with Arabella picking us off in the water one by one." He spoke loud enough for the whole crew to hear. I could feel their opinion swaying away from helping a stranger.

It wasn't too long ago that I'd been a stranger, kidnapped on an island, and Pearl had saved me from the men who'd tied me down. Then there was Serena, who rescued me when there was nothing in it for her, and helped me rescue everyone on my crew. And Raven had freed me when we were imprisoned together in the king's cells.

If I turned away now, it would make me the exact kind of pirate that I dreaded becoming.

"We need to help," I said more firmly.

Ontario's face was set, and I knew he was about to say no when Raven shouted from below, "I see them! There!"

We all swung around to look and gasped.

It made sense now. *A net for a big fish.*

There, against the rocks, with netting tying her down, Arabella had trapped a mermaid.

Not just any mermaid. Coral was strung up, meters above sea level, her wrists tangled in the net and body pressed tight to the stone. Her fin flapped for water but came far too short. Her skin was turning a sickly blue shade, and her coral-colored fin was draining of color. "Please help," she cried out. Her sound was muffled from exhaustion and almost lost to the waves.

"Ontario!" I pleaded.

He was already turning for her. "Starboard side, keep your weapons up. Port side, prepare to cut her free."

Emric was at the helm in moments, his face stoic and tone sharp. "Why are we going toward her?"

My mouth dropped open, and Ontario stared at him. "Have the seas turned you heartless?"

That was rich coming from someone whose first instinct was to leave her.

"She has a note in her hands." Emric pointed out. "It's only another trick from Arabella."

"Likely leading us to whatever other victim she's tied to a rock," Ontario said. "Truly, your mother is one of a kind."

We were closer to Coral now, but her pleas were fading. Weakness was apparent in every part of her—the sag of her head, the draw of her shoulders, the limp way her tail hung. Her skin turned bluer with each passing moment. I didn't know much about mermaids, but I knew if she didn't get in the water soon, she'd die.

A fact that should concern Emric greatly. But instead, his comment was calloused. "I've never trusted mermaids."

What had happened between him and Coral?

"Please." We could hear her begging now. "I don't . . . have much time."

"Drop the rowboats. Bring rope." Ontario shouted and we obeyed. Emric was the first in the boat, but his expression was flat. He was only proceeding because his captain had given the order.

Before the rowboat could fill, I flung myself from the helm and into the water beside them. Emric helped drag me in.

"I wish you'd stayed," Emric said, displeased.

"Why?"

His eyes were searching the rocks as he began to row. "Because if Mother is here, I'd rather both of us not be so accessible."

Although we could still hear Coral's faint pleas, he was more worried about Arabella. I shook my head and drew the blade from my pocket.

Coral had looked up at last, and her sea-green eyes latched onto Emric. Her whimpering stopped. All her movement had stilled. There was a sadness there, one completely separate from her current circumstances, and it ran deep. She didn't look away even as our rowboat hit the rock she was pinned to.

The net stretched tight over every inch of her, and she had a note tied to her wrist. I started the painstaking task of cutting each thread of the net, starting at the bottom. "We are going to get you down." I assured her as I began to cut.

Her *thank you* was the tiniest whisper.

Clarice worked on the other side, while Emric continued to scan for Arabella. But if she was here, she would have revealed herself by now.

I got enough net free that Coral could move her fin, which was a sickly shade of gray. "I'm going as fast as I can." Her eyes began to flutter shut. I moved faster.

"Ask her what sort of trick this is," Emric demanded. "Ask her where Arabella is."

Coral could likely hear him perfectly fine, but she didn't respond. I checked to see if she was still breathing. Barely. My hands worked faster over the ropes, the blade sawing them free until, one by one, they snapped. She shifted downward some, then with a few more slashes, she slid off the rock entirely and into the sea.

Water splashed into my face, and I blinked through it, staring after her. She didn't come up for a minute. Then two.

I looked to Emric. "Do you think she's okay?"

He gestured impatiently for me to get back in the boat. "She'll be fine. But now we'll never get that note."

Reluctantly, I swam back to the rowboat and let Emric and Clarice navigate us to the *Royal Rose*. Just as they grabbed hold of the rope to climb up the hull, Coral dragged herself back atop the rocks. She had more color now, both to her fin and to her skin, but she still moved slowly.

She needed to be in the water to live. She came back to tell us something.

I instantly dove back into the water to swim to her. Emric yelled out my name, but I didn't listen. Soon, I was at Coral's side, pulling my soaking body onto the rock next to her, where she kept her entire fin submerged.

"Are you alright?" I asked. I reached out my hand. "Who did this to you? If it was my mother—" Despairing anger filled me. "I am so, so sorry."

She turned her head to give me a faint smile. Her voice came weakly. "I'm just grateful you showed up. I was supposed to give this to you."

I knew what it would say before I opened it. After a while, my mother became predictable. Sure enough, I opened it to find a threat.

Never forget that I can easily kill anyone you love. Join my crew, and I won't have to.

The threat was for both Emric and me, but this attack was targeted at him. Yet, it seemed to pain me deeper. For some reason, he appeared not to care. I looked back to Emric in the rowboat, his hand on the hilt of his pistol like he thought I could be in trouble. Coral now seemed to be deliberately looking away from him.

I tucked the note away. "Coral." I hesitated. "Why is my brother acting like he doesn't know who you are?"

A tear came to her eye. "How much did he tell you about the island he was trapped on with Arabella?"

"Just that it was miserable and lonely."

"Did he say how he escaped?"

I thought back. "He and Arabella made a raft and sailed away until they found a ship to join."

She looked at me sadly. "They made a raft, but it crashed. They hardly survived."

My eyes widened. "He didn't tell me that."

"He doesn't remember," Coral said quietly. "I saved them and helped him leave the island. But the island takes something from you when you leave. For Emric, it was his memories."

I was speechless. That was cruel beyond understanding.

Arn would see the poetic nature of it, for the island to keep a piece of them, but I doubted Coral saw it that way. "It took away all his memories, everything he knew about you?"

"No," she whispered softly. "It stole all his memories of you."

She was giving answers, but nothing made sense. "But he remembers me. Emric knows who I am."

"He faked it," she said, "hoping the memories would return. But they never did. The only way he could get them back was if he traded them for his memories of me. The price of the island had to be paid."

I sat there, frozen, trying to fathom facing such a choice, yet panged at him pretending to know me when I'd been so relieved to see him alive, mixed with awful guilt that he'd traded away Coral for me. "I never would have asked him to do that," I told her.

She propped herself up on her elbows. More color had returned to her complexion. "I know. But it didn't matter. He looked at you and decided whatever life he had with you was more important than whatever life he could have with me."

Her words dug the guilt further into my chest until it was all that I felt. And it felt horrible. In a way, she had traded her life for his. For ours.

"Is there a way to undo it?"

She looked over at Emric, and he stared back blankly. "No. He's gone to me." When I checked, her gaze had slid from Emric to Raven as she stood on deck, watching. "He was made to sail, though. Not live under the waves," Coral went on. Truthfully, I believed that. I couldn't see Emric under the sea where the sun couldn't reach. He belonged here. And if Coral had made her peace with their separation, then perhaps his lost memory was really a heartbreak prevented. "And besides, there are politics going on under the sea that I didn't want him tangled in, for they have a way of ensnaring people until their spirit is drained. He's happy here." Coral slipped herself further into the water until it reached her neck. "Take care of him, Emme. And if you see your mother, tell her to leave me alone."

"Coral, wait." I reached for her before she could move away. "I know this is a wildly inappropriate time to ask you for a favor, but I'm desperate to know where Arn is. He was the old captain of the *Royal Rose*."

Thankfully, she didn't leave. She pulled back up and looked at me. "If I tell you, I need a favor as well."

"Anything."

"Soon, I'll need a letter from a captain. I want that to be from you."

I frowned. Back on the *Royal Rose*, they were calling for me to hurry, but at the chance of finding Arn, I wasn't moving. "I'm not a captain."

"Not yet, but you intend to be, yes?" I nodded. Raven and I were to be captains together. "Good. When I write, I need you to answer."

Simple enough. Almost too simple. "Deal."

"In that case, I do know where Arn is, and I know where he's going."

Relief flooded me. "Can you tell me? Please?"

She nodded, but her expression was solemn. "Though you should first be aware that the man you once knew is now very different."

I tried to keep my heart from sinking. "I just need to find him."

"Follow the trail of destruction" were her ominous words. "He serves a new master now, and that master has him heading for Kwoli."

She disappeared into the water, leaving me to wonder who this new master was and if it was worth chasing after something that might not exist anymore.

But all those questions fell away when I swam to Emric, and he pulled me aboard. "What did the mermaid say?"

In that moment, I was highly aware of how I'd just chastised Raven for keeping secrets from him. I opened my mouth. Then closed it.

My eyes trailed up the expanse of the ship to see Raven, watching us over the deck with worry. She didn't know anything about Coral, of course. She didn't know that Emric was in love with someone else when they met. She didn't know that if he remembered Coral, he might choose her. But I didn't know that either.

And what would I say? I couldn't offer him resolution. I could only offer confusion.

"She was warning me about Mother. But we can handle her."

He gave a wary look back to the seas before tugging on the ropes to check they were secured to the ends of the rowboat. "Let's go then. I don't care to be around all these rocks when the sun goes down."

We pulled our tired bodies overboard and wrung out our jackets, reaching for tunics that crewmates passed to us. Before Emric left, I grabbed his arm. "Thank you."

"What for?"

"For always having my back."

He knew how rare that was in our lives. He covered my hand with his. "Always."

Ontario waited at the helm. "What did the note say?"

"It was a threat." Then I thought quickly. "But Coral said that Arabella sailed for Kwoli."

He turned the wheel. "Then we go there."

When I was alone in my cabin, the image of Coral on the rocks came to mind. I thought what it would be like if that had been Arn of whom I had no memory. Or if he was truly so different that the man I knew was gone.

I wept.

I unfolded Arn's note for the hundredth time to compare it with the other letters he had written me over the years. We'd only been friends when we'd written to each other, so there weren't any sweet words to hold onto. But I had his unmistakable writing.

I couldn't find any discrepancies.

Raven was scouring over them with me by the candlelight in the main cabin.

"Can you get out the inventory reports?" I asked. "Check for the files from three months ago."

Raven shuffled through a box. "Inventory stops two months ago, right when he left."

"That's not surprising," I said. "Any folder will do."

She brought one to the table and set it down. I went through his writing meticulously once more, comparing every curve of the letters, every stroke that he'd made, trying to find proof that the letter he'd left me wasn't written by him.

I turned one page. Then another. Raven stayed diligently at my side.

"It appears the same," I confessed.

"Then we will keep looking." She took another folder of inventory reports and dropped them on the desk.

We could go through ten files and find a few letters that looked different, but for each of those, a thousand more were the same. It was his writing.

Yet, I kept going through.

"Thank you," I said to Raven after we'd gone over another stack of papers.

"For what?"

"For believing me."

She rested her back against the wall, propped one knee

up, and scrolled another page. "I didn't know Arn, but I got a glimpse of him. Two, actually. Do you remember?"

I nodded. "When we escaped the castle."

"That was the second. The first was when you were arrested. A crowd full of officers, you being carted away, and he flung himself at the bars to try to free you. When that didn't work, he oathbound himself to you in a promise to find you again."

I wrapped my arms around myself. That was the morning after he asked me to marry him. I still had that ring in my pocket.

Raven flipped another page. "Someone doesn't do something like that one day, then walk away the next."

I needed to hear that. I'd been doubting what Arn and I had over the past few months, but it was healing to hear someone else acknowledge that it was something real. I went back to the notes he'd written me during my time at the Banished Gentlemen tavern, my fingers going to my pocket to feel the curve of the engagement ring he'd stolen for me. He loved you, I reminded myself. Arn loved you.

I brushed my other hand over his signature at the bottom of a page. He had such a fine signature, with the A curved to take up half the page. Above it was the formal tag of sincerely. Always the same tag in each letter.

I straightened. Was it always the same?

I scrolled through the other notes quickly, checking the ending. Sincerely, Arn. Sincerely. Sincerely.

"I think I found something," I said, trying to control my excitement. Raven scooted to my side to see. "He always ended the letters the same way, with this word here. But look at how he signed off in the last note."

She looked. Yours forever, Arn.

Raven didn't look convinced. "You were more than friends

when he wrote this last letter, so it's reasonable that his words changed."

"Maybe. But it's not in the same format. He always breaks it into separate lines. But here, it's all together. That's not his style. The letters are written the exact same, but the format of it . . . that's not Arn."

I'd spent so long looking at how he'd stylized the words that I'd ignored this aspect. Any doubts washed away. Arn wouldn't leave me or his ship behind. Nor his compass, which I'd just found in his room.

"I have the proof I was looking for." I felt absolution now. "Arn didn't leave me intentionally. Something happened to him. If he's in trouble I need to save him. I have to help him."

I took out the ring from my pocket to look at it. He'd found one with blue that reminded him of the sea, but to me, it looked like his eyes. I pretended that was what it was, and that I was looking at him as I promised, "I *will* find you." I slipped the ring on my finger.

20

ONTARIO

I was losing control. The crew was a mess, going through their chores, pausing near each other when they thought I didn't see. I more than saw, I heard.

"We can't win against Arabella."

"She'll drown us all."

"I heard this crew is cursed."

We might be cursed, but we would not fail. I knew that deep in my bones, that the *Royal Rose* would sail away from this unscathed, but raising morale was never a forte of mine. So I strode into my cabin as the sun set to write the one who was causing all this uncertainty.

I skipped the pleasantries.

> *What in the name of the dark seas was that? If you ever try anything like that again, our deal is off, and I'll make sure you never see your children alive.*
>
> *- Ontario*

When my messenger hawk came next, I gave him the note and sent him away.

A week passed before I got a reply. I opened the note.

You will be left alone for a bit. I've got bigger
fish to fry.

After I'd read it, my messenger hawk bent his head to slip a second note out of the pack on his back. This one bore golden wax, pressed by the royal seal, and had parchment so thick it was a wonder it didn't weigh the hawk down.

"You've been busy," I told him.

The glint in his eye was knowing. I'd never stop marveling at the ability of his race to find anyone despite where they hid. No matter how far to the ends of the seas someone had ventured, the hawks could find them. It seemed this time, the hawk had been called to the castle.

I was far more nervous opening this one than Arabella's.

I breathed a sigh of relief at the words.

You have my alliance.
Her Majesty, Queen Isla.

21
ARN

A tenuous friendship settled across the *Commander* over the next few weeks, fragile and illusive, threatening to break with the next wind that filled our sails. Jakob moved in circles around us, not crossing the barrier but not pushing us either. We were fed. We trained like brothers. We had no further mysterious assignments from King Isaac. All the while we watched our backs for the moment the reprieve would snap.

Jakob would watch us, and we could tell he was thinking of his loss. The navigator stood by us once when this happened.

"You look like his son," he said, indicating Landon. "That's why he's hated having you aboard our ship. It's like seeing the ghost of his son at every turn."

"I didn't ask to be here," Landon said plainly, arms crossed, watching me at the wheel. I shot him a glance. "What? We didn't. And I can't help it if I look like anybody. We were following his king's orders like any soldier worth his salt would. He hates us because we are pirates and because we worked for King Unid, and not for any other reason."

I turned to the navigator. "Forgive him, he just lost his father."

Landon glared.

"You and Jakob can mourn together," I told him, then I

turned back to the navigator. "Why did you tell him we were in that battle?"

"Because he deserved to know," the navigator replied and started down the steps.

From the crow's nest, came a shout. "Ship ahoy!"

A bell rang out, and the crew flooded to the starboard side to see where he pointed. It was merely a black dot on the water, far in the distance. I remembered the last time a black ship followed us. It led to our minds being haunted and many going mad.

This one moved closer.

I veered into the wind to pull us quicker. "Men to the oars!"

In the same breath, Jakob commanded, "Ready the cannons!"

Landon was flying down the helm to fill his gunpowder pack. He swept up a dagger and drove it into its sheath beside his cutlass. The other men grabbed broadswords. "You really mean to fight?" he asked Jakob. "Look at the size of that thing."

The *Commander* was much larger than a pirate ship and should frighten any who crossed our path. But the ship chasing us grew every moment it got closer, until it dwarfed us in size. Now we were the ones frightened. If this were my ship, I'd say we turn and speed away. Next to that, I'd feign a surrender. But as it was, we were running out of time to raise the white flag, and I doubted we had one of those anyway.

Jakob didn't bat an eye. "Az Eloians don't run from a battle."

"We'd be unwise to not try an escape," I insisted.

"We fight. Hnoll!" He raised his fist in the air, and the crew chanted his words back. Like they were barbarians who lived for this.

Landon took a more brazen approach. "It's that attitude that killed your son. When his ship saw we weren't a merchant vessel, they never should have fought us. Do not make the same mistake."

Jakob's eyes flashed, and his chest rose heavily. Landon had courage of steel to not only say that to him, but to stand close enough that Jakob could whack him upside the head.

I was surprised when he didn't. If I had said that, he definitely would have.

"We do not run from a fight. Especially one from the queen of Julinbor."

Landon stepped back. "The queen?"

Jakob thrust a spyglass in his hand, and when Landon looked through it, his face paled. He tossed the telescope back. "The queen is on a warpath right now. She won't care that we aren't pirates. She won't care if it angers your king. She will destroy us happily."

"Her men are not going to win today," Jakob snapped. "Are cannons ready? Pistols loaded? Blades sharp?"

The crew shouted in return. They stood in formation at the starboard side, grappling hooks in the hands of those at the front, and pistols raised from the others. Belowdecks, cannons thundered while being rolled out.

"Keep us steady," Jakob shouted to me. "Keep us facing leeward. Let them come to us."

I hated it, but I obeyed. I checked that my own pistol was loaded, my cutlass in its sheath, and that my hook was screwed on tight.

"Men ready!" Jakob bellowed. The ship drew closer, its every cannon visible, every soldier waiting on deck to attack.

"Fire!"

Our cannons went off. They hit the side of their ship with only a hollow clank. I looked closer. The wood wasn't lacquered black, it was crafted of steel.

Cannons were no good here.

Their crew dropped into rowboats, coming from both sides

to attach their grappling hooks to our bow and stern, all the while firing their cannons at us to keep our focus divided.

They fought like pirates.

But their jackets were the blue and cream colors of Julinbor, and they didn't bear the cutlasses of pirates.

I let go of the wheel, not caring where the wind pulled us now. Enemy soldiers dragged themselves aboard behind me, and Az Eloians crowded the helm to keep them at bay for as long as they could.

Men had already infiltrated the deck, but the crew worked in beautiful formation to take them down one after another, and when one enemy slipped through, the second line of defense was there to finish them off. But men were coming too quickly, and we weren't going without casualties. Bitter screams were enough to picture the sickening sight of crimson blood spilling on deck.

I found Landon and pulled him into the cabin.

"What are you doing?" He jerked away from me. "We need to be out there."

I grabbed his shoulder. "This is not our fight. Let's take a rowboat and get away."

Every part of him in constant motion, he edged back to the door where the fight was. But we could row to land; I knew where we were, and I knew it was close enough that we could make it. We'd find a way to Julinbor on our own.

"We can't leave them here."

"We owe them nothing."

"We've trained with them."

"That does not make them our concern. Landon, I don't want to leave you, but I will. You think Jakob will let you stay on crew if you fight with them? You think anyone here will have your back? Come with me."

That got his attention and he relented. "It'll be hard to steal a rowboat right now."

"We'll have to try." I sounded more confident than I felt.

At that moment, Jakob burst through the door, eyes raging. He was panting as he looked between the two of us.

"You're both here." He filled the doorway, and his pistol was raised. I didn't want to test how likely he was to spare Landon's life based on his resemblance to his son, but I knew he wouldn't spare mine.

"Let us by." I moved my hand to my own pistol.

Jakob held up his hands. "You don't need that."

Behind him, Kao approached, gun drawn. Jakob swung around and, in one motion, aimed his gun and fired through the man's chest.

I stifled a choke as Kao's body fell to the floor. Jakob took a deep breath, then faced us again. "He was going to kill you. The whole crew planned to kill you tonight, even before the attack."

Now I did take out my pistol, and Landon leveled his. "And you?"

"Not me," he said. There was a wound in his expression as he looked over Landon. "But you can't stay on crew and hope to live."

"Then let us by, and we'll escape," I said hastily, taking advantage of this turn of events. We stepped out the doorway. The deck was crowded with men falling overboard, bodies dropping, and gunshots echoing in every corner. I tried to trace a path through it that led to the rowboats, but it would be a tricky one to survive, and even trickier to untie the boats once we got there.

I was too busy mapping it out that I missed Jakob as he raised the end of his pistol and collided it against my head.

I fell. My vision blurred, and I sensed Landon struggling beside me before falling too.

The noise of battle drowned into a ringing tone. Before

darkness set in, Jakob whispered in our ears, "This was the only way."

I woke some unknown time later to more darkness, the unsavory scent of rats, and a wavering beneath us to say we were still on a ship. But so far there was nothing about it I recognized.

I looked around and cursed. We were in a cell. Jakob had handed us over to the other ship as prisoners.

Something dug into my back, and I maneuvered my bound wrists to feel the edge of my hook tied there. *Jakob.* I had no other weapons, but that one Jakob had snuck through on me. Landon still lay on a stiff cot, unconscious.

Somewhere outside the cell, a door opened. I swiveled my gaze that direction as buttery light seeped in from the passageway. A woman strode toward us, light catching on her long, braided hair.

Her long, *red* hair.

I stood. "Arabella."

"You remembered my name." She put her hand to her chest, covering over a black amulet necklace, and grinned. The way she smiled was disturbing. "Pleasure to meet you again. Plus whoever this is." She glanced at Landon.

I tried to think through my lingering fog. "You attacked us?" *I knew they fought like pirates.*

"I carry many flags." She gave a wave of her hand. "I even have one for Az Elo, which is what I almost flew to get to you. But as it was, things turned out nicely."

I was only half listening. So this ship was still afloat and very much moving by the feel of it. There was no porthole to check through to see what had happened to Jakob and his men, or even note what time of day it was. All I had to go off was the warm glow coming down the narrow stairwell, which could be evening light or lamplight.

And I wasn't injured. Only a dull throb where Jakob had knocked me out. Was he working with Arabella? For most men, I'd assume so, but Jakob seemed the type who wouldn't want anything to do with Arabella the Ruthless. He might be rough around the edges, but he wasn't crooked.

Which begged the question of why we were here.

"What do you want?"

Arabella's lithe hand came through the cell bars to stroke a finger down my cheek. I flinched. "Oh, but you are mistaken. I don't want anything from you," she said, voice dripping with fake pleasantry. Her nail slipped from my cheek, as sharp as any blade. Her tone turned just as sharp. "You are nothing but bait."

She turned to walk away.

I knew who she would need me as bait for. "She won't come!" I yelled after her. "Emme is too weak to sail. She's probably dead already."

Arabella only laughed. "Oh, she'll come." Then she slammed the door she'd entered through and left us in darkness once more.

My heart leapt. Her reply gave me both hope and dread at the same time for the one I missed, the one I'd been fighting to return to . . .

"She'll come."

She was still alive.

22
ONTARIO

The emerald stars glowed brighter. Someone was bound to notice them tonight. But I doubted anyone knew the prophecy like I did, unless all fathers were obsessed with reciting it over their children like a twisted bedtime story.

The sea had been quiet recently. It concerned me. There was a saying that went *small waves mean something malicious is brewing beneath.*

Plenty was brewing right now.

I dipped my quill into ink. Trade licenses were scattered across the table in my quarters, and I sorted through them, filing requests for renewals where needed and asking for expansions into other territories. When Jackson launched his company soon, we would be prepared to take his shipments all over the world.

The communication pod beeped two hours before Jackson said he'd make contact.

I turned it on.

"Did you get the information?" I asked, continuing through the papers, though these didn't need to be shipped for another week.

Jackson was sitting at his own desk, but the surface of it was clean. He didn't answer the question. "This feud between

Queen Isla and the pirates is heating up. Perhaps we should push back our timeline until it ends."

"No," I said too quickly. "That business is with the queen and Arabella the Ruthless, not us. It shouldn't hurt our plans."

There was a strain in Jackson's voice as he spoke. It was the first time I'd seen him look something other than put together. "I've planned this for fifteen years, most of that spent with long nights in the workshop, making sure every detail was right so when we launched, it would be flawless. I don't want to be derailed by a war. If I have to wait another fifteen years to do this right, I will."

I stood, so he could see that he had my full attention. "You won't need to wait. This war will be over before a battle is fought. It won't be an issue for our company."

As he studied me, I sighted the emerald stars again. The power they spoke of was ready now . . . not in six months. Certainly not in fifteen years.

Jackson might be willing to wait. I was not.

"We've nothing to worry about," I repeated.

His shoulders relaxed the slightest, but there was still an edge to his voice. "If you say so. In that case, Arabella is arriving on the island of Kwoli as we speak."

So the mermaid was correct. I mulled over the location. "What business does anyone have at a small place like that?"

"I don't know. Even I don't have contacts there."

I repeated the name to myself a few times until remembering why it unsettled me. "There is a war outpost there. She could be recruiting."

"Possibly." From the even-keeled way he said that, the thought had already crossed his mind. "If she's amassing an army, you should make haste. But remember," he stressed, "it was a military outpost and could very well be reinforced again. I can't guarantee what you'll sail into."

I gave a reassuring nod. "We will be on guard." Then I turned off the pod.

23

EMME

Emric and I were leading the crew through training when Tess shouted from above. "I see her ship!"

We flocked to the port side. Emric peered through a telescope. "At last," he said. "There she is."

A ship settled in the distance, perched off the narrow shore of Kwoli. The island was tiny and overgrown and seemingly deserted—other than the several men who walked along the strip of sand between the dense forest and the ship, carrying supplies with them.

My pulse sped. Coral had told me Arn was headed here, and here was a ship. I'd found him. My thumb fidgeted with the ring on my finger as excitement built inside me.

"What could they be taking from the island?" one of the crew asked.

"Lumber," Emric replied, lowering his telescope. "Their ship is broken."

Soon, we saw it too. A harrowing crack split their main mast, what remained of their sails was in tatters, and large holes riddled their hull. They'd been attacked.

Excitement collapsed into fear. Arn's having only one hand put him at a disadvantage. Easier to kill.

"Flank them," Ontario shouted. "Amass into three groups,

two in rowboats and one here, and approach from all sides. They can't escape."

We didn't need three groups to take this ship. We only needed to sail up to their side, and they would be ours. But Ontario didn't know that I hadn't led us to Arabella—I'd led us to Arn.

Then Emric sucked in a breath. "It's not her flag." He passed me the telescope.

I peered through to find the torn flag, made of black canvas with gold threads and the image of a bear. I'd been expecting to see the *Dancer*. This was not it.

I passed the telescope to Raven. "It's a ship from Az Elo." She paled.

What was Arn doing on a ship from Az Elo? I thought of Coral's warning. *"He serves a new master now."*

"Is Arabella here or not?" Bo asked beside us.

"I don't think so," I told him. "But the Az Eloians are."

The energy on deck dulled, but Ontario continued surveying. "Arabella has to be here."

But we could see almost the entire island. There was no other ship.

"I'm not getting close to Az Eloians," Ontario declared. "Even if they are weakened." He moved the wheel.

"No." I flung myself at the stairs. "We have to go to them."

"Why?"

I debated telling him I'd led us here solely because I believed it to be where Arn was. I'd risk his wrath if it got me to that ship.

But it was Raven who spoke. "I'd like to go." She was messing with her necklace again, watching the ship from Az Elo.

Ontario stopped turning the wheel. He narrowed his eyes. "The Az Eloians are on a mission right now to find the missing princess," he told Raven. "If they find her, they will bring her straight to their king. They won't make exceptions."

I tried not to gape at his words.

She twisted to see him. He had a straight look in his eye, and an undertone that said he knew more than he was saying. He said again, "They will not go on missions to find a ship of orphans. They will go straight to Az Elo."

He knew. Raven handled this revelation deceptively well, with a casual stance and slight nod, then returned her focus onto the other ship. They were taking down their sails. They might want to bring her to Az Elo, but they wouldn't be going anywhere right now.

Raven's voice was firm. "I know their mission. I want to go anyway."

"Are you certain?" I whispered to her.

"I need to make these seas safe for my children," she whispered back. She pointed to the ship. "There is an entire ship of warriors, and they will fight with me if I command it." She turned her head to me. "We can find your mother and end this war."

Even at a whisper, she had power to her voice. It was easy in times like this to see the leader she was bred to be. "I will come with you," I said without hesitation. "I need to be on that ship."

"Once done, this cannot be undone." Ontario's voice cut through our whispers in a stern warning. "Are you certain you want to go to that ship?"

Raven stood, head held erect. "I am certain."

Emric's brows were low. "Why do you need to go? Those men are heartless thugs who care for nothing other than the glory found on the other side of a blade. We should have nothing to do with them."

I winced. Little did he know that the girl he kissed was from those heartless thugs.

Raven gave a sad smile. "They will not hurt me," she said. Then speaking quickly, as if it was against her better judgment, she let the words fall loud enough for the crew to know the truth. "Because I am the lost princess they are seeking." Her declaration rang through the deck. "I am Calypso, daughter of King Isaac and rightful heir of Az Elo." Emric's face went slack. Raven turned to Ontario. "Take me to them. Now."

"Yes, Your Highness."

Emric brushed past her to go belowdecks, the shock evident in the jagged way he moved. When he was gone, she glanced at me. "Now I've told him."

"He'll cool off."

"There's no time to wait for that," she said and turned to go after him.

A hand was at my elbow. Ontario had turned the helm over to Clarice. "Before you go, there's something I need to show you."

The *Royal Rose* sailed closer to Kwoli, and I watched from the porthole inside Ontario's cabin. "They are dangerous men," he warned. "You'll need to be on guard."

"What did you need to show me?" I'd left my cloak in here earlier, and I put it on now, tying the string together at the top. I kept my cutlass at my side.

I shouldn't rush. Walking into a band of An Eloians was never a fond thought, and Emric had Raven's focus right now, but all I wanted was to fling myself overboard and swim through the sea until I found Arn on that beach. It took all my control to steady myself in that cabin and not run to find him.

As I shifted, Ontario opened an old trunk and pulled out a locked box, opened it, and removed something. "I want you to bring this with you, so we can keep in contact."

He passed it into my palm. It was a relatively small, round device with one button on the side. "What does it do?"

"Press that," Ontario pointed, "when you need to talk to me, then set this on the ground. I'll appear."

I squinted. "Is it magic?" He'd managed to capture some of my attention as I studied the deceptively simple trinket.

"Technology."

Technology? We weren't engineers on this ship, crafting new developments in our spare time. "Where did you get it?"

Ontario grinned. "You know what I like about you? You're tenacious. The Az Eloians aren't ready for you."

"That's not an answer."

"It's not." Ontario leaned his frame against the wall to study me, and I could see him mulling something over. He made his decision. "I've been working with someone who produces these to set up trade routes. In a few months, we will take this technology to the world, and our ship will become the richest on the seas. It won't harm you," he added, "but it is expensive so don't lose it."

I examined it again, then placed it into my pocket. He'd omitted names and details, but from his voice, this meant a lot to him. At least it explained some of why he'd been so distant recently. He was working on something big. I wondered when he was planning to let the crew in on it, or if we'd even have heard about it until after the product had been distributed.

But I had my own mission to worry about right now. "Any other advice before I go?"

"Be careful."

"You already said that." I crossed the room and opened the door.

"It's the most important one," he called after me. His voice was dulled by the pouring of ale in a cup, and he swished the liquid around the tin. "There's no goodness in men like Az Eloians."

"There's goodness in Calypso. That's good enough for me."

Plus, they had Arn. They could be the most dangerous men in the world, and I'd still run toward their ship, just to find him.

24

EMRIC

My heart was contorted in a way that was unfamiliar. It was a blade pressing into my chest—not enough to kill me, but enough to hurt. I wasn't used to heartache. I wasn't used to someone stealing my breath away simply by coming into the room, or making me want to become a better man.

Tell me who you are, I'd said. *I want to know everything about you.*

Right now, the most important parts about me are the parts that are drawn to you.

And I'd accepted that, never pressing for more.

I had sworn to never be like my father: settling for someone who would never truly be his. I'd either have someone's whole heart, or I wouldn't want anything at all.

In the end, I fell for someone who hadn't even told me her real name.

Footsteps entered the cabin behind me, then a tender hand touched my back.

"I wanted to tell you." Raven's voice was soft. Or Calypso's. I had just gotten to know Raven. I didn't know where to start getting to know the princess from Az Elo.

"I wish you would have." I turned to face her. I saw her differently now. Her stoic nature was her hiding something.

Her confident movements were her upbringing. Her skill with a blade was royal training.

"There is a generous reward for anyone who returns me to my father, one that I'd rather no one collect." She gave a wary look behind her like she expected someone on crew might try to collect it this moment.

I'd protect her before that happened, but no one on this crew would dare harm her. We'd all seen what she could do with a blade.

"What part do I belong to?" I asked her.

"What do you mean?"

"Which side do I fit into? Raven or Calypso? Because you can't be both, and I suspect Calypso will win in the end. So, I'd like to know which version of you I fit into, and which I don't."

My resolution was cracking. It was impossible to hold bitterness against her when she was so good-hearted, and having her here, all I wanted to do was say that we would sort it out. But if she'd kept this from me, she didn't see me as a viable part of her life.

Which would be unfortunate, because I saw her as a part of mine.

She gazed at me for a long time, then lifted her hands to my face. Her touch was warm against my cheeks. "My life is not a certain one. But however it goes, I want you in it." She hesitated, then pressed a gentle kiss against my lips. "Is that enough for you?"

With the kiss, the last of my resolve snapped, and I sank into her touch.

I couldn't see myself with a princess. I definitely couldn't see myself as a king, learning all the stiff rules and regulations befitting a monarch and having so many people looking up to me. But I could see myself with her, so I murmured, "It's enough for me."

My selfish hurt drifted away. Whatever part of her life she

wanted to spend with me was more than enough. I should be grateful she wanted to spend even a day with me, and would take anything more that I got.

Over Raven's shoulder, I saw Emme tread lightly into the cabin. She reached for her bag. "We should go. We are coming upon the ship."

"You're going too?" I asked her. Raven let go of me to pack her things.

Emme fiddled with the strings of her bag. "I believe Arn is on that ship."

I very much wanted to be there when she found him, if only to strangle him for leaving her when she was so ill.

But Raven gave me a look. "I think you should stay. I don't like leaving Ontario alone."

He wouldn't be alone, but I knew what she meant. He'd be without someone who knew he was untrustworthy, and we'd be blind to his movements.

"I'll stay," I sighed. "But you two stay safe."

As I said those words, Raven loaded her pistol. She flashed me a smile. "You too, sailor. We will see you when this war is over."

25

EMME

We came to shore a distance away from the other ship, barely able to make out its name painted on the side. *Commander.* The *Commander* was a beast, able to carry a large crew that would come in handy if they joined with us in battle. They would also be difficult to escape if they decided to oppose us. Raven didn't appear worried, though, as she climbed out of the rowboat.

"Keep on the lookout and be safe," Emric told us again.

We promised him we would, and he rowed back to the *Royal Rose.*

"What will you do if your pirate is not on board?" Raven asked as we trekked across the sand.

"I haven't thought about it," I admitted. "I'm just hoping Coral gave good information."

Raven accepted the answer and brought up the hood of her cloak, masking her features in darkness. I followed suit.

The Az Eloians must have seen us coming from the ship, but they continued regardless, sculpting a new mast from forest lumber. On deck came the loud clang of a hammer and the snap of lines as old sails were replaced by new.

I scoured through the mass of men, searching for Arn.

If it wasn't evident from the ship that they'd been in a fight, it was evident from the sailors. Some limped, some nursed weak arms. Some were bandaged and bruised and bloodied. But they were all massive enough to make me shiver.

Once we got halfway to the ship, all work stopped. They formed a line in the sand, clearly showing how far we were allowed to come and at what point we would not get past.

Raven's steps did not slow. Neither did mine.

I was very aware of the sheer number of weapons on them. They'd just been through a fight, so they were fidgety and restless and would be too eager to pull a trigger. It didn't matter how small we were to them, Az Eloians saw everyone as an enemy. It was a wonder they hadn't shot us already.

The one in the middle had an especially piercing face, twisted and rough, with a scar down his cheek.

It could be only that man standing in our way, and it would still give me pause.

They didn't speak, instead letting a deep silence stretch between us as we drew closer, until we were ten paces away.

Then the one in the middle barked, "Business?" His booming voice broke the stillness.

Raven halted and threw back her hood. "I'm taking control of your ship," she announced. "I ask you all to fight beside me the way you fought with my mother years ago."

A jolt snapped through the crew, and a murmur ensued. "Your name?" The middle one peered closer at her.

"Calypso."

I kept like a shadow behind Raven's shoulder, watching every glorious moment as recognition took hold of them. One by one, knees dropped to the sand. The one in the middle raised his head first. "Your Majesty. You've returned to us."

"I've returned to ask you to fight with me."

The man stood. "We should deliver you to your father. He isn't well, and the kingdom looks to you to rule."

I saw her shoulders tense. She hadn't told me her reasons

for not wanting to go home, but I knew her reasons for staying at sea. If they decided to drag us to Az Elo anyway, the *Royal Rose* was too far away to help us. "I'm not sailing home yet," she declared. "And neither are you. We have a war to win."

The men of Az Elo stood. "It is not our fight," the middle man responded.

"And yet," Raven stepped closer, "we fight anyway. We fight and take the victory that we were denied five years ago, when Julinbor forced us from their seas. We prove to the world that we are leaders, on land and on sea. I will not stand by as power shifts and let Az Elo end on the bottom. Are you that placid that you'd let the world move on without us? Or will you fight?"

As she spoke, she neared the crew like a general speaking to soldiers. They straightened at her presence, until they didn't look broken down anymore. They looked ready to sail for their leader.

"Who is with me?" she asked. "Who will battle at my side?"

"We will fight, Your Majesty," they rejoined. The ragged one at the front didn't appear pleased, but he gave his princess an obedient bow.

She raised a fist in the air. "Hnoll!"

"Hnoll!" They shouted back.

"Good." She gestured to the one in charge. "Now show me what happened to the ship. How soon before it can set sail again?"

He cast a cagey look my way. "And your companion?"

I came to Raven's side. "I'm looking for someone." I took a breath. "His name is Arn Mangelo."

There was a ripple that went through the crew, and for the first time, their focus went to me. But there wasn't reverence in their eyes. Rather, it was something I couldn't pinpoint. Caution, perhaps. Hints of distrust.

The man in the front appeared unshaken, but he took his

time before answering. "We were in a battle recently, and he's gone."

The words sank into me like a bitter poison. Raven reached for me, but I pulled away.

"He died?" The words sounded far off. My stomach was uneasy, but there was nothing to grab to steady myself. "How?"

"He is not here anymore." The man turned back to the ship, but I couldn't move as the world tilted around me.

"Where is he?" My voice was tight, and it was all I could do to keep upright.

The man sighed. There was undeniable pity when he looked at me. "I don't know what became of him."

My hands clutched my own heart, as if that could do anything to ease the pain. It didn't help.

"It's not too late for us to signal the *Royal Rose* to turn around if you want to go with them," Raven said quietly to me.

I blinked hard. The *Royal Rose* was almost gone. It was like watching him sail away. How many times had I seen that ship coming to port from the tavern where I'd met Arn, and watched it sail away again? I always knew it would return and bring him back to me. Now I might never see him again.

Now its sails were too far away to see the bleeding rose, and soon the ship was lost over the horizon.

"I'm fine," I said. I might throw up. "We have work to do."

I didn't walk to talk to anyone, but when the communication pod flashed, I set it down and pressed the button.

Ontario's image came above the pod, as if he stood in front of me.

My sorrows dissipated briefly as curiosity took its place. "How is this possible?" I asked.

"I told you," he said. He wore his jacket unbuttoned, and I could see the edges of his table. He must be in his quarters then, though I couldn't see the full room. But I saw him clearly. "Technology."

"How much of me can you see?" I asked. I was in one of the many cabins on this enormous ship, Raven urging me to take time to recollect myself in private. There was a small cot here, though the rest of it was crates of inventory. I had Arn's note open in front of me as I sat on one now, the words of the man, Jakob, throbbing in my head.

"Gone. Not here. I don't know what became of him." All things that didn't quite mean dead, but didn't mean he was alive and well either. Arn could be anywhere. He could have fallen in battle. He could be at the bottom of the sea. Wherever he was, I had no inkling how to find him, and if he was alive and looking for me, he'd be looking in the wrong places.

I should have searched for him as soon as Ontario had told me he'd left, especially when he'd said Arn was with Landon. That should have been my clue that Arn was in trouble. Instead, I'd easily believed he had gone away on his own. But it was I who had deserted him.

"I can see that you're reading that note again," Ontario said, drawing me back to reality. "Did you find him? Or hear of his whereabouts?" There was a hesitancy in his question, and I had a similar one in my answer.

"Not yet. How is Emric doing?"

"He's training the crew, so I'd say he's okay." He took a sip of something, then squinted at me. "How are you?"

I pushed the note away. "I'm fine." It was an obvious lie when my face must be blotchy, but he accepted it. I cleared my throat and pulled my shoulders back, as if the action could pull the broken parts of myself together. "The Az Eloians have welcomed us warmly, and Raven convinced them to fight with us. When we corner Arabella, we will have the might of Az Elo behind us."

He seemed pleased. "Very good. I wasn't convinced she

could sway them, but it's coming together nicely. Do they have many weapons?"

"I haven't looked yet. But it will take two days to fix the ship, so I'll have time to search. Have you made contact with the queen?"

"I have," he replied. "She's willing to accept Arabella in exchange for letting us sail as before."

"And did she say what she intends to do with Arabella?" I asked. The plan was coming together, the pieces falling into place, one after another, just as we'd hoped, but I was hardly processing any of it. My mind was too distant, somewhere where Arn was.

When Ontario didn't answer right away, I looked up. "I can't promise that she won't kill her," he said finally.

I'd had my fill of death. But at this point . . . "It's out of our hands."

He couldn't move closer through the communication pod, but he tilted his head. "Are you certain you're okay?"

From behind him, Tess came into view. Her small frame was dwarfed by his, and when she saw me, she kept back. The door to my own cabin opened, and Jakob stepped in.

"I'm fine," I told Ontario hastily. I didn't want another seeing the communication pod and risk it being taken from me. It wasn't worth as much as their missing princess, but it must be worth a lot.

Ontario had noticed Tess behind him. "I'll see you later," he said. "And Emme? I really admire you for your strength over the past six months. You're an amazing woman."

"Thank you. I'm grateful for your friendship."

He nodded and disappeared.

Jakob stood stoically in the doorway. With all the crates I didn't know what he had seen, if anything. He made no remark about it.

"Thank you for granting me passage on your ship." I gathered Arn's note and the communication pod in my hands.

Jakob closed the door behind him. I froze. The only light in the room was a small lantern, and it made his eyes glow. I eyed the pistol at his hip, noting how difficult it'd be to get past him if he reached for it.

But he didn't move for his weapon. Instead, he lowered his head. "I know where your pirate is," he said. His voice spoke truth.

I sank to my knees. Without warning, tears flooded my face.

The next thing I felt was his hand on my back. "But he is not safe."

I lifted my eyes to him. Relief was pounding through my veins. "Where is he?"

"He was in danger on board our ship," Jakob said. "He and his crewmate, Landon, were sent by our king to find Calypso, but the crew didn't care for foreign men aboard. So I traded them away to the queen. If I hadn't, my men surely would have killed them."

I took a shuddering breath. "Where did the queen take him?"

"The ship sailed east, but that's all I know." He watched as I wiped my eyes dry, my heart still racing, my mind telling me not to hope too much, and other thoughts suggesting he might still be dead after all. Though, the people in my life had a habit of coming back from the dead. Jakob's voice pulled me from the spiral of thoughts. "You can't let the crew know that he lives. I risked my reputation saving the lads."

"I won't tell," I promised. I was on my feet now, seizing my bag and muttering a new concern, "I swear, if Landon hurts him before I get there, he'll have to deal with me." I reached for the door and said more loudly, "I need to talk to Raven."

Jakob rapped his fingers against a crate as I moved past, then spoke. "Why would Landon hurt him?"

My entire focus was on how we could track the ship that

took Arn and how to convince the queen to release him. If he left recently, he couldn't be far. The western winds would be against them. But I refocused enough to say, "Landon is always at the root of Arn's troubles."

"Not this time."

"Trust me," I said, turning the handle. "Those two have been at odds for a long while."

"No." Jackob's tone stopped me. "Someone betrayed them both." He had all my attention now. I let go of the door. "I heard them talk about it late at nights, cursing the other bloke's name and swearing they'd set things right. It was an old friend of Arn's who handed them both over to the king."

Numbness set over me. He didn't need to say the name for me to guess who it was. The one who had been there for me when Arn had left, the one who had handed me the note in the first place and told me Arn had sailed away. The one who'd offered me a home on his ship as if he hadn't stripped away the one with whom it felt like home.

"Ontario?"

"That'd be the name I heard."

Emric was right then. And Raven and I might have been very, very wrong to leave Emric alone with him. I swung open the door. I needed to find her.

After I talked with her, Raven reached for the communication pod. "Emric should have come with us. I might have underestimated Ontario by a long shot. If he's been doing business with my father, then I don't trust him." She pressed the button and stepped back.

It flashed for a long time before Ontario finally appeared.

His eyebrows went up. "I see you've shown Raven the device." His jacket was buttoned, but his cheek was red, as if he'd been hit, and he was breathing hard.

"Is Emric there?" I asked as nicely as I could. "We'd like to speak to him."

Ontario's expression faltered. "He's sleeping now, but I'll tell him you've asked for him."

"He slept on the night shift." Accusation was clear in Raven's tone. Any faked friendliness between us and Ontario was now gone. "He wouldn't be sleeping now."

"And yet." Ontario shrugged.

Raven drew close to the image. "You listen to me. I do not trust you at all. If Emric is harmed while I am away, I promise you I will send the entirety of my father's army against you and make both Arabella and Queen Isla look weak in comparison. Do you understand?"

Ontario didn't appear threatened. In fact, he smiled. "Try."

Then he shut the pod off.

26

ONTARIO

EARLIER

After expressing my concern about Emme, I shut off the communication pod and Tess shut the door behind her. "Emme is significantly harder to kill when she is not on board," she said. Her black, knitted cap, wool tunic, and black canvas doublet was a mirror of what Raven wore that garnered an air of mystery about both of them.

She even sounded like Raven as she pressed. "Do you have a plan?"

But there was a shake in her voice that surprised me. She was nervous, I realized. The task I'd given her wouldn't be so easy after all.

I sat at my chair and watched the flame of the candle flicker, trying to piece together a new plan in my mind. We could chase Arabella forever and never catch her, and she could turn on us at any moment. I was done going after her. She would come to me.

"Let me take out Emric at least," she went on. "Then half the job will be done."

"No." I put my hand up to still her. "We won't kill him yet. I want to wait until we have Arabella in our grasp to finish him off." I stood and selected a long-tipped dagger from my collection. "Find rope," I instructed. "Thickest lines we have."

She left to do so, and I called Emric to the cabin.

This part of the plan would be easy enough to carry out. When he entered, I feigned exhaustion, sitting slowly down on my cot. "Would you captain for a while? I need rest."

Predictably, his eyes lit up. "You sure?"

Someone moved outside the cabin, and I waited for them to pass. It was pertinent that no one overheard my request. "Of course. You'd be doing me a favor." I patted his arm, letting my cufflink dig into his sleeve so it tore when he moved.

I apologized immensely, but he'd been so eager to captain that he hadn't given it notice.

The next part of the plan was not pleasant, so I did it quickly. I took my telescope and bashed it against my cheekbone.

The pain was instant, with a heat that spread over my skin as the spot throbbed. I gave it enough time to redden before stepping out of the cabin and climbing to the deck. Emric was at the wheel, enjoying his taste of being captain again.

"I thought you were resting," Emric said as I approached. He didn't even look my way.

Emric was the only person left whom I feared would take my position as captain from me. Arn and Landon were gone. It would ease my worries to remove the last threat.

I planted myself next to him and threw a punch.

Emric staggered back, but I drew my pistol and let him stare down the barrel.

I'd been surprised that he hadn't demanded the ship back the moment he'd returned from the grave. It'd been rightfully his. Instead, he'd been loyal. Even so, none would be surprised if he asked for it back, and I knew they wouldn't question when I claimed that now.

"What is this?" he growled.

I let my voice ring out. "You dare try to take my place as captain?"

We had the attention of everyone on deck now, and I spoke to them. "Just a minute ago he threatened to kill me if I didn't let him have the ship back."

"I did no such thing, and you know it," Emric said grimly. But my crew saw the tear in Emric's sleeve and the red on my cheek, and my story was believable.

His hand inched toward his hilt.

"Careful now," I said through my teeth. "Think of Emme."

"I'm thinking of how I'd like to kill you," he spat. His voice and eyes were both filled with fury as he slowly raised his hands. I took away his cutlass, then led him to the deck, all the while keeping my pistol against his back.

"To the mast," I ordered. "You'll be tied there."

He stopped. "I'll freeze if you leave me overnight."

"Go, or I shoot."

"I know you will."

Emric took one step forward, then spun around, ramming his elbow into my hands to point the pistol away. The crew on deck scattered. I fired, but the bullet went harmlessly into the sea. Before I could fire again, he wrapped his hands around my neck and squeezed. I slammed the pistol into his temple. He didn't waver. I fumbled to aim the gun, and it wasn't until he saw it turn at him that he let go, grabbed the barrel, and pointed it away again.

I punched his gut. His fist collided into my jaw with a force that shook me. He hit again. Then he drew my own cutlass from my sheath and held it below my neck, keeping his other hand on my gun to render it useless.

"I've been watching you for a long time," Emric rasped. "And you know what, Ontario? I never trusted you."

He would have ended me there, but instead, he crumpled to the ground.

Tess stood behind him with the hilt of her dagger raised. She tucked it away calmly. "Are you certain we don't kill him now?" she whispered.

I was tempted. But I had use for him still. "Let's tie him up."

His wrists were bound behind him and strung to the main mast while the crew watched in silence. "He is not to be released," I ordered. I received solemn mutters of agreement.

Tess was inspecting Emric oddly, and it almost looked like regret. It wasn't long ago that I'd knocked her unconscious when I'd traded Landon and Arn away to the king of Az Elo, and I wondered if she thought of that. When it came to loyalty, Tess seemed to go where the money was and where the tides turned, and recently that'd been with me. She was smart in that way, that she knew which path to take to align herself with powerful people. It wouldn't surprise me if one day she was a partner in Jackson's business as well. I'd put in a good word for her.

I placed a hand on her shoulder. "You've done well."

"Let me know when the job needs to be done," she said firmly, then slipped away like a shadow.

After being choked, I staggered back to my cell to grab a flask of water. I hadn't much time before I ought to reappear to the crew, who would undoubtedly have questions. Those questions might grow when Emric woke and pled his case. I needed to work quickly. And I should gag him.

On my desk, the communication pod was flashing.

I had hoped to not see Jackson again until I had news that Arabella was captured, and the bruise on my cheek was hard to hide, but it wouldn't look good to ignore his call. I smoothed my hair down and answered.

It wasn't Jackson. It was Emme . . . and Raven.

"I see you've shown Raven the device," I said. My voice was hoarse, and from the accusation in their eye, they were no longer friendly. That was fine. I was burning bridges today anyway. All necessary in order to forge the new empire—one that would be built from the wreckage I created.

After Raven's speech, I almost laughed. I knew who she was, but she had no clue who I was or what I could do. "Try," I taunted and pressed their image away.

It was almost midday, yet I felt as drained as if it were midnight. There was still one more person to contact, and I greatly wished I could do this one over a communication pod as well so I could see her face when she found out I had captured her son. As it was, a note would have to do. I could picture her wrath, though, and hear her ordering her crew to find us.

No more chasing. No more running. This would end now, before the winter thawed.

> *Arabella,*
> *You will turn yourself over to me, or I will kill Emric before the sun goes down on the third day.*
> *You want your son? Come and get him.*

My father had always foregone signing his name at the bottom, letting the threat speak by itself. I'd found it dramatic, but now I adopted his style as I sent it away.

Things were coming together nicely.

The next morning, I got her reply.

> *I'll be right there.*

27

ARN

We bided our time with our escape, but at least we had a plan. We'd use my hook to pry the window from its frame, sneak through the porthole, and scale the hull to the deck, preferably at night when the crew would be less alert. The climb wouldn't be a pleasant one, and it would require a grappling hook.

Landon was on the cot, tossing a rock that he'd found and letting it fall into his palm, over and over. "Or you pry the hinges off, and we go that way."

"We aren't prepared to fight our way out," I told him. As much as I enjoyed the simplicity of his plan, mine allowed us to find a rowboat and escape, while his left us bleeding out in the passageway.

Or, we'd starve first. They greatly neglected our needs in this abysmal cell.

A distant door opened, and footsteps came our way. "Are you still alive?" Arabella called out before we saw her. Then she stepped into view, holding a note in her hand. Landon stopped tossing the rock to lean forward, but I kept on my knees, facing her so she'd have no chance to see the outline of the hook hidden on my back.

Her eyes took in the dreary sight of us, and she grinned.

"Of course you are. You're resilient." She took a key from her pocket. "Besides, I wouldn't kill you. I've got special plans."

She fit the key into the lock. At the sound of the bolt unclicking, Landon and I both had the same idea, and without so much as an exchange of glances, we both abandoned our earlier plans in favor of a new one. We lurched forward.

As we knocked the door opened, Arabella stepped aside, and in a fluid motion, she had a dagger drawn.

But she didn't put it to our throats. She twisted it before her face. "Before you try anything," she began. The glint of steel held us at bay. "I am your only chance to live. If anything happens to me, the entire crew is ordered to kill you. But if I live, then so do you."

"I'd take my chances against the crew," Landon said with an edge in his voice.

In the same breath, I demanded, "Where is Emme?"

"Close," Arabella said. "I hope." She tapped the note against her arm. "However, it seems I have unpleasant matters to attend to first. I will be leaving for a brief time and," she pointed at us, "you will make yourselves useful as part of this crew until I return."

Now Landon and I exchanged looks. This kindness, if it could be called that, was unexpected from Arabella. I'd expected exactly what we'd gotten over the last few days: poor provisions and cold lodgings.

She headed down the passageway to climb back above deck. "Now before you think of leaving, all the rowboats are bolted down, and you don't know who has the key. No one leaves unless I say so. Furthermore, I only employ crew that I trust, so you will not be able to turn any of them against me. And lastly, if I hear you've been an ounce of trouble in my absence, you will not survive another day. You are part of my plan, but not vital enough that I need you alive. Understand?"

There was the ruthless.

She didn't wait for an answer but let the threat hang in the chilly air.

Then she was gone, and Landon and I were standing outside the cell, free but still trapped.

"Looks like we don't need a break a window," Landon said. Neither he nor I made a move to go above deck. I didn't trust what we'd find there.

"Once more, we're asked to join a crew that doesn't want us," I said. "And I don't care about being a pawn." Now freed, I screwed my hook on its base and savored the strength it gave me.

"What's our plan?"

"I'll come up with something," I mused. "But I won't let her use me against Emme. That's a promise."

28

EMME

It had been agony thinking Arn had left me. It was worse knowing he was in trouble. Raven felt it, too, as the one she loved was in danger. Yet neither of us could go to them.

The nerves came out in small actions, incessant pacing, and jittery movements. Raven and I were at the helm now, staring over the water with preoccupied minds.

"How do the seas look, Captain?" Raven asked. We were slow to move at first as we tested out the new sails and mast, but now we picked up speed.

Jakob straightened happily at the title. "Fair seas. We travel quickly."

"Good," Raven said, though her tone was displeased. She paced around the helm. Her pale blonde hair was tied up with twine, so every twitch of her eye was seen.

"He'll be fine," I said as she prowled past me.

She gave no reply. The wrinkles in her brow deepened.

Sometimes it was me assuring her, sometimes it was her assuring me. Both of us handing out promises we couldn't prove and hope we couldn't fulfill. But we gave it anyway. It provided less and less comfort with each time.

I turned my eyes back to the seas, eastbound, the direction Jakob said Arn was taken. The queen knew she was getting

Arabella, so she shouldn't have need to kill Arn. But she was unpredictable, even less so than Ontario, and I couldn't guess what she would do.

I could guess. I tried not to. None of those visions were pleasant.

In the distance, a messenger hawk descended. Raven's relentless pacing finally stopped. "At last," she breathed, and shoved her hand into her pocket to pry a letter out.

"Finest one we've got," Jakob said proudly.

"I remember."

The hawk settled on the taffrails before Raven, his head bowed. In turn, she stroked his neck. "This is important, Abago," she murmured to the bird. "Find the *Nightingale* and deliver this to the children on board. They need to know where I am." She whispered the coordinates.

She removed the twine around her hair and tied the letter to Abago's leg, and he flew off. She watched until he was out of sight.

It was silent for a while, then Jakob spoke. "You never gave a reason for leaving us."

She dropped her eyes. He didn't push for an answer, but he waited for anything she would give him. Raven's hand went to her necklace. "I didn't think of it as leaving everyone. It wasn't about Az Elo or anyone there. It was about searching for my true purpose, and I found it."

"You had a purpose," he responded defiantly. "With us."

"I had a father who had his own designs and sent his whole army scouring the seas to drag me home and bind me to the castle," she said. "I don't want that."

From the tight draw of Jakob's lips, he didn't approve of her abandoning her home country. Raven stood there in the stiff air to acknowledge whatever he had to say to her.

"There isn't anyone else to rule us," he argued. "Not well, at least."

Raven held her ground. "I can list ten advisors who would be more than adequate—they'd be wonderful."

"I can list a hundred who are crooked, and I bet yours are on there." Jakob held the wheel with one hand so he could face Raven fully, looking at her less like a beloved princess and more like a reviled deserter. "Your father fell apart after you left, and what remained of his council scrambled to establish themselves as rulers of small territories, leeching any resources from the capital as possible." Raven went slack. Jakob continued, "Your kingdom is fragmented and aimless. We need you."

It wasn't fair to her. She wasn't born to rule—her brother was. But he'd died shortly after the princess from Julinbor was killed en route to him, thrusting Raven into a position she hadn't prepared for. Now, she also had a crew of children depending on her, ones whom she didn't want to walk away from, and a kingdom looking to her, asking her to come home.

"If my country needs me, I will find a way to help," Raven said. "But there are others depending on me as well."

Jakob didn't ask what she'd been getting into since she'd left, but he looked at me as if I were the one who'd dragged her to sea. I turned away.

"I will not force you home. But I beg of you to leave behind what life you have here and return to us."

Raven went to the rails to stare the direction the messenger hawk had gone, keeping her back rigid. "I protect the people I love," she said, and she left it at that.

29

ONTARIO

There was a strange sense in the air, almost like a living thing that fluctuated in accordance to our surroundings. Dropping when there was danger about. Thinning when there was fright. Thickening when tensions were high.

Now, it seized up. The moisture was sucked from it, leaving behind a brittle thing with uncertain energy. I felt the change from the helm, where I steered us through the dark of night, and didn't have to turn to know what it meant.

Arabella had arrived.

She approached from the east, single-handedly crewing a skiff, with a white flag raised and lips turned down.

Tess watched from above, and as Arabella's skiff drew near, she let out a low whistle like a bird's warning call. The warning settled over us all like a haunting melody, awakening every survival instinct. At the sound, Emric woke.

"Someone is here for you," I told him.

Emric's lips were turning blue and his cheeks pale, but he used what little strength he had to struggle against his bonds as he tried to see over the rails. His mouth was still gagged.

"Tell me," I said as I gathered rope in hand. "What must it be like to have someone fight this hard for you? She's come, alone, in the middle of a freezing night, to your aid, no matter how many times you tell her you don't need her."

His eyes flared wide as he realized who I meant was coming. He thrashed harder, though I couldn't be certain if he fought to keep his mother safe from me, or to keep himself safe from her.

Tess moved around the deck, knocking lightly against the various crates we'd set up in a perimeter, cueing our crew to be on guard. For a bit, it was the only sound until we could hear the water breaking beneath Arabella's skiff. I moved to the rails.

Her hair was wet, her eyes raging, and her voice gruff as she spoke. "I came. Where is my son?"

"Glad you could join us." I threw the rope to her. She made quick work of tying it around her mast and scaling to the deck like a spider searching for a victim to inject with her poison.

It was a dangerous thing to have someone like her on board, and as soon as her boots hit the deck, the energy in the air heightened. I tried to keep myself steady through it, as my father would have done. He wouldn't be fazed by Arabella the Ruthless, especially not if he had a plan like I did.

It was dark tonight, and I'd only allowed one lone oil lamp to be lit. Arabella peered through the inky darkness.

"Where is he?"

She'd hunched her back like a lion, scouring for danger. Her focus snagged on her son, weak and tied down. Her frown sharped into a grimace. "Let him go." The words were short and came from a deep place within her, like a beast waited there, eager to jump.

"This is a trade situation. You for him." I held up additional rope. "Just say the word, and he goes free."

My eyes took in the details of her, from the sparrow-tailed jacket with double rows of brass buttons, to the loose, cotton pants, and the golden glint off her cutlass's hilt and the curve of her pistols. A bump along her thigh indicated a dagger. Those long boots were perfect for hiding two more. Her red hair was twisted up with pins that were likely lethal. She was armored to the teeth.

Arabella hardly looked at Tess. Last time they saw each other, Arabella had been impressed with the young girl, but now she made no indication of that. Tess had a blank expression on her face.

A true, worried mother might cross to her son. But Arabella did not go near Emric. She just looked at him warningly as she spoke. "Once I set you free, take my skiff and find my ship. The crew will take care of you."

There it was, her plan to get Emric on crew with her. And thanks to how poorly I'd treated Emric over the past few days, he'd likely take the deal. She'd get him, and later Emme would come to their rescue.

Emric watched his mother, but there was no pleading there. His expression was empty. With his pale skin, it made him appear lifeless.

I undid his gag.

He wet his lips before replying, "No."

She jerked like he'd slapped her. "I am not your enemy here."

"I've no interest in joining your crew. I would only take your skiff and sail away."

At least he was honest.

I expected her to fight to free him. Instead she turned to me, whipped out a knife, and placed it under my chin. "This was not how the deal was supposed to go." She spoke quiet enough for only me to hear.

"It was. I just skipped a step."

Her lips twisted in a snarl. "I wasn't ready to come yet."

"It is not my fault Emric doesn't want to join your crew," I told her. "No matter how long you waited, his reaction would not have changed."

Her eye swept back to Emric, and I saw her debating leaving him.

"You go now, and he will never trust you," I whispered.

"I don't need him to trust me. I needed you to break him enough that he would be grateful if I freed him."

I thought I had broken him. He'd gone days with little food or warmth, and every bent angle of him showed how exhausted he was. But she'd ruined him far worse than I had.

"Here's the plan: You agree to be bound if he goes free, but I'll keep him tied up. Then I will give you the key to the cell," I said, slipping her the key to my cabin instead. "You can stage a great breakout and see how grateful he is then."

She mulled over it, all the while keeping that blade pressed uncomfortably against my neck. Then she tipped it away. "I've got my own plan."

With striking accuracy, she threw her blade and severed one of the bonds that held Emric back. The blade teetered in the wood, just beside his arm, as the ropes unwound themselves and fell.

"Grab the blade and fight for yourself," Arabella challenged. "Join me or stay here to die."

Then she threw herself toward the rails.

Sensing her intention, I let out a sharp whistle. That was the cue.

Barrels lifted, cracks opened, and tarps were thrown back as crewmembers emerged from hiding with cutlasses drawn. I seized Arabella's jacket before she could throw herself overboard, then ducked to avoid her punch. She drew another blade, but my cutlass was already poised under her chin.

One by one, other cutlasses followed suit, forming a circle around her.

None would move on Emric, but he didn't move on us either. Instead, he yanked the dagger from the mast and slipped it into his pocket.

"Do you desire to fight?" I asked Arabella. "Your life is worth very little difference to me dead or alive."

"It makes a difference to me." She flicked her arm.

A dagger from her sleeve fell into her hands, and with a second flick, she sent it straight into Tess's shoulder.

The girl sank to her knees.

A blind anger came over me. I twisted my cutlass and bashed the dull end across Arabella's forehead, and she fell.

"Someone grab me rope," I shouted. "Medic to Tess now!" It was the first time I missed Arn. His medical knowledge would be valuable. It was hard to see Tess through the crew that had gathered around, but she was moving, which was a good sign.

Arabella wasn't quite unconscious, so I hurried to tie her arms behind her back and drag her belowdecks. She stumbled as she moved, but was alert enough to curse at me as I yanked her into our only cell. We'd cleaned it out earlier, which was why we had the influx of crates on deck. The first prisoner the *Royal Rose* had carried in years, and it was a big one.

I removed all the weapons I could find on her and locked the cell door.

"I grew up hearing stories about you," I remarked. Now that she was locked in, it was easier to speak. She was on her knees, hands on the bars and head bent low so I couldn't see her expression. "I heard some pretty vicious things. I expected someone a little rougher."

She glared as she looked up. "You haven't heard the half of it."

I bent to be on her level. "But I've seen all I will ever see. When it comes to your children," I pointed upward, "you will always be divided. You should have forgotten about them and moved on with your life. They've certainly done so in regard to you."

That menacing look wasn't one I'd soon forget.

"Can't you see that they do not care for you?" I pressed. "They want absolutely nothing to do with the parent who neglected to raise them or show a sliver of affection. And now you are reaping the benefits of that."

She surprised me with a sly smile. "I am not the same as Admiral Bones."

I flinched. Foolishly, I hadn't reckoned on the research she would have done upon returning to the seas.

I stood and straightened my jacket. "Thank you for making this easier for me to capture you. I must admit, I thought we'd get you on Kwoli, but you evaded us again."

I said it so she'd know she wasn't the only one with detailed information, but her expression gave me pause.

My chest sank. "You were never on Kwoli." It wasn't a question. It was a revelation.

"No." She was standing now. "But it's curious that you think I was. Perhaps you should think twice about who you partner with. The old man doesn't know everything."

I controlled my reaction this time, but her awareness of Jackson was far more concerning than her knowledge of my father.

I started to walk away.

"What about the key you were to give me?"

I laughed. "The plan has changed. I'll give you a key when I'm ready."

Above deck, I was relieved to find Tess sitting up. A fair amount of blood stained her clothes, and her shoulder was wrapped, but she seemed alright. Emric was sawing through the last of his bonds as most of the crew watched him uncertainly.

"How are you?" I asked Tess.

Her voice was detached. "I could have died."

She could have, but it'd bring her no comfort to say so.

"You are a fighter," I said instead. "You aren't taken down so easily."

Yet by the distant look in her eye, the dagger had hurt more than her shoulder—it had hurt her confidence. "If she had killed me," she gestured awkwardly, "this is all I would have become."

I was trying to think of something to comfort her, but Emric's voice shouted out at me. "If you wanted me as a trap, you could have said so!"

I remedied the situation. "Tie him back up."

Emric tugged on his feet to try to finish loosening the bonds. He glared at me. "Why? You have what you want."

"No," I snapped. "I don't. I want Arabella gone, and I want my ship safe. But as long as your mother remains on deck, I need something to keep her in check. You are my ticket to do that, so I need you exactly where I can see you at all times."

"If you're worried I'm going to free her, I won't," Emric said, swinging his dagger at any who attempted to bind him. Bo, Bishop, Collins, and Timmons were the only ones who didn't even move to try—those who still remembered him when he was their captain. The rest were paid by me, and that made them bolder.

I swung my finger to point at the four. "I have concerns that one of them will free you, and you'll try to take my ship again."

"I didn't try in the first place," Emric roared.

I advanced through the circle of the crew, my cutlass raised. They backed up, leaving only Emric, still bound by his legs to the mast, his gag fallen around his neck. He slashed as I drew closer, blade meeting my cutlass with a sharp clang.

I swatted his blade away and cut downward. It tore through the skin of Emric's shoulder, the same place where his mother had shot Tess.

He let out an ear-shattering cry, but kept a hold of his dagger.

I pried it from his fingers.

"Tie him," I ordered my crew again. They were faster to obey this time.

When his wrists were bound together, he sank to his knees once more. "What has happened to you?" His voice was hoarse. "What have you become?"

I didn't owe him an answer, but I thought of it all the same. I'd become someone very different from the loyal first mate he'd first met. In five years, I hoped to be different again. Stronger, wiser, more respected. But for now, this was who I had to be.

A tinge of guilt pricked me as I looked him over—pale skin, weak body, bloodied shirt. It was a hard feeling to swallow. To do so, I tipped my head upward to see the emerald stars.

"The path I was on before would have led me to nowhere," I said, more to myself than to him. "I was nothing. But now?" I surveyed him, then my ship and crew. I was a captain. I was the one who had captured Arabella. I was about to forge a personal relationship with Queen Isla upon turning Arabella over. I was in business with a man who was about to change the world. Those were things to be proud of, and everything I had to do to get what I had now—it was worth it.

"I've become *someone*," I replied. Then I walked away with an order to bandage his shoulder so he didn't bleed out on my deck.

I wasn't certain if Emme would answer, but after five flashes, her picture came into view. She was in that small storage room again, but this time she didn't look like she'd been crying. The white of her cloak made her dark hair stand out, which she left wild and untamed. Her jaw was set as she spoke before I could. "May I ask to see Emric?"

Better not.

"I have your mother," I said instead.

That got her attention. Her stiff demeanor dropped. "Where?"

"Locked in a cell," I said proudly. "Tomorrow, Queen Isla will meet us at these coordinates. Bring the men of Az Elo as well, in case of a fight."

I'd be surprised if a fight didn't happen, though by this point, I didn't trust Emme to be on my side. But if Arabella's crew came searching for her when she didn't return, I wanted the appearance of an army there as we handed Arabella over to the queen.

One more day, and the seas would be declared safe again—from the queen and from Arabella.

"We will be there. But first," Emme said, "I want to see my mother."

I hadn't let anyone see Arabella. I didn't trust how she could spin words and twist alliances.

"Why?"

"Because she's my mother, and it might be my last chance," Emme responded evenly. "Before we hand her to the queen, I'd like a final word."

It was such a simple request, and it did fulfill my end of the deal with Arabella, so I nodded. "You can see her tonight if you wish."

"Thank you. I'll be waiting."

Then she disappeared.

30
EMME

Raven was there in the shadows of the crates, the entire time, watching as I spoke with Ontario. When I hung up, she moved from the position with a frown. "Something isn't right."

"Emric will be okay," I assured her. I was as worried for his safety as she was, but there was no indication that Ontario planned him harm. "Arabella holds all of Ontario's focus."

Raven picked up the communication pod to inspect it. "And you trust that Ontario is being honest? What if he intends to unleash Arabella against us?"

"What purpose would he have for fighting Az Elo?"

"There is much bad blood there."

"Queen Isla is coming as well, and she wants Arabella more than anyone."

"She also wants Az Elo, and killing me would be the perfect way to do that. And if Ontario knows who I am, she probably does too."

I hadn't considered that. And I could picture him using Emric against Raven. "Then we keep you away from the fight."

She set the communication pod down. "I can't stay away." She crossed her arms, but her fingers wandered up to her necklace again. It was a gamble when it came to trusting Ontario, but ultimately, he wanted Arabella out of the picture, and everything he did would be in favor of that. So long as she was on the *Royal Rose*, his focus would be there.

"And Queen Isla will come to the *Royal Rose*?" Raven asked.

"Usually, I'd doubt the queen would come personally, but she seemed determined to prove herself to her captains. I wager she'll board."

From the way Raven nodded, I could tell an idea had taken root. I was about to ask what it was, but she had a question of her own. "What will you say to your mother?"

Before I answered, the door opened behind her.

Jakob filled the doorway, holding a note in his hand. "It just arrived, Your Highness," he said with a little bow. "With a child's writing."

The question there was obvious, but she ignored it to snatch the letter and scan its contents. She gasped and her eyes met mine. "They've located Arabella's ship."

"Ask them to keep an eye on its movements and alert us to where they go," I said. "If Arabella's crew goes to her aid, we'll need to know."

Jakob arched a brow, and Raven looked at him squarely. "Arabella is captured belowdecks of the *Royal Rose*. If we play our cards right, we will also have the queen."

Jakob's eyes widened. "The queen?"

"You told me our kingdom is falling apart." Raven tucked the letter away. "Queen Isla can fix that, and we know where she's going to be."

She skirted past him, leaving me to wonder how we could possibly make it out of this week unscathed with so many plans in the air. We had an agenda, Ontario had an agenda, Arabella had an agenda, and the queen would too. Someone was bound to be foiled, and I could only hope it wasn't us.

31

ONTARIO

I called for Jackson. Either he'd lied to me about Arabella being on Kwoli, or he'd been mistaken. If he'd lied, I needed to know why.

When he first asked to be in business, I'd said no. Perhaps I'd been wrong to change my mind.

It wasn't Jackson who answered, but Zara. Her dark hair was curled into delicate ringlets, a gold ring gleamed from her nose, and silver painted her eyelids.

"I've captured Arabella." The words tumbled out.

She was taken back. Then a lithe smile crossed her face. "Truly?"

"She's in my cells now," I said. "If you listen hard enough, you're certain to hear her screams."

Arabella had been intolerable. Half the crew signed a petition to throw her into the sea and be done with the noise, and I was more than tempted to take it. I suspected it a ploy to mess with our minds until we couldn't think straight and were willing to do whatever she wanted to make it stop. She was relentless, I'd give her that. But I was too.

Zara made a noise in the back of her throat and threw her feet on her father's desk to lean back in his chair. "I'm impressed. You're more than I thought you were."

I tried not to take offense to that. "What did you think I was?"

"A boy who inherited more than he could handle. Someone who was all talk and no action." The words pierced but were quickly smoothed. "I was wrong. You're quite something."

Quite something.

I grinned. "You're not too bad yourself. Designing technology like this?" I gestured to the communication pod. "It's impressive."

She sat straighter and glanced around her. "You think that's good? I'm working on something new." Her voice was low, telling me this was information that wasn't freely shared. It touched me that she'd do so with me.

"What is it?"

"A water cleaner." She scrambled through the desk until finding drawings, which she held up for me. They showed two boxlike structures connected by a tube, with meshing between them. "You'd attach it to your ship so it pulls water from the sea as you sail, which then gets cleansed through this tube, and stored here. A whole stock of these, and you'd have enough water to keep your crew hydrated even on the hottest days."

Now that she'd said it, I marveled how it hadn't been done before. "That's brilliant. Will your father manufacture it?"

"He will. And you'll distribute it."

There was a light in her eye as she spoke, one that I didn't see often. It was pure passion and nothing more, like she'd do this for free if only someone would hand her the materials. I imagined she could get lost in the workshop for days, bent over designs, creating things from the genius of her mind. Her joy wasn't from money or power or respect. It was from creating.

Zara shouldn't be hidden in the background of the company. She should be the face of it. People would be drawn to her products, but they'd be more drawn to her.

"You're going to make us rich," I proclaimed. It was hard

not to dream of my new life already. "What will you do with the profits?"

"I'd like to travel and explore the world. I've wanted to see the southern lands and follow the Unending Land to see where it goes. Explore the Moving Islands. Just . . . see it all." There was that light again. Such eager joy. "How about you?"

"I don't need to see all the islands. I just want one. I'll purchase it for myself and spend a whole month there, with nothing but the waves and the sand, and enjoy the world from there."

Unabashed, she asked, "Room on your island for one more?"

That took my breath away. I smiled, and managed to say, "For you? I'll make room."

Her return smile was infectious. "When this business with Arabella is finished, come visit us. I'll show you the workshop and give you a tour of the factory. I know my father is eager to meet you in person."

At the mention of her father, I remembered my reason for calling. I did my best to keep my tone light. "I look forward to that."

If she noticed my change in tone, she didn't say anything. "Good. Did you need anything?"

"No," I said as smoothly as I could. "I was calling to speak with Jackson, but seeing you was much better."

Her nose crinkled with her broad smile. "I hope to see you again soon."

Zara's image faded away, leaving me grateful that I hadn't been met by Jackson after all. I'd find out later whether or not he had lied, but his relationship with me now included collateral.

I picked up the communication pod. Someone else needed it tonight.

32

EMRIC

The wind was harsh, but the battering within me was worse. There was a void that tangled inside, leaving me feeling hollow and stripped. When the wind snapped for the hundredth time against my back, I closed my eyes, begging for sleep to bring much-needed rest.

And quiet. My mother's shouts were unyielding.

I focused on the rhythm of movement around me—the slow tap of Bo's finger against his glass bottle as he sat across the deck, the swipe of Bishop's rag on the rails, the creak of the wheel as Clarice stood at the helm. She'd avoided my eyes the most, and I knew she suspected Ontario had lied about my intention to steal the ship back.

But she didn't do anything about it, so her thoughts did me no good.

I'd worked the gag down, so a mere flick of my tongue would push it away from my mouth. But I allowed it to stay put for now, so no one would see it. It wasn't freedom, but it was something.

Besides, I had nothing to say. Unless I cared to join my mother in her unyielding chorus.

I would have something to say to Ontario if he bothered to come above deck.

Sleep wasn't happening. I peeked one eye open.

Four people were still on deck. I had hoped for less. Mother's skiff was still bound to ours, and if I could make it off deck, I could sail away in it.

Maybe. I was injured and weak, after all.

A stronger option would be to free my mother and give way for her to sail for me, though I hated that idea with every fiber of my being. But I hated the idea of dying more, and I was unsure what Ontario planned for me.

Freeing my mother, it was.

In the earlier scuffle, no one saw me lift a dagger from Bo, and now I worked it out of my sleeve to start the long process of sawing through the ropes. With each scratch, I feared someone would look over and notice, but it seemed guilt kept their eyes at bay.

Though it wore on me, I made quick work of it, keeping my head lowered and eyes shut—as if I were asleep. My ears tuned to the crew as they moved around the deck.

A creak came from behind, one of aged wood giving way to weight. I froze. The silence that followed was too empty. Too purposeful.

Slowly, I eased the dagger back into my sleeve, not daring to move otherwise.

I opened my eyes to the dark night. Someone had snuffed a lantern. I could make out Bo and Clarice on deck, but a prickly feeling told me there was a third.

Another noise came, one so soft that, if I weren't straining, I wouldn't have heard. It was the barest movement of a cloak as the fabric moved against itself.

Someone was advancing, and they didn't want to be heard.

Before I had time to flick out my blade again, someone else's was against my wrists. I would bleed to death, then. That would be my fate.

But they didn't cut me. They cut the ropes.

"Don't move." A small voice came, soft as the wind.

"Tess?" I realized.

Her hand rested against mine. "If you move, Clarice will know you are free." She withdrew her hand, and there was a sawing sound. I felt the bonds tighten around my legs before they gave way altogether. I was free.

"Why are you doing this?" I whispered, resisting the urge to look at her. Bo glanced my way, then took a long swig of his drink and faced the sea again. Tess must have been so hidden in the shadows that he couldn't spot her.

She was quiet for so long that I wondered if she'd gone away. "Tess?"

"I'm here," she said softly.

"Why?" I asked.

I heard her sigh. "I lost track of what was right. I want to find that path again."

She said it like there was some great sin she was atoning for, but I heard her retreating before I could thank her or ask anything more.

My first plan came to mind: get Arabella and leave. But as I looked over the deck, my mind changed. I didn't want to leave. This ship was too much a part of me. I had become fond of it. And I liked this crew. I didn't want to run.

Ontario had falsely accused me of trying to steal back his ship. But now, I was going to. The *Royal Rose* would be mine to captain again.

I held my dagger tight in my fist as I shifted until the ropes all dropped. My plan came together slowly. I didn't know who else on the crew was against me. I could only guess from their expressions as they'd bound me that Ontario worked alone. But it wasn't a chance I liked to risk. I studied the distance between me and the hatch to belowdecks. I'd need to pick the perfect moment.

It was Tess who gave it to me. She no longer lurked in the

shadows but strode down the deck and went up to the helm to stand by Clarice, angled at such a way that when Clarice looked at her, she was looking away from me. Over her shoulder, Tess gave me a small nod.

Bo was still facing the sea. This was the best chance I'd get.

I peeled away from the mast, treaded to the hatch, and slipped belowdecks.

At the bottom, I swung to find Ontario. Instead, a voice stopped me, one that should not be on this ship. Was that Emme? Surely, I was hearing wrong. I turned away from the captain's cabin and glanced around the corner to where Arabella's cell was.

Sure enough, Emme stood there.

She wore a white cloak lined with fur, a thick dress beneath, and her hair was let loose. She stood daringly close to the cell doors where Arabella glowered before her. I was about to call to her when she spoke.

"Did you ever love me?"

The question swallowed her pride to leave Emme looking vulnerable before Mother, waiting to hear the answer. Silence stretched between them, one that was more painful by the moment. I could feel the pain, too, and I saw it in the glint of Emme's eyes. She spoke again. "When did you lose love for everything other than yourself?"

"Blame it on the cursed island," Arabella replied. "It stole sentiment from me."

"No," Emme said staunchly. "You lost it well before that. So I wonder, why do you want me and Emric to sail with you so much? It's not love for your children that drives you, so what is it?"

Arabella didn't reply, but Emme didn't need her to.

Emme drew herself up. "I know what it is," she said. "It's fear. All this time, I've thought Arabella the Ruthless was invincible, but actually, you're afraid of what Emric and I might become. You keep us close so we can't grow beyond your shadow."

"I keep you close to keep us a family,"

"Emric is my only family," Emme snapped. "I lost my mother to the sea six years ago, and she never returned. And you," she gave a mirthless smile, "you lost your daughter the day you saw her in the prison cells and you *turned and walked away*." Her words were coated with disdain. "When you looked at me and decided I was nothing, and you abandoned me. You lost me then, and you know what? You won't get me back."

I wanted to reach for her, but she didn't need me. She needed this. This was how she said goodbye.

"You won't leave me," Arabella said. "Even now, you come looking for a mother's love. You'll never stop wanting that."

Emme leaned close. "I promise you this: I will hand you over to Queen Isla and not look back."

Arabella's eyes flickered and she stepped back. The determination in Emme's face was clear. There was nothing she could do to change our plans to give Arabella over.

"Look at you now," Arabella mocked. "Ruthless, just like me." Emme didn't respond. Arabella shrugged. "If I've lost my daughter, then so be it. In that case, I can still slay my enemies."

Without warning, she produced a dagger and drove it through the bars and into Emme's stomach.

33

EMME

When Arabella stabbed me, Emric cried out. I had seen him, but I hadn't seen Arabella's knife. Her lips curved in victory, but killing me would accomplish nothing for her. She was still trapped. The queen was still near. Her fate was bound.

But there was the answer I'd come here for, and now I knew my mother was gone beyond all hope of decency. She was twisted, broken, and dark. We were making the right choice by turning her over to Queen Isla.

All those thoughts skimmed my mind as I looked down at the blade and then back up to Arabella.

Her smile disappeared. She pulled out the dagger and thrust it forward again, but just as before, it passed effortlessly through me.

I lifted my arm through the bars, showing her. I was here, but I wasn't really here. Ontario had placed the communication pod outside the cell for me while Arabella had slept, so I could speak with my mother once more.

And my mother had tried to kill me.

Arabella blinked, trying to make sense of it.

My voice was thick with emotion. "I am not real. But the fleet waiting outside for you is."

I shed one last tear—the final tear I would shed for my mother.

"From this moment forward," I said, voice taut, "you are banished from the seas. If by some mercy, the queen spares your life, you will spend it on land, as the waters will be barred from you. You will no longer plague them with your destruction and cruelty. They are mine now, and you are not a part of my future." I watched as her face grew slack, then added the final blow. "I, Emme Jaquez Salinda, oathbind myself to you with this promise, that if you return to the seas, you will be shown no mercy."

Pain etched over my left foot as the binding tattoo marked itself, crawling its way over the skin and leaving a burning feeling behind. Thanks to this tattoo, I would know if she touched land, and I would know just where to find her.

We could have oathbound ourselves earlier, but we hadn't been desperate enough to try that before. But looking at the dagger in her hand that she'd just thrust into my belly—I was desperate enough now.

I reached to turn off the communication pod, but not before Arabella said quickly, "If you give me to the queen, Arn dies."

I stilled, then straightened. "What did you say?"

"You heard me. I have Arn, and if I'm not back to my ship in two days, they have orders to kill him. Tell Ontario to release me, or your love dies."

My heart pounded like thunder. There was no time to waste. "Don't release her," I ordered Emric, and I shut the device off.

My mind was racing. We knew where Arabella's ship was, but it was far away. If it received news of Arabella's capture before I got there, Arn would be dead.

Queen Isla was expecting to take Arabella in the morning. But I needed longer than that. We needed to delay the transfer until he was safe.

My mind became a blur. I ran to find Raven.

"Raven!" I tore through the passageways of the ship, searching for her cabin. "Raven!" I yanked open her door. She was awake still, staring out the porthole, the darkness of the room diminished by a lone candle flickering on the desk. Her eyes widened when she saw my face.

"What happened?" She reached for her cutlass.

"It's Arn," I gasped. "Arabella has him on her ship. If she doesn't return," I bent to catch my breath, "she's going to kill him." My words came in panicked puffs. "I have to save him."

"We will free him," Raven said. "He won't die." She pulled on her cloak and strapped her belt around her waist, as I tried to figure out a plan.

"I must speak with the queen first. She's expecting to receive Arabella tomorrow."

News of her capture could already be reaching her crew, and if we give her to the queen, that news would fly even faster. I couldn't risk it reaching Arabella's crew before I did. My best chance was keeping her on the *Royal Rose* until Arn was safe, then turning her over.

My foot still hurt from the recent oathbinding, and my mind was tormented by a picture of Arn bound in a cell as Arabella's men attacked and ran him through. It was a gruesome image that I couldn't move past, and it only knotted the worry inside me tighter.

Raven pointed out the window.

"Then it's your lucky day. The queen is here."

I looked out. We'd traveled all day to be near the *Royal Rose* in preparation for morning, giving Ontario the appearance of a fleet by his side as we took Arabella down. Queen Isla said she would come, and she'd shown up in full glory.

Her ship was bedecked in sparrow-tailed banners along the taffrails, fitted with forty cannons, and topped with crisp, cream sails, trimmed in cerulean blue. The carved figurehead depicted the queen herself, majestically guiding the ship with a dagger in one hand and a crown in the other. A name had been painted onto the side: *Isla's Revenge*. The oak gleamed with fresh polish, the sails hung clean, and the sheer size of the ship entranced me.

Looking at it, there was no doubt to whom it belonged. She didn't try to hide her identity or her wealth—she flaunted it. Bold, considering the pirates.

Beyond her ship, at least fifty ships lined the sea. Queen Isla appeared to be looking for a battle.

I bit my lip. Even with the Az Eloian's strength, we were wildly unmatched if friendly relations broke.

The *Royal Rose* waited in the distance, the three of us making a triangle. But the queen's fleet was in movement, slowly circling. They'd surround us before morning came.

"I'm taking a rowboat," I said. "I must speak with the queen." I climbed to the main deck where the air was cool and the atmosphere silent, as the crew kept an eye on the new arrivals. It wasn't too long ago that their country fought Julinbor.

Our flag had dropped its Az Elo sail in favor of a plain black one. We'd appear as pirates, and for now, that's what we were. Pirates trading away one of their own to end a war.

"I don't care for this." Jakob stood at the helm, inspecting the fleet around us. "We're too close."

"We aren't close enough," I countered. "Raven and I are going to the queen.

His face shut down. "No."

"Jakob," Raven said calmly but in a commanding tone, "we must see and speak to her."

His eyes were defiant, but his hands obeyed. Raven and I worked with the crew to adjust the sails and pull up the anchors until the light wind drifted us to *Isla's Revenge*.

The queen's fleet noted it right away. Their bell rang, dull and deep, alerting the other ships. Bodies moved on deck, and one by one, ships angled themselves toward the south, their bows pointed right at us.

When we were still a fair distance away, Raven lifted her hand. "That's far enough. I don't care to be shot at. We will take the rowboat from here." She started to untie it.

"I don't like this," Jakob said again.

"You don't have to come," Raven told him, using her teeth to rip open a knot. "Stay with the ship."

His expression seemed pained. "I don't want to lose you. We just found you."

She paused as she held the ropes. I hauled myself overboard, and she yanked the rest of the boat free. "I will be just fine." She slid down the rope to join me.

I hadn't the time to grab more weapons, but they'd likely strip us of them all anyway. Still, I was highly aware of how vulnerable we were as we rowed our tiny boat to their ship, their crow's nest eclipsing the moon and leaving us in shards of pale light.

Some of the queen's men had loaded into their own rowboat, and they met us halfway.

"Business?" one shouted. There were four men in the boat, all with hands on pistols.

"We ask to speak with Her Majesty," I called as I purposefully kept my own hand away from any weapons to show we meant no harm.

"On what business?"

"I am Arabella the Ruthless's daughter, and I have information about my mother."

They exchanged looks, then inspected us. We were two young girls, clearly not coated in weapons, and could do little harm. They agreed. "Come with us."

Two boarded our rowboat and took us all the way to *Isla's Revenge*.

My stomach turned as I thought of the last time I'd seen Isla. She'd been willing—eager almost—to kill me. Hungry to start a war and prove herself tough to her captains. She'd killed her husband with no warning, and she'd ordered my mother's death.

She was going to get my mother no matter what. But as I climbed aboard, all I could think was how, if she wanted, she could have me too.

"We have two pirates," one of the men said to the captain at the helm. "They seek to speak with the queen."

The captain had dark skin and a gold jacket that gleamed in the moonlight. His eyes scrolled over us—from our tangled hair to the tattoos on my arms. "Take them below. Alert Her Majesty."

Our arms were not bound, but eight men flanked our sides after we were brought down a ladder into a wide passageway, leading directly to a cabin marked by a crown. A man went before us to rap on the door.

A second later, the queen answered. "Yes?"

The sound of her voice gave me shivers. The officer went inside the queen's room, assumedly to inform her of the two washed-up looking girls who wanted a word, as the other seven men patted us down for weapons.

"You don't have to do that." Raven flipped a knife from her sheath. "This is all I have."

I drew one from my boot and one from the loop in the back of my pants. "I have two."

They checked us anyway. When they were satisfied, they stepped back and waited for the queen to summon us.

I tried not to think of all that could go wrong and instead focused on those I was helping. Arn. My brother.

My brother.

"I saw Emric by the way," I whispered to Raven. "He's fine."

Raven swung to me. "What?"

"He's fine. Perfectly fine."

She put a hand to her chest and gave a little laugh. "And you're just now telling me?"

"I forgot to tell you earlier," I confessed. "I'm sorry about that."

She faced the door again, but her frame was more relaxed. "Thank you, Emme. I know Emric and I have had little time together, but I really do care about him."

I was learning something about Raven: That when she loved, she did so deeply. When she fought for something, she did so with all her heart. From the children on the sea to my brother to winning this war, she put her full self into it and never wavered.

She didn't waver now as the door before us slid open.

"Her Majesty will see you," the man said, standing at attention. We both moved forward. His hand flicked. "Only you, daughter of Arabella."

Raven gave my hand a confident squeeze. I crossed the threshold alone and heard the door shut behind me.

The queen's cabin was unlike any I'd seen before, as if she was determined to forget she was on the sea. Thick curtains were draped over all the portholes, the cot had a true mattress with fluffed bedding on it, and almost every wall was covered with a painting of some sort, until it looked like a slice of the castle had drifted off land. A thin rug had been rolled out, the doors to the cabinets lacquered blue, a slim chandelier hung from the ceiling, and an extravagant desk with lion-like legs stood in the room's center.

Queen Isla sat behind the desk, her eyes fresh and alert. Her smile, as I took everything all in, transported me back to the night where she'd sentenced my mother to hang. She looked the same now as she did then, as if she'd won a great victory.

"You're brave to come here," she said smoothly. She crossed her legs. Instead of a dress, she had on a cream-colored tunic and wide pant legs, flowy enough that it looked like a gown but free enough that she could run if needed. A belt was around her waist, and a pistol sat there. She played with a curled tress of hair.

I went straight to business. "We have Arabella trapped and ready for you."

"I know." She touched a letter on the desk. "Captain Ontario informed me as such."

I took a gulp of breath. "I need three days before we hand her over." Her eyes narrowed, and I continued quickly, "She's trapped someone important to me, and if I don't free him before she's turned over, her crew will kill him."

She studied me before laughing. *Laughing.*

It was the same as when I'd begged her to spare my life when she knew I was innocent—she didn't care. Humanity had no place in her soul. Her words now were equally cold. "I owe you nothing."

"Not yet," I said. Luckily, I wasn't here to appeal to her virtue but her greed. "But I can offer you something better than Arabella."

A spark ignited behind her eyes. But her voice was calculated. "What?"

"If you find this new information of value, you will agree to my terms? We delay giving you Arabella by three days."

"If," she laid heavy on that word, "I like what you have to say." She stood. "If not, you and your mother will hang together."

My hand shook, but I didn't give myself time to be afraid. "You'll like this."

I drew out the communication pod and set it on her desk. She flinched at first, but when it was clear the device wasn't going to explode, she leaned closer. Before she could snatch it away, I put a hand over top. "This is technology unlike anything in the world, and it's being produced right under your nose. In a few months, this product will be delivered all across the lands and make its manufacturers rich beyond all desire. But"—I tapped it—"you can beat them to it. Put together a team to dissect this until they know how to replicate it, and you release it first. You'll make your kingdom rich."

That's what she wanted—not necessarily for her kingdom to be rich but that she was the source of it. I knew from our first meeting that she craved the approval of the captains of her army, and this would give it to her. She would be the one to change the world.

"What does it do?"

I had expected she'd want demonstrable proof. I set it on the ground and turned it on. "Watch." I purposefully set it so the queen wouldn't appear in the image with me, and hoped my background didn't give me away. After a few flashes, someone answered.

It was Emric.

"Where is Ontario?" I asked.

He was studying me then his feet as he figured out how this worked. "That dirty scoundrel is tied to the main mast," he replied. "Are you well?"

Behind him, the queen's eyes were wide. He couldn't see her, but she was staring at him like he was a ghost. It truly was unlike any technology the world had ever seen.

I wanted to go into details about what Ontario was doing tied to the mast, but I didn't have long, and I needed to convince the queen of what she was seeing. "I'm well. Where are you?"

He frowned. "On the *Royal Rose.*"

I put a finger to my lips and listened. From behind Emric, someone was shouting. "Is that Arabella screaming?"

"Aye, she won't stop."

I made sure the queen heard that, then grinned. "That'll be all. Please inform your crew that we will be delivering Arabella in three days, not tomorrow morning. Arn needs saving first." I turned off the communication pod.

Queen Isla was still for a long time. She twisted a strand of her hair, staring at the communication pod, piecing it together. "Did he have one of these too?" she eventually asked.

I nodded. "That's how we communicate. Each conversant needs one."

She faded back to silence as she thought.

"Think of how this will change things," I pressed. "You can speak to your army directly, instead of through captains. You can hold meetings with all your lords without having to travel. Families will all want one so they can stay connected to each other."

I could go on, but she lifted a hand. "I know how valuable this is. I'm trying to think of a team who can replicate it."

I picked up the device. "Do we have a deal?"

"We have a deal. I will wait three days for the *Royal Rose* to deliver Arabella, and no more."

I hated giving up my only way to communicate with Emric, but I passed it over. "Thank you."

Things were almost set right, and I could feel the success brimming in my chest, a hopeful feeling that I hadn't had for a long time. I opened the door to leave. Upon seeing me, Raven strode past before someone could stop her.

"Your Majesty," she declared, "I request an audience with you."

Queen Isla put the communication pod into her desk. "And who are you?" The guards stood aside, waiting to see what would happen.

Raven held her chin high. "I am Calypso, daughter of King Isaac, and I have a proposition."

Queen Isla's eyes went wide, and she gestured for the guards to shut the door. "Leave us."

There was a draw to Raven's shoulders almost like defeat. She'd worked so hard to keep her identity a secret from everyone, and since she'd met me, she'd lost that time and time again. But even now as she lay herself before the queen, there was a glint in her eye that said she was getting exactly what she wanted out of this. Meanwhile, Queen Isla was soaking in the sight of the lost princess from Az Elo here on her ship, and likely plotting what this could mean for her.

Rough hands took hold of my arms to lead me out. Raven only had time to give me a reassuring nod before the door was closed between us.

I wasn't privy to Raven's plan with the queen nor to their conversation now. All I got was muffled echoes through a door as the guards and I stood silently, all pretending that we weren't trying to listen in.

Before I knew it, the door swung open again. Raven strode out as confidently as she'd strode in, her expression unreadable.

I peered at the queen. She was sitting at the desk with one leg crossed over the other, a finger stroking her cheek in thought.

I looked at Raven questioningly.

"I guaranteed us peace," she said. "Peace for you and for my country." Then, without asking permission from the guards who watched us, she headed above deck and climbed aboard a rowboat. Whatever had just happened, she wasn't in the mood to tell, and this wasn't the place to speak of it. She lifted an oar and said, "Are you coming? Arn is waiting." Suddenly all I could think of was him. Once in, with droplets of misty sea in the air and the pinks of morning at my back, I grabbed hold of the oar and rowed.

When we'd almost reached the *Commander,* Raven broke the silence. "How are we going to get onto Arabella's ship?"

I instantly thought back to the stash of henna wrapped in my belongings. "I will play the part of my mother once more."

34

EMME

Jakob was glad to take us anywhere that was not near the queen of Julinbor, and it was smooth seas that took us to the coordinates Raven's crew had provided. On the morning of the next day, we found ourselves in the green waters of a shallow bay off the coast of a jungle island.

My heart ached at the sight, though it took a moment to realize why. It looked very much like the Island of Iilak. From that correlation alone, it looked like death.

Perhaps it was an omen. But Arn was here, so I wouldn't turn back now.

Raven's ship was nowhere in sight, but Arabella's was. The name *Nightshade* had been painted onto the side in large letters. It didn't surprise me that Mother named the ship after her old one. She'd jumped right back into her old life.

From the looks of it, the Fates had blessed us today. Only half the crew appeared to be actually on the *Nightshade*, the other half at the edge of the jungle with their socks rolled down and rowboats staked to shore. That meant we only had half the crew to worry about at one time.

Fewer pirates to trick.

I'd colored my hair last night with the henna leaves, and now it was bright red. The vivid locks kept catching my eye and making me feel not quite like myself, but that was perfect for today. To complete the look, I'd traded my warm cloak for a black tunic that showed my tattoos to make her persona more believable, then topped it off with a large hat to hide the details of my face. A cutlass at one hip, pistol on the other, and I was ready.

Raven looked at me on deck. "If we lose Arabella, we can hand you over instead."

"Ha," I said dryly. My mother's courage was the hardest costume to feign, especially as we drew closer to her ship. They'd noticed us now, and their cannons rolled out.

"Raise the white flag," Raven ordered.

Jakob frowned, but did so. It snapped in the wind as it was lifted.

"Are you nervous?" Raven whispered.

I rolled my shoulders back. "Do I look it?" One speck of nerves, and they'd know I wasn't Arabella.

"No, you look perfect. I meant, are you nervous he isn't here?"

Her words picked at my fears, but I hadn't the time to let them out. I swallowed hard. "I'm starting to wonder if he's even real, or if everyone's just playing a trick on me," I confessed. I grabbed hold of the main mast. "But worrying will solve nothing."

I started climbing. The ship swayed beneath me as we kept moving, making climbing trickier, but it was important that when they looked at us, they saw me.

He saw me, I thought, letting my hopes out a bit. *Please be on board.*

When I was near the top, I drew my cutlass and posed so it would gleam in the sunlight and leaned out on one foot. My red hair streamed over one shoulder as I lifted the cutlass higher. Every eye should be on me—not on the crew of Az Eloians, not on the missing princess, but on their captain returning to them unharmed.

They hadn't fired at us yet. That was a good sign.

But the men on shore had gathered along the beachfront with weapons drawn, and the deck was crowded with the remaining pirates, all watching us. We were evenly numbered, assuming they didn't have a large company belowdecks. I looked to Raven and she nodded at me. We could take them. If I got us to their deck without a struggle, we could take them easily.

"My crew," I shouted, imitating my mother the best I could. "We bring you another ship."

We were close enough to hear their murmurs. "Drop your plank," I ordered. "And see what I have brought you." I put as much of Arabella's unbridled authority into my voice as I could. By now they could see my tattoos and my hair, and the barrels of their pistols lowered.

"Captain?" someone asked.

"Don't just stand there," I snapped. "Lower the plank."

I knew our crew must be itching for their weapons, but they held back. We'd left most of our men belowdecks, waiting for the orders. The ones above did their best to make themselves appear small and unarmed. But they were ready to strike.

There was a whistle. "You heard the captain. Lower the plank." They lowered it to hit against ours. "Grab the ropes to keep them close, clear the helm, and do we need cuffs, Captain?"

"That won't be necessary," I said. Inside, I was relieved. I started scanning their faces for Arn. "They will come aboard peacefully." I dropped to the deck and watched as Raven led a small group across the plank. "No need to come in," I shouted to the men on the beach who waited by their rowboats. "Carry on as you were."

I should have kept my face lower as I called out, but as it was, one of their nearby men caught sight of beneath my hat. I watched as his eyes narrowed.

"How was carnival?" he asked.

I stilled. My heel was already lifted to knock against the planks in signal to our men below, but now it wavered.

Arabella hadn't gone to carnival. I knew that, and the crew knew that. She'd left them with a code for when she returned.

I thought fast. What association would mother have with carnivals that she would make her coded answer? She'd only gone once when I was little and had come back grumbling about how it wasn't half as interesting as anything she saw on sea. That was the best I had to go on, and I hoped it would be enough.

The man had put his foot on the plank, blocking more of the Az Eloians from crossing. Raven, Jakob, and three more had already passed over and were now alone on their deck. If we were caught now, they'd have a hard fight.

The tension swelled in the air, like the sky was holding its breath. Raven kept deceptively calm, but Arabella's crew had stiffened as eyes latched onto me for an answer I didn't know.

"It was dull," I replied as carelessly as I could. "Not half as interesting as anything we see on the sea."

I rapped my heel against the deck, giving the signal to our men, then stepped aboard the plank to cross.

The man regarded me as I approached, and I hoped he couldn't see the nerves beneath my stoic expression. He might not have, but whatever he saw was enough, for he let out a low chuckle. "So," his voice rumbled under his breath, "you are the daughter she is trying to reunite with."

My stomach dropped to my feet. I hadn't fooled anyone.

I reached for my cutlass, but his was drawn in an instant, and he swung at me. I flew back, but a sting told me he'd clipped my skin. It wasn't deep, but it tore a long line down my arm.

Raven drew her blade. "Now!"

Our ship came to life. The crew threw open the trap doors, storming out with their cutlasses raised. I hurled over the plank to the enemy side, leaping past the man who'd recognized me as he faltered at the sight of our men.

Jakob led his men in attack. Within moments, the full force of the Az Eloians had boarded their ship, and the sound of steel cleaved the air.

Arabella's crew adjusted well, but half of their men weren't on board, and the Az Eloians fought like beasts. It only took them one swing to bring a man down, one punch for someone to buckle under the weight, and one swift kick to send someone flying. They worked their way outward, men dropping like sand between fingers, none able to hold against their size.

I worked alongside them until I'd pushed my way to the helm. Sweat clouded my brow. I climbed the creaky stairs to find a single man there, his eyes wide and knees trembling.

His words were immediate. "I surrender. I'm not dying for her."

For my mother. I wasn't surprised she hadn't found loyalty yet. All across the ship, the gesture was the same—pirates dropping their weapons, asking for mercy.

"We will give it to them," Raven commanded our men. She was breathing hard but unscathed. "We are not here to draw blood."

At the knowledge that their surrender would not mean death, the remaining crew surrendered almost in unison. Their weapons clattered to the deck. Their hands raised. Their knees bent.

The ship was ours. I stood at the helm overlooking it all.

Arn was not here.

"Where do you keep your prisoners?" I demanded the man at the helm.

"We have none," he said. He still trembled slightly, and his eyes only grew wider as I advanced.

"No. That can't be right. You have two."

He shook his head. "Every hand on this ship is part of the crew."

My patience wore thin. I'd been searching for Arn, chasing him, told where to find him just to be informed he was gone, then searching some more. By now I was used to the feeling of hope being stripped away, but the dull pain of it was turning into a sharp frustration. It was like Arn had turned into an idea instead of something tangible. Someone I'd reach for but never touch.

I sucked in a deep breath. I grabbed hold of the wheel with both hands and faced the crew, all of them on their knees as the Az Eloians removed their weapons. I hollered to get their attention and waited until every head turned to me.

I was tired. I was irritated. I was *done*.

My knuckles where white as I gripped the wheel. In my loudest voice, I shouted, "Someone find me Arn Mangelo, now, before I tear this ship apart plank by plank."

At that moment, a blade slid over my throat. Someone held me from behind, bundling my tunic with a tight fist and pressing a cold knife against my neck. His gruff voice breathed over my skin. "Careful what you wish for."

35

ARN

Our opportunity for escape came two days after Arabella left. Half her crew departed for the jungle to gather provisions, and the half that remained was guideless without Arabella. Landon and I played our parts, bided our time, until the morning of the second day.

I eyed the remaining rowboat through the porthole. It had been left unlocked.

I dropped a bag of tools on the desk in the cabin on deck. "We'll scrub the hull today," I told the acting captain, Milo.

Milo wore the captain's hat in Arabella's absence and looked at us from beneath it. He was a fair man as far as I'd seen, but quite comfortable handing out orders and watching the work be done.

Landon and I stood on the deck, waiting for his permission.

He looked back to his papers, his voice dry. "I've already got the tackles out. We'll be careening her later." He carried a thick northern accent that reminded me of Emme and Ontario.

Landon let a bit of his own seep into his voice as he replied. "Too much work. We'll dive."

Milo lifted the flap of our satchel to glance at the stone scrapers and scrubs. "Shall we heel it?"

"No," I said quickly. Heeling the ship would tilt her to

make scraping the sides easier, but it would make it nearly impossible for anyone to stay on deck. The last rowboat would be taken to shore, and we needed it. We weren't scraping the hull for the fun of it. "No need. We were divers for our other crew, so we're used to holding our breath."

He gazed at the two of us. "Divers, eh? I thought you were captains."

Landon covered quick. "Arn here believes the crew should split such unpleasant tasks equally." He shrugged. "Thus, we dove." He lazily leaned his back against the shelves with one foot crossed over the other, soaking in the strand of light that came through the porthole and looking like he didn't care whether we cleaned the hull or not. He had a knack for looking disinterested in almost every situation, and this time that came in handy.

I had no such talent, and as such, Milo's eye rested on me longer.

"We don't have to." I swiped the tools away. "Perhaps Arabella likes to scrub her own hull. There'll certainly be plenty of barnacles for her to clean when she returns."

That got to him. "That's fine, you can do it. Blankets are in the second storage room for when you're done."

"Splendid." Landon tipped his head at Milo.

I followed him out as calmly as I could. We were quick to tie ropes around our waists, tackle them to the main mast, and clip our tools to our belts. The crew's attention slid past us without interest. It wouldn't be unusual for Milo to assign such a dirty task to us, and none would question how long we were down there. The biggest trick would be cutting the rowboat away.

"Ready?" Landon asked.

"After two months, how sweet do you think freedom will taste?"

The thrill of it lived in the curve of his lips. "Gloriously."

We dove into the waters. I clenched at the sudden cold, but forced myself to stay underwater until I'd acclimated to it, not letting myself come up for air until the shivers had stopped. Then I kicked, lifting myself toward the green hue of the surface, where the light hit against small waves. The jungle loomed behind us and the ship to the other side. We'd need to cut down the rowboat quickly enough so the men in the jungle didn't notice and stealthily enough that the men above didn't hear it. We'd have to row as fast as we could to escape, and if spotted, we'd have to add bullet-dodging into the equation.

"Pst." Landon's gaze flicked upward. I followed it to the watchful eyes of a crewmate eating their lunch along the rails.

I sighed. "Dive," I instructed. "And hope he's gone when we come up."

Landon grimaced. "I don't really care for this chore."

"We're not captains anymore."

"Had we found Calypso, I could have been a king."

I was already filling my lungs, letting the air out in puffs, preparing myself. I did this several times until I was ready, sucked in the last gulp of air, and dove.

Landon came after me, and we kicked our way beneath the ship. We removed our scrapers and worked to peel the barnacles off the wood and scrub away the worms that ate their way through. As I worked, my mind kept going back to how we would possibly escape, where we would go, how we would survive on our own to find help, and how I could get a message to Emme through it all. I didn't have any of that figured out yet. All I knew is that we couldn't be here when Arabella returned.

When we could hold our breath no longer, we surfaced for air. I looked up. "The man's gone," I said, wiping my face dry. "We can go now." I reached to trade my scraper for my blade, but Landon stopped me.

"Something's not right," he said. He was looking behind us.

I circled to survey the scene. Every crew member on the jungle was looking our way. No, not our way. Something past us.

We couldn't see what, because the ship blocked my view, but something approached. Fast, by the sound of it. As the ship came nearer, the mutterings of the crew grew.

"Move!" Landon shoved me, and we barely had time to get out of the way before the last rowboat came crashing down.

"Did you cut it?" I kicked wildly to keep my head above water.

But he hadn't. Two of the crew had, and they were stowing away to the jungle on it. In mercy, they reached for us. "Come in, mates." Fear vibrated in their voices. "Get away from whoever is coming."

We could sail with them and escape through the jungle, likely with twenty other men. No one would ever bother to come looking for us.

But I held back, and Landon did as well. The jungle wasn't our aim. "Who is approaching?"

"I don't know, but they're too big for us." Before we could change our minds, the two men drew their hands back to row with ferocity, taking away both our opportunity to go with them and to escape.

I was less concerned with the approaching vessel than with our chance to leave, now sailing away.

"What's the plan now?" Landon asked, putting away his scraper roughly.

"That was it," I said in frustration. "That was the plan. That was our only way away."

From above, there was a shout, and we heard the reply. "It's our captain."

I cursed. Arabella had returned.

Landon was already cutting himself free from the ropes we'd tied. "We swim to that ship then, and as they attack, we sneak away in one of their rowboats."

"Didn't you hear? They are led by Arabella. The incoming ship won't attack."

He scoffed. "They might attack her."

I brightened. He was right. They might. Likely, this new ship was one she'd taken over, by killing their captain and giving orders to sail. They would be eager to be rid of her. All they needed was a spark to set that in motion. At my face, Landon shook his head. "I recognize that look."

I clapped him on the shoulder. "Your idea, mate."

From the sound of it, the plank had now dropped, and pirates were crossing over to our ship. Whatever mutiny was led, it'd need to be aboard this deck. "We'll have one chance at this—to sneak aboard and take charge of a rebellion. With luck, we can get enough men over to the new ship to take off." I worked to lengthen the rope in my belt and pushed against the hull. "You take one end; I'll take the other. Wherever Arabella is, we find her."

I could see Landon weighing the options out. It was risky. But I wasn't surprised when he nodded. "See you on the other side then." He took off.

He aimed himself to come up the bow, so I went the other way. I grabbed hold of the rope that we'd tied and started to climb.

From above, shouts erupted. I froze.

They didn't need us to start something. They were fighting anyway.

I tried climbing faster, but it was tricky with the hook. I had to twist the rope around it to pull myself upward, then hold myself steady with one arm as I managed to get the hook free, just to do it again. Inch by inch, I worked upward, until at last I could grab onto the bowsprit.

The tip of my hook sank into the wood, and I clawed my way overboard.

I was dripping wet, freezing cold, and on high alert as I

searched for Arabella. I suddenly realized the fight had died already. Large men held swords over Arabella's recent crew, forcing them to their knees. My eyes roamed over the scene until snapping back to a face.

Jakob?

I blinked. That was him, burly beard and chilly eyes, standing over hostages. His snarl was the same one I'd seen time and time again, but he wasn't leading training now. This was a real fight, and somehow he was here. Once I recognized him, the faces of the other men came clearer.

It was the *Commander* that had come, and this wasn't just any crew. It was our old crew.

Our old crew that had wanted us dead.

We might have been better off swimming for land and escaping from there. But I stayed, bracing myself against the prow to see how things would unfold. My hook was raised and my other hand on my cutlass if needed.

A woman's cry split the air. I turned my face to the helm and saw Arabella there, shouting at the top of her lungs.

She had tight hold of the wheel. Behind her, Landon eased himself onboard, his blade drawn.

But then Arabella shouted again, "Someone find me Arn Mangelo, now, before I tear this ship apart plank by plank!"

It wasn't Arabella at all. I saw through the red hair, through the dip of the hat, through the outfit. That wasn't Arabella the Ruthless.

It was Emme.

She was here. She was alive.

More than alive, she appeared to be thriving. Her body was strong again, her skin warmed by the sun, her stance sure and not wavering. She didn't shake. She didn't hunch. She was healed. And she was looking for me. A heaviness lifted from my chest, swelling with delight, wanting nothing more than to stand here and soak in the sight of her forever.

I felt like after months, I could breathe again.

But Landon appeared at her back and slid his dagger to her throat, and my muscles convulsed.

"Landon, stop! That's not her," I shouted. I didn't care if the Az Eloians saw me now—I had to stop Landon before he slit Emme's throat. "That's not Arabella!"

I tore through the crew to throw myself at the foot of the helm. I looked up at her, panting. "It's Emme."

I saw Landon startle. He lowered his blade, giving Emme enough room to look down. Her eyes found mine, and time stopped.

I'd forgotten how beautiful those eyes were. Time had a funny way of glorifying things that you hadn't seen in a while, sprucing them up in your memory until the real thing could never live up to the image you'd created for them, but she did. She exceeded it. My heart was pounding.

Her mouth fell open, and she went to the railing to get closer to me. "Arn?" Her voice was weak. "Are you real?"

"I could ask you the same thing." I took the stairs two by two until I'd reached her side, then paused there, just out of her touch. Savoring the look of her. The distance between us was so thin, but neither of us crossed it. After months of a sea between us, now there was nothing but the space of one breath.

There were tears in her eyes. "I have looked everywhere for you," she whispered.

My hand moved to her cheek to wipe it dry. Touching her at last. "I've been trying to get to you every day," I whispered back. "I never stopped trying to get back to you."

Her body swayed my way, but she stopped herself from getting closer. "Do you love me?" she asked. The question was so vulnerable that it shook me. I hated that she doubted that.

I wrapped my arm around her and drew her close. The space between us closed. "I love you more than I love anything in the world." I kissed her, and it was as if I was whole again. She leaned into my touch and didn't pull back until Landon led the crew into applause around us.

I shot him a look but couldn't control a smile.

Emme's cheeks were flushed as she eased away.

"Looks like you don't need to pull apart this ship plank by plank anymore," I told her.

She laughed. I'd been wrong. With that sound, *now* I was whole.

Emme cleared her throat and faced the crew. "We've no desire to take over your ship," she informed them. There was an audible exhale. "I'm not Arabella the Ruthless. You won't be seeing her again, so I suggest you select a new captain."

The hostages were released as cutlasses were sheathed, yet they were slow to stand. Each man looked to another as the uncertainty of their next move hung between them. Milo would likely take the position, but there was always a chance another would step up, and I didn't envy how unstable the chain of power would be for the next few months. Thankfully, I wouldn't be here for that.

Emme moved from the helm, and I followed her to the main deck, where she stopped in front of Jakob. "Thank you for helping."

He gave her a nod, then looked at me. There were a hundred unspoken words between us. Finally, he gave a polite bow. "It was an honor to sail under you, Captain."

Emme's eyes went wide, but I chuckled.

"You never followed my commands, and you know it." Still, I bowed back. "It was an honor to sail with you." A month ago, all I wanted was to be off his ship. But now I could find the appreciation in the lessons he had taught me and the strength he had driven into me. Most of all, he had helped Emme to find me, and I could never repay him for that.

"I will let the king know that you have fulfilled your mission."

I opened my mouth to remind him that we hadn't, in fact, found Calypso, until I followed his gaze. Raven was leading the crew of Az Eloians back to their ship before taking her place at the helm of the *Commander*. She didn't veil her features behind a cloak like before, but was trussed up in leather with knives strapped to her arms and hair braided back, standing tall as she welcomed each fighter back to the ship. It was a wonder she'd managed to keep herself hidden for so long, because looking at her now, it was clear she belonged to them.

Her gaze found mine and then flicked to Emme before coming back to me. The warning inside was clear. Leave her again—by accident or purpose—and I'd regret it.

I didn't know her well, but from what I saw, I knew enough to take her seriously.

It wouldn't be a problem though. Now that I'd found Emme again, I never planned to leave her side. I'd abandon the seas for her if she desired. I'd find a ring and propose to her all over again. I'd spend my days being grateful for every moment I had with her and guaranteeing that she never doubted my love again.

Landon approached, drawing me from my thoughts. "Never thought we'd see you again." He extended a hand to Jakob. The big man looked at it, then gripped it firmly. "I trust if we board the *Commander*, we won't be killed by the crew?"

Jakob's mouth twitched. "I'll alert the crew you are to be left alone."

Emme stepped on the plank. "We must return to the *Royal Rose*. The queen is waiting."

Landon and I shared uneasy looks. "The queen?" If Queen Isla was there, it was the last place I wanted to be.

But Emme was already crossing over. "I'll explain later, but there are still things to sort out."

From the helm, Raven cried out. "There!" She pointed across the seas. "I see them!" I expected to see the *Royal Rose*, but instead there was a small ship peeking around the bay, with its sails trimmed and a blank, yellow flag flying. Raven ushered the remaining Az Eloians to cross quickly, while directing the crew to approach this new ship.

"The orphans," Emme explained as we stepped aboard the plank. "Raven's original crew. They told us where to find you."

"And they will be how we get back," Raven said. "I've been gone from them for long enough."

I swept my eye behind me to see Milo already walking to the helm. The crew was more interested in who would be their new captain to bother mounting a counterattack on us, so we were allowed to go effortlessly.

An eerie sense filled me as we boarded the *Commander*, one rooted in my old desperation to leave, along with a surprising thread of joy to see it again. If I looked to the left, there was the place where Landon and I had trained every morning and every night until our limbs barely held us up. To the right, there was the wheel I had stood at as I tried to get us back to Emme. There was the path up the stairs I'd tried to take, time and time again, as Jakob let Koa and his crew beat us down. There was the mast I'd fallen from.

From every side, this deck was stained with memories, each one of them already tinged with Emme, though she hadn't been here. She was all I'd thought about. And now she was here. With me.

At my side, Landon was roaming his eyes over the deck too. Though his expression had a thoughtfulness to it like he wasn't just reliving old memories. He shook his head slightly, then went to pull up the anchor.

"Forward, crew! They are not to be attacked!" Raven commanded.

Wind caught in our sails, and from below, men rowed us along the coastline to reach Raven's ship. With every second, she grew more and more active and vibrant, until she was leaning along the bowsprit and calling out to them.

At the sight of her, their whole deck exploded in whoops and cheers. Some beat their chests, some threw their hats, and many scrambled up the masts to lean themselves outward in a likewise manner, shouting with joy.

They were children, I realized. All of them.

"How did they survive without Raven?" I wondered out loud.

Emme watched them with awe. "Raven taught them how." She looked ready to jump overboard to swim to them. Raven did too.

We reached them at last, and Raven quickly grabbed hold of a line to swing herself over. As soon as she landed on deck, she spread her arms wide and was lost in their swarm.

"She educates them," Emme told me. "She is their teacher, their mother, their provider, and their friend."

"All by herself?"

"For now."

I caught the shift in her tone. I looked down as the wind pulled Emme's hair away from her face so I could clearly see the admiration there. She used to look at ships with disdain but now . . . it was like she looked at home. Realization hit me. "You want to join her crew."

"I think I can do good there." She looked up at me. "I want us to both go."

I knew I could never deny Emme anything. But even if I could, I wasn't sure I'd deny her this. The idea of it stirred something in me.

"Tell me you'll come too." She breathed like her very essence was hanging by a slender rope, waiting for me to agree to propel us into a new future.

Her words felt like adventure. While I didn't know my next steps, if they were with Emme, then they were in the right direction. After all, it was similar to the leadership I'd implemented on the *Royal Rose*, educating the crew so they would have options for their lives. I pulled Emme close and rested my head on her chin.

I could see it clearly. Me teaching the children mathematics, writing, reading, and Emme teaching them how to fight and be decent. We could do good there.

Somehow, we'd found a way to have goodness and the sea together. The perfect blend of her and me.

"Yes," I said with all certainty. "Let's do it."

"You mean it?" Her voice caught, but her eyes sparked.

"With all my heart. If you're there, I'm there."

Emme slid her hand into mine, turning her face to see the ship. Our new home.

On their deck, Raven had pulled away from the children to come to the starboard side rails and look at Jakob. "Thank you for helping us," she said. In each of her hands was a child's grip, and her lips stretched into a wide smile.

I knew Jakob's expressions well enough to know he wasn't too pleased, but he gave a low bow. "Of course, Your Highness." Behind him, the Az Eloians prepared for another long journey, adjusting sails, checking inventory, and plotting the navigation. He'd be joining them soon, and odds were, I wouldn't see him again.

As I was looking at him, his eyes came to mine.

I wasn't certain how to say goodbye to the one who'd broken me down but saved my life. In the end, I offered him my hand as Landon had done. "Safe travels."

His calloused hand met my own. Through shadows over his eyes, I caught a hint of respect. "Farewell."

Emme stepped up to the plank, and I followed, but there was a hollow sound behind me that made me turn back. It was like an echo of what should be there, a void that wouldn't be filled. A tension rose in the silence, and I found Landon in the midst of it.

He should be following. But he wasn't.

He gave me a long look, then purposefully planted himself before Jakob to stand at attention. "Sir," he said. "If you'll have me, I'd like to join your crew."

Jakob's chest filled as he looked over my friend. "Are you certain?" He kept his voice brusque, but there was a wistfulness inside.

Landon jutted his chin toward the sea. "There is nothing else for me out there. No family, no crew. I've never sailed with such dedicated soldiers as yourselves. If you'd have me, I'd like to stay. I'd like to work alongside you, and I'd like to hnoll alongside you."

Jakob trained his features back to their austere manner. "You fight well. We'd be honored to have a warrior like you."

The crack in his voice gave away his true emotions, and it was a crack in me as well.

I'd just gotten Landon back as a friend. A trust had been built between us that I doubted would fall again. Trust was in short supply these days. But there was a longing in his eye, roaming over the *Commander,* and I suspected that where I saw us being broken, he saw us being built.

He would work here, train here, and fight alongside his new crew with honor.

Landon's gaze landed on me.

"I never thought I'd be grateful for what Ontario did to us," he said. "But if we hadn't come here, I'd still be chasing my old ship and working to undermine you."

I dropped back to him on the deck. "I'm not ready to thank Ontario quite yet." I clasped my hand in his. In that moment, I saw my childhood friend, the boy I'd enlisted with, the one who ran with me to become pirates, the one who then turned on me, and every moment after. And now, I saw a new man. An Az Eloian. A loyal sailor.

"Life has a way of throwing us in each other's paths whether we like it or not."

He chuckled. "That it does. No goodbyes then. Only a farewell."

"Farewell. I will see you again, my friend."

He nodded, and we let go.

I roved my focus across the deck, across Jakob's hard-set face, across the stack of weapons along each side, to the navigator at the bow, and again to Landon. He was already falling in line to work beside the Az Eloians, and this time they didn't give him a wide berth to move. They folded seamlessly around him. He was one of theirs now. Jakob was watching him work, and his expression split into softness. He'd watch over Landon.

I gave my old friend a final look before stepping aboard the plank by Emme. We crossed to the other side and watched as the Az Eloians pulled their plank back.

The *Commander* sailed away.

"I'd like that story later," Emme mused, looking after the Az Eloians.

"I'll give it." I turned to her. "I'd like your story too, most notably how you were healed."

"Stories later," Raven ordered from where she stood nearby. "For now, we have a queen to find."

"Another story I'd like the reason for," I added.

Beside me, Emme paled. "No, I have dibs on the first story." She reached out to my arm and pulled up the sleeve. My iron hook gleamed in the wan evening light. "What in the name of the high seas is this?"

"Ah, yes. Perhaps you'll hear the first story after all."

36

EMME

I was still obsessed with the view of him. As we worked among Raven's crew, I'd catch sight of Arn and do a double take, having to remind myself over and over that he was really here. I couldn't get over it.

There was more to look at now. He'd grown stronger over the last few months, his hair longer and twisted into a knot behind his head, and his beard had come in, making him appear ten years older. It was taking some time to adjust to this new version.

Then there was the hook. He worked naturally with it, but I couldn't stop staring.

The children on crew looked at it often too, but with fascination, not fear. Arn had to stop working several times to let them touch it.

"Does it hurt?" a small boy asked.

"Only the bad guys." Arn grinned. The children squealed at that.

Raven closed her eyes to smile at their laughs, and I knew she was soaking in the sound.

Night fell around us, darkness creeping to the rails until we lit the lanterns. "Captain, would you take over the helm?" the boy behind the wheel asked. He appeared to be the oldest of the bunch with tangles of copper hair, dark skin, and a lanky build, coming in at maybe eighteen, but no older. There were others in that age range as well, two boys and a girl, but then a steep drop to the next set at around twelve.

Honestly, I was surprised they'd survived on their own.

Raven sorted through their inventory. "You keep control, Bryce," she told the lad.

Bryce shifted. "But you're here to stay, right? Shouldn't you captain us?"

Raven's hands slowed, and she took a while to meet the boy's eyes. "I'd like you to continue operating like I'm not here."

That caught everyone's attention. I glanced at her, puzzled. The older set looked at each other. "But you're back," the oldest girl said. "And you're here to stay, right?" Everyone stopped their work to wait for her reply. I waited as well. That was our plan all along. Return to the children.

Raven plastered on a smile, but her tone was bleak. "The seas are an uncertain place. You never know when I might be taken from you again."

A young girl with hair as pale as Raven's came to Raven's side. "Don't leave," she pled.

Raven brushed the girl's hair back from her face, her fingers moving in slow motions before going to her own neck to unclasp her necklace. She draped it over the girl's head and tied it there. It settled halfway down the girl's chest before she grabbed it with two, tiny fists. "Everything I do is for you," Raven promised. "I never want to leave."

The girl smiled as if that meant all her worries were gone, but I knew that wasn't a real answer.

"The ship is in good condition," Raven announced, changing the tone. "Amaranth, did you patch the sails?"

Sitting on the bowsprit, a slight girl with a crystal necklace and a scarf over her head kicked back her feet to look at the sails. "I did. They're holding up nicely."

Raven looked impressed. "And did you get a fair trade for supplies at market?"

Now it was Bryce who answered. "Better than fair. We told old Daryl that we were orphaned and had lost you, and he gave us half the price he usually does."

Raven smiled, but an eyebrow raised. "You used the extra to buy sweets, didn't you?"

Bryce beamed. "Yes ma'am." From Raven's burst of laughter, she didn't mind. "Not all of it though," Bryce amended. "We saved the rest."

From across the deck, I watched Arn take this all in, and I knew he would love it here. I knew *I* would love it here. But actually being here, it put a feeling inside me that I couldn't have imagined. A sense of belonging, strong and sweet, curled inside my chest. The view was splendid. The lanterns swayed softly, casting golden hued light over the small ship, and the children worked seamlessly upon it, each with their own sense of purpose. The stars had come out above, and the seas were fair enough to offer a gentle rhythm to sail over. It was innocence and beauty at its finest.

It took me a long time to love the seas. But this right here, was perfection.

"And, Honey, last time I was here, we were working on arithmetic." Raven continued through her checklist. A dark-haired girl, who couldn't be older than seven, sat at her side. "Have you learned your numbers yet?" Everything about the girl was the shade of sweet honey, and I wondered if that was how she'd gotten her name.

She bashfully shook her head.

From the helm, Bryce cleared his throat. "Let's focus on how nice the sales and inventory books look, shall we? Lessons may have gone downhill since you left."

"I didn't do any lessons," Honey admitted.

"Good to know." Raven was smiling. "That'll be remedied. But not tonight. Tonight, it's time for bed."

The younger ones groaned, dragging their feet and pausing to squeeze their little arms around Raven, as the older three ushered them to the hammocks belowdecks.

Honey paused in front of me. "Are you staying too?"

My heart melted. I knelt next to her. "I hope to, if that's okay with you."

She straightened as if she were the captain. "That'll be alright with me." Then she wandered off to bed.

Raven watched us. "She's a sweet one," she said once Honey was gone. "She has a tender heart. They all do. They're too good for me."

That was ironic, because Raven had been too good for the Royal Rose. "They are lucky to have you. And I'm lucky to have been arrested with you."

Raven cleared her throat. "Let's keep the details of my absence quiet please? The young ones are impressionable, and I'd rather them not think it a virtue to get arrested to be like me."

"That's fair," I said with a laugh, then hesitated. "They really seem to love you. It's good that you're back." I was looking for assurance that she was here to stay.

Like an anchor falling, her smile dropped. Darkness veiled her eyes, but she kept her thoughts shielded from me. "You and Arn likely want to see each other. You have much to talk about. The on-deck cabin will be empty and will do nicely."

I did want to speak with Arn, desperately. But it was only because Raven moved away so adamantly that I didn't press about her comments. I found Arn's eyes and nodded to the cabin. He dropped the halyards and moved that way.

I gave a final look to Raven, now at the helm speaking

in low tones with Bryce, before slipping inside the cabin and closing the door behind me.

And, at long last, I was alone with Arn again.

37

EMME

The only sound was his breathing as he stared at me. As soon as the door shut, he reached for my hand. He tugged me against him and leaned his lips to mine, gently kissing me.

"I missed you so much," I uttered between kisses.

"You've no idea." His movements slowed, until he eased away. There was only a small porthole of light to see Arn by, the rest of the room clouded in inky black, but I could still see the shine of his eyes on me. "I missed you," he repeated my words, and I could hear how much he meant them. He stepped away to fumble through drawers until coming up with a stubby mold of wax.

All I wanted to do was pull him back. The distance between us had been too great for too long, that now even a few steps felt like miles.

There was the *snick* of the match as he lit a candle. Light brightened the room. "So," I started as he blew out the match. Smoke billowed in whorls. "You look different." My gaze dropped to his hook again, where the candlelight gleamed off the iron arch.

"You've changed too. Your hair is red."

That wasn't on the same level. Not even close. "You're gone for a few months and come back partly made of metal."

He ran a hand through my locks. "It's like a bright fire."

"And you have a beard," I added.

"You walk straight."

"Your arms are twice their usual size."

He laughed. "Fine, I've changed a little. But it's still me underneath, I promise. And I don't think either of us are upset about the beard. Stars know it took its time."

I let my fingers work their way through it. It was rough under my touch. "No," I murmured, "not mad about it at all. But what will I poke fun at you for now?"

He grinned. "I'm sure you'll think of something." He lifted the hook and rubbed his hand against it. "It is odd." His tone grew serious. "I hated the thought of this at first. It makes me look like a weapon instead of a man. But it's useful, and I manage much better with it than without."

Tenderly, I traced a finger down its side. "I don't mind the hook," I told him. He breathed out like he needed to hear that. "And the children seem to like it."

"I'm glad they aren't frightened. When Jakob first gave it to me, I was worried how it would make me appear."

"Tell me about Jakob," I encouraged. "How did you come to know him?"

His smile sagged, and a war raged behind his eyes before he answered. "Landon and I became King Isaac's henchmen. He put us in charge of Jakob's ship, and we spent the past two months on crew with the Az Eloians."

There was something in his voice I couldn't discern. When he interacted with Jakob earlier, there was nothing but respect between them. Their time couldn't have been that bad if Landon had asked to join their crew. This whole time, I assumed his proximity to Landon would've been the hard part, but from the edge to his words, it wasn't that at all.

"What happened to you there?"

"Everything that happened on that ship—the jobs we did, the

people we . . . it's in the past." His voice was distant. "Landon saw the honor in their routine and their dedication to their king. And I suppose there is honor in the devotion of it. But it was just like when we served for King Unid—following orders without asking questions. Becoming nothing but soldiers. I already lived that life and was eager to get away from it." He shifted. "Then as captain I tried living for myself instead of someone else." Arn looked at me. "Emme, it was self-indulgent and didn't fulfill me." His face brightened. "This, though." He gestured around the room, the schoolbooks on one side, and the maps on the other. "Raven has it figured out and you tried to show me that all along. I wouldn't be living selfishly here, and there would be no blind following of a king. To live for those children, and their future, is an honor greater than anything else I could find."

I drew near to him, and he rested his forehead against my hair.

"And I would be living for you," he whispered.

There was an odd juxtaposition to him, more pirate in his appearance than before, but also more philosophic. Before, he could hardly think around his engulfing need to be captain of the *Royal Rose*. Now his rough edges had softened, and the cold areas had melted. It left behind the parts I loved best.

He saw the way I was looking at him. "Do you miss your hardened pirate who wanted nothing other than his ship and the glory of captaining?"

He knew I didn't. "I like this change."

"I'm glad. Though I hope you never change." He rested his head against my shoulder. "You are everything someone should be."

I swallowed. "I oathbound myself again."

Silence fell like a rock. He pulled back. "You did what?"

I peeled back the top of my socks to show him the curve of the oathbinding. "I banished my mother from the seas, and this oathbinding will burn if she returns to them."

His mouth opened. Then it shut. Then it opened again. "I feel like I missed an exciting few months for you."

"They were certainly chaotic." I blew a long puff of air through my cheeks. "Every moment since I agreed to get on your blasted ship has been nothing but chaos. I don't mind though," I hurried to assure him. "I'm becoming quite fond of it."

He quirked a smile. "One of these days we need to stop oathbinding ourselves. We've each done it twice. Though," he looked directly into my eyes, "I don't regret one of those."

Warmth spread through me. One of those times had been for me.

"I'd oathbind myself to you if you asked," I said.

He used his hook to wrap my wrist and tug me closer. "Really? Because I seem to remember asking you to bind yourself to me, and you said no."

My smile was wide as I lifted my hand. "Did I?" I wiggled my finger.

Moonlight caught on the glint of my ring, and his face went slack. Arn had stolen this ring for me months ago, saying the blue reminded him of the sea. He'd asked me to marry him, and I had told him there was too much happening at the time.

Things were still happening. Many more things. But none of them would change how I felt about Arn. I loved Arn more than I'd ever loved anyone, and I was ready to promise that love for the rest of my life.

"I gave you the wrong answer before," I confessed. His eyes were glassy, and my own were tearing up. "But I'm ready to give the right one this time."

"I slipped that into your pocket before I left you," he said. His voice was uneven. "I'd forgotten."

"I held onto it. Angrily so, at first, I have to admit." I looked at it fondly. "Then as my symbol of hope."

I slowly slid the ring off my finger and passed it to him. He closed his fist around it. I seemed to have stopped being able to breathe.

Arn lowered himself to one knee. He looked up into my eyes. "My dearest Emme. The Fates brought you into my life at the perfect time. You have been my friend, my comfort, my dependency, and now my whole heart. I have lived life without you and have spent everything inside me to get back to you and am now certain that life without you means nothing." He held the ring up. "I have sought after treasure, but you are the greatest treasure I have ever found. Emme Jaquez Salinda, will you be my wife?"

My heart was so full that it could burst, and I could barely get out the word. "Yes."

He twisted the ring back onto its place on my finger. It had meant hope before, but now it meant everything. It was the first sign of a beautiful life that we would share together, and in that moment, it felt as if all was so beautifully right nothing could go wrong.

That ended quickly.

Raven nearly flew through the door just as Arn was standing. "I've clearly interrupted something," she said. "I'm sorry. But this can't wait." She pointed to the southern seas. Smoke plumed in the distance. "The horizon is on fire."

I sucked in a breath. "The *Royal Rose* was that way."

"One ship against the queen's fleet?" Raven's eyes were full of anxiety. She might be back with her children, but there was one person left on the *Royal Rose* whom she cared for as well. "It would be a miracle if she still stood." Our sails were already adjusted to pick up speed, and we were headed that way. Whatever the fate of the *Royal Rose* was, we would find out soon.

38

EMRIC

Waking to the smell of smoke was never a good sign. Before I'd drifted to sleep at the helm, Ontario was in clear sight, his arms still bound around the main mast and his head long since drooped to his chest as he slumbered.

At some point, he must have awoken and decided to let it all burn.

His ropes lay in a haphazard mess around the mast as vicious flames furled themselves around it, licking their way higher. They'd spread over the deck soon and be upon the sails.

Ontario stood at the side, rubbing his wrists, watching with a triumphant smile.

I dove for the compartment beneath the wheel for our brass bell. "Wake up!" I yelled to the crew as I rang it urgently. "Fire!" I kept ringing as I dashed down the stairwell to find buckets and tie them to ropes. The air was warm at my back. I lowered the bucket as the crew came above deck.

Tess was first, her eyes alarmed. She ran to my side to grab another bucket. "What happened?" she asked.

"I'll give you one guess." I grunted as I pulled the bucket above deck. Its water doused what was crawling nearby, but the mast would be hard to save.

Truthfully, I couldn't figure out how Ontario had started a

fire. But from how he stood back as the rest of the crew threw themselves into fighting the flames, he was happy to let the *Royal Rose* sink.

I filled another bucket. "You will make us lose everything," I shouted to Ontario.

"No," he shouted back through the heavy smoke. "I have an empire to fall back on. *You* will lose everything."

I hadn't the time to think what I could have done to offend him, because the flames were growing out of control. Around us, the queen's fleet was coming to life—most drawing away to keep from the wreckage, but one coming nearer. The queen's ship itself. The image of it was hazy through the flames, but it came right alongside us.

I threw another bucket of water.

"It's too late for the mast," Tess yelled. "Douse the deck, and we can control where the mast falls. If it falls on another mast, we will lose more sails."

It felt like giving up, but she was right. The fire had already eaten through too much wood to make the mast stable, and the best thing we could do was make sure it was the only casualty. The bucket clattered at my feet as I dropped it and crouched to fetch some rope. I handed one end to Tess. The other, I held tight.

"We'll have to be quick or else the fire will eat this too." Clarice saw what we were doing and rushed to help. "When I finished looping," I instructed, "we pull as hard as we can."

They nodded, and I circled the deck with the rope until it was well wrapped around the mast. When I returned, I shouted, "Pull!"

We pulled, and the mast creaked.

But it didn't fall.

"It's not breaking fast enough," Clarice said. "The rope will give way first."

I handed her the rope. "I'll break it free." I filled my lungs with air before diving toward the fire, feeling its intensity across my skin as I drew out my cutlass and whacked it against the side of the mast. My skin burned with heat, and everything within me shouted to pull back, but I stayed put to hit it again. And again.

At that moment, someone threw water over me, providing a sliver of relief as I went for a fourth hit. Finally, it gave way. Tess and Clarice immediately pulled, navigating it over the side of the ship. It splintered against the rails with a sickening crack.

"Douse it now," I called. "Before it eats away the hull."

Using my cutlass, I hacked at the remaining shards of wood that held fast, until the mast was fully freed.

"Now push!"

Everyone, except Ontario, lent a hand to push the remains of the main mast into the sea. It sank beneath dark water as the last of the fire went out, leaving behind smoky remains and a broken ship.

But we were alive. Thankfully.

I pivoted to search for Ontario. He was gone.

"Where is that snake?" I asked. No one questioned who I meant. I paid little regard to the pain of my burnt arms as I scoured the deck for the vile scoundrel who'd almost sunk us all.

Bo gave a shout and pointed. "He's taken a rowboat."

I stormed to the side of the ship. "Ontario!" I roared. "You are a coward!"

He stopped rowing long enough to stand. He had his bags at his side, and I wondered how long he'd been free and walking the deck before he started the fire. "I am not running from you!" he shouted back. The cloudy air made it hard to see anything, but I could hear the snarl in his voice. "I am running to something greater than you could ever imagine." He was almost too far, but I still heard his taunting words. "You should have been more like your mother—maybe then you would have become something. You'll never be anything more than an ordinary sailor, Emric, while I will be one of the leading men of the entire world."

Then he was too distant, weaving between the fleet as they left him alone, off to chase whatever satisfied him next.

And I was left here, with a ship that couldn't sail. There was a low chuckle of a woman behind me.

I turned to see Queen Isla on deck, completely unbothered by the frantic crew running about her and her guards as we tried to piece our ship back together.

"Never a dull day with you pirates, is there?"

"What do you want?"

"Arabella," she replied without hesitation.

I was looking over the ship for extensive damage. "We still have one day," I replied. "Emme isn't back yet."

"I've grown tired of waiting."

My eyes darted to her. There was a restless movement beneath her surface that said she was more impatient than she let on. She swept her arm out. "This is not reliable. I trust neither you nor your ability to keep my prisoner safe."

"Your prisoner is not in any harm," I told her. Though as I said it, I became aware of her hysterical screaming from belowdecks. She could likely smell the fire and would have heard the crack of the mast and felt the rock of the ship as it tipped. She probably thought we were all going down.

"Regardless," the queen said. "I am not leaving here without her."

Upon her words, each of the eight guards surrounding her drew out their pistols and pointed them directly at me.

The crew froze in the background. My eyes narrowed. "We had an agreed-upon deal."

"That deal changed."

I bristled, wondering how badly Emme needed the extra day and what my odds were of surviving eight pistol shots.

Ontario wasn't around to pay the wage of our crew's doctor, and even so, I doubted he could bandage eight holes at once. Though if I ducked, perhaps I'd only take four. If I stalled here long enough, Clarice would attack them from behind. She was already moving into position behind them. If she could take out some, maybe I'd get away with only two holes. Two didn't sound so bad.

Then, over her shoulder, I saw a new ship in the distance. A slender one with yellow sails.

It was exactly as Raven had described it to me.

Relief swept through me. If she was coming, then Emme was safe.

I stepped aside. "You can take Arabella. She is all yours now."

The pistols lowered. "Thank you," Queen Isla said, her eyes wary.

To show my good faith, I held up a key and tossed it to one of her men. "Just follow the shouting." Half of them moved, while the remaining four stayed at their queen's side. Clarice took a wide arch around them to reach my side. Thankfully, she'd put her weapon away.

"Emme should be here to say goodbye," she said.

"My sister already said her goodbyes," I told her. "And I don't need mine."

Arabella's shouts stopped, and I guessed they'd opened her door. It wouldn't have surprised me if Arabella appeared on deck having taken them all out, but when she did appear, it was with her hands bound.

Her eyes found mine instantly, and they glowered.

But there was less fight in them now. I'd be foolish to hope for regret, and I got none as she was dragged past me.

What I did get was a low snarl.

"Without me, you will always be nothing." Her hair was matted to her head, and her eyes yellowed. She yanked on her bonds to pause in front of me.

"Encouraging, as always," I remarked. "Goodbye, Mother."

She gave no response, and the ship was eerily quiet as guards dragged her across the plank and onto Queen Isla's ship.

But the queen stayed behind, her gaze drawn out to the sea and fixed on Raven's ship. "Calypso is returning," she whispered.

"You have what you came for." I tried to hide the edge in my tone.

Queen Isla lifted her skirts in one hand to step aboard the plank as her guards waited for her. "I am not after your precious princess," she said with scorn. "I don't have to chase her. I own her now."

My stomach dropped. "What do you mean?"

She was on her own deck now, their plank wrenched back. I went to our rail. "What do you mean you own her?"

She gave a lithe grin that twisted my insides. "Farewell, son of Arabella."

39

ARN

I'd dreamed of seeing the *Royal Rose* again many times, and in each vision, it looked far better than it did right now. I stood on deck with my mouth gaping. "There isn't even a main mast. Where could that possibly have gone?"

"It was there when I left," Emme said, shakily. The sun was rising, and the light brought out the hazel flecks in her eyes. She wore a maroon, capped-sleeve tunic and creamy-white cloak, which still allowed me to see the tattoo along her arm of the falling stars. Every time I looked at it, I remembered that night where we danced, and how I knew then that I'd love this girl forever. "But at least she's still standing."

I brought my attention back to the sea. "She's hardly standing," I corrected her. As light broke through the sky, I saw the generous-sized hole in the top of the starboard side. A suspicious amount of smoke clouded the air. "She's not able to sail like this. She'll need a month to repair." Yet somehow, I felt nothing but relief. These were problems I knew how to deal with, and they hardly felt like problems at all. No one was trying to kill us. We weren't running from something. We didn't owe anyone anything. Repairing the ship would feel like a holiday.

Emme drew a quick intake of breath. "I see Emric. Raven,

I see him!" A figure at the helm was shouting out orders as he rolled up his sleeves to get to work.

Raven was at the helm, directing Bryce to the *Royal Rose.* "Do you see Ontario?"

The sound of his name was like a fuse that sparked within me. Time might have healed the wounds between Landon and me, but things were beyond repair with Ontario.

He was a liar, and there was one lie that he had hidden well. "Did you know he was Admiral Bones's son?" I asked Emme.

She nodded. "I did, actually. Queen Isla mentioned correspondence from him and had an envelope sealed with Admiral Bones's insignia, but I never had the chance to confront Ontario about it. Though," she winced, "I suppose that means Ontario must have watched me unintentionally kill his father."

I gripped her hand. "He had no love for that man. Any remorse he had for his death was faked."

She tried to smile but searched the deck with her telescope instead. "I don't see him. He might be in the cell."

"As long as he's locked up, that's fine for me."

Emme's telescope shifted. "The queen's ships are leaving, so they must have Arabella." Her voice wavered.

I couldn't guess her emotions with this. I knew mine—elated to not have to deal with Arabella the Ruthless ever again—but it felt insensitive to say such a thing. In the end, I found something softer to say. "I'm sorry things didn't end better in that regard."

She shoved the telescope away. "They ended as well as they could have, given who my mother is." She fell quiet as we continued toward the *Royal Rose,* then spoke. "Is it crazy if I still hope Queen Isla doesn't kill her?"

"Not at all." I assured her.

At last, we were close enough to engage with the *Royal Rose,* and Emric was the first at the side to wave us down.

"Ahoy there! Care to assist?" The rest of the crew drew near to check our ship as if we were a potential threat. There were murmurs upon the sight of the crew of children, which rose in volume when they spotted me.

It was the next moment that I cared about. I watched on edge to see if the atmosphere shifted into happiness or anger. It was subtle, more of a cautious optimism, but it was there.

"We thought you'd abandoned us!" Bo shouted. If leaving them was the worst lie that Ontario had told them, then perhaps it would all be just fine.

"Never," I shouted back. "What have you done to the ship?"

Emric patted the hull. "She's a fighter. She'll pull through."

"Did the queen attack?" Emme asked.

"No, the fire was set internally."

He didn't have to say by whom. It surprised me though, that he'd try to burn down something so valuable. All that fight to keep his place as captain of the *Royal Rose* and he was willing to burn her down. I shook my head. We dropped plank between the two vessels, and I stepped up.

"Permission to come aboard?" I grinned at Emric.

"Granted, but I'm not captain."

I dropped to the deck, soaking in the feel of it under my foot again. It was broken, charred, and without an important mast, but it was still standing. No thanks to Ontario. "Where is the fire-setting captain?"

Emme boarded behind me as Emric jutted his chin to the seas. "Scallywag rowed off. We won't be seeing him around here anymore."

My emotions came in two parts. The first was regret that I couldn't have seen him off. I wanted to show him that he hadn't broken my relationship with Emme, and that I'd found my way back. But mixed with the regret was a sliver of comfort. He was gone. At last. We were done with him, and there were no loose ends to tie up now.

Raven came aboard next as the children waited tentatively on deck. Without hesitation she went to Emric, grabbed his shirt by the collar, and brought his lips to hers.

I looked to Emme. "You left out that part of the story."

She smiled. "It's new."

But there was a hesitation in Emric's reaction and a shake in his voice as he spoke. "Can we talk?"

Raven's expression changed. "Of course."

Suddenly, the rest of us made ourselves appear very busy with the ship. I gave Emric and Raven a wide berth as I picked up some questionable planks of wood. "How can we help?" I asked anyone within hearing.

Collins answered, with a friendly tap on my back. "We need to get this side patched up before we send a crew out to build a new mast."

"On it."

And just like that, Emme and I effortlessly folded back into the crew like no time had passed. They handed us tools, we held nails, and together we started putting the ship back into one piece. Raven's children came aboard slowly to offer their hand at working, and they were readily given various tasks.

I spotted Tess watching from afar, focused on the youngsters that were about her age. Then focused on me.

I gave her a small wave. Without Ontario or Landon to drag her into trouble, she might turn out alright.

She returned the gesture, then disappeared belowdecks.

"She's been odd ever since you left," Emme said.

"If she spends time around Raven's crew, I wager she will liven up again. It'll be good for her to be around people her own age."

"I hope so." She held a plank in place so I could hammer it to the existing hull. "Why do you think Ontario set the *Royal Rose* on fire?"

"Who knows?" It was Collins who answered, as he came

carrying more planks. "This is the last of what we have on deck, by the way. We haven't had our usual man to keep inventory in line."

"Then I'll look over the books when I'm done here," I told him. The lull of working together was easy, but it still felt like there were unspoken things between us. Collins, Timmons, Bishop, and Bo were around us the most, and I paused to look them in the eye. "You know I never meant to leave you, right?"

They lowered their tools to look between each other. "We do now," Bishop said. "Just glad to see you back and glad to see Emme smiling again."

I could have given a detailed account of why Ontario had pulled me away and the things I did to try to return, but no more words were needed at this time.

Emme was mulling over things with Clarice, but she would peek at me here and there. I caught her eye and smiled. I hated to think of what she went through here when she thought I'd left her behind.

I pushed the thought away and raised my voice as I picked up my hammer again. "Let's get this ship fixed!" I grinned. "Because I want her shining if I'm to get married on deck."

40

EMRIC

Raven led me back to her own ship to speak, and all I wanted to do was be guided through the various rooms and listen to everything about her life on board here, learn the children's names, hear what their days had been like.

But the queen's words were caught in my mind, and I couldn't be rid of them. So as soon as she closed the door to the cabin, I asked the question, "What deal did you make with Queen Isla?"

She recoiled. "How did you hear about that?"

"The queen mentioned it. She said she owns you."

Raven gave a dry laugh. "No one owns me. The decision I made, I did for myself."

I waited for her to tell me what it was. Instead, she drew herself close and slipped her warm hands in mine.

Instinctively, I leaned my chin against her head. I'd missed her so much over the past few days, and the relief at seeing her well was immeasurable, but I'd had this thought in the back of my mind since we'd met, and it only grew by each day. A fantastic girl like Raven was hard to keep. For some reason, it felt like she was already slipping away.

"I asked you before where I fit into your life," I breathed into her hair. "Do you still see me there?"

Her eyes lifted to mine. The blue of her threadbare scarf made the similar hue in her eyes stand out like small storms captured inside them, that settled when they found mine. "I don't often see my future clearly," she said. "But with you, I do."

Her lips touched my own, so gentle that I hardly felt it, then she leaned back. "I promised the queen that I would return to Az Elo and rule."

I flinched like she punched me. "Why?"

There was determination in her voice. "Because there is still strife between Julinbor and Az Elo, and as long as there is bad blood between our countries, the seas will never be safe. I need to do this to ensure the children's safety."

In one moment, she wanted me in her future. In the next, she said she's leaving. I struggled to adjust to the changing tides. "When do you leave?"

"Soon," she said. "A ship called the *Commander* is returning for me, and they'll take me home. But," she said, holding tightly to my hands, "I will only rule for a few years as I search for a suitable successor. Then I'll be right back."

A few years was not *right back*.

But for Raven, I'd wait more than a few years. I'd wait a hundred. "I'll be anxiously awaiting your return," I replied, but it took everything in me not to ask her to stay.

She licked her lips before speaking. "Actually, I was hoping you'd ask to come."

That sucked the air out of me. "Come? To Az Elo?"

"It's not as bad as the stories make it sound," she said quickly, with a little smile. "And you could train our soldiers or join the fishermen or do whatever you like. Anything that keeps you close by."

I was too slow to answer, and she withdrew. "Emric, you don't have to. Perhaps it is more selfishness on my part."

"No—" I collected my thoughts. Az Elo was filled with

unknowns, and a thread of fear crept along my spine at the prospect, but a wave of intrigue followed that drowned me with exhilaration. I'd been lost on the seas, searching for a ship to captain and a crew to guide while trying to prove myself worthy of the title son of Arabella. It'd been futile, an endless stream of turmoil. Then I'd met Raven, and it had all settled. She was my breath of fresh air in this world, and I knew that even a place like Az Elo wouldn't be bad if she was there.

And I could see myself training the men as she ruled.

"I want to go," I told her.

Her expression flooded into relief. "Really?"

"Definitely." I took her hand and drew her close. "I'd go anywhere with you, though I suppose this means I'll have to start calling you Calypso."

Her mouth curved into a smile. "Actually, it's Your Majesty."

41
ONTARIO

I dragged my tired body through the bleak town, feeling my way through the darkness over chipped cobblestone streets and beneath dim oil lanterns. The streets were widely spaced, yet walking was difficult since they were packed with people in fur-lined cloaks who held their bags close as they vanished through slits to smoky parlors. I tried to look like I belonged among them, but I was doing all I could just to keep moving. I hadn't stopped. Not when I rowed the small boat to the rocky shore. Not when I stowed away on a larger vessel to this shore. My stomach felt as empty as the sky, and my body as weary as a frayed rope ready to snap, but I kept on.

My hand brushed against a black, iron fence where the gratings were starting to rot. Behind it lay a twisty path, lined with bare, thorny rose bushes until giving way to a stretch of patio and double, wooden doors. The oil lamps weren't lit, inside or out. The house was still.

Even in the dark, I could make out the size of the manor, so big that I had to step back to see it all. Time had worn away at it, softening the edges and breaking down the stone, but it still held like a lighthouse beside the sea, overlooking both the water and the busy town. It was the kind of town that appeared to never sleep, the kind you could get lost in if you weren't careful, which made the silence of the house all the stranger.

I fumbled my way to the gate and let it creak open. It gave way easily, yet the house was different. It bore three locks on the door and bars over each window. Anyone could sneak into the yard, but no one got past the threshold unless the owner wanted them to.

Luckily, Jackson knew I was coming.

I lifted a hand and let the door knocker fall.

My limbs protested as I pulled myself to full height and cleared my voice, holding my meager pack close and hoping my coat hadn't gotten so tattered that they'd send me away with one glance.

The door opened, and I was looking at Zara.

"You came." Her eyes took in the dreary sight of me, but her voice was pleased.

"As quickly as I could."

She stepped aside, and I entered the home. Zara held a candle in one hand, shedding light on a grand entrance room with marble floors and stone gargoyle statues along the sides. She had on an amethysts cloak over a silver dress, both thick to protect from winter's final chill. She pulled a second cloak off a hook for me.

I draped it over my shoulders. "So this is where you operate from," I said in awe. I hadn't given them many details on how I'd left things on the seas, just that I was ready to put myself fully into the business and desired to come right away. Zara had given me the coordinates, and here I was. Being here was exactly what I needed—to see the proof of a successful business and throw myself into work to forget about those I had left. I'd make amends down the road, once I had rebuilt myself.

But I didn't want Zara to see any failures of mine, only a man whom her father had trusted enough to bring on as a partner. "It's impressive. Is the workshop out back?"

"It's everywhere," she replied, then turned to cast the candle's glow across the hall. It danced into the furthest corners. "Every room is dedicated to the business in one way or another, though you'll have to get the full tour in the morning. Tonight, let me show you to my father's office. He'll be home soon."

I tried to wonder what business Jackson could have in a city such as this at this hour, but Zara let her cloak slip off her shoulders as she held a hand out for me, and I could think of nothing else other than the warmth of her hand over mine. My exhaustion slid away bit by bit until by the time we reached the tall door to an office, I was feeling like myself again.

"Which one is your office?" I asked. "For surely you deserve the biggest one."

She laughed. "Tell that to my father."

The lock unclicked as she opened the door, and the scent of sandalwood seeped out. Everything was constructed from birchwood, some left pale and others lacquered blue until the entire room was shades of either the land or the sea. A symbol of the world in its entirety, how it lay for us to claim. We crossed through a sitting area with sumptuous sofas until it gave way to an arched desk and highbacked leather chair, stubs of candles spread throughout. Zara moved through the room to ignite them, and I watched her.

"Is Arabella handled?" Zara asked when the last candle was lit. She perched herself by her father's chair, which I now saw looked more like a throne than anything.

"I personally captured her and handed her over to Queen Isla," I said proudly.

Her eyes lit. "Impressive."

"Not as impressive as designing these." I went to the table to tap my finger against Jackson's communication pod. "Though I fear I ruined mine with water."

"We have more." Zara glanced to the door, then back

at me. Her tone lowered. "Tell me, what was it like to hand Arabella the Ruthless over to Queen Isla?"

My mouth dried with the lie, but it wasn't fully dishonest. It was me who'd locked Arabella away. It was me who had summoned Queen Isla there. Without me, the crew wouldn't have been able to do anything. I focused on that as I ran a hand along Jackson's chair, thinking of what it would be like to sit in it someday, when he passed the company over to me.

"Thrilling," I responded. "Arabella did everything she could to escape, but we held her fast. Then Queen Isla thanked me and let me know she'd be open to further dealings down the road, so I have her trust. And soon the whole seas will know I was the captain who took down Arabella, and they'll want to be on my side."

Zara absorbed every word like a sponge. "So powerful," she mused. "I knew I'd chosen the right man for Father to join." She had a way of looking at me when I spoke like she would be satisfied if she never heard another sound. It was an intoxicating feeling.

But her words settled uneasily. "You were the one to tell your father about me?"

"I was."

"But how did you know who I was?"

"I worked with your father." She said it so causally, but it was a sharp strike to my gut. I stepped back, but she wove around the desk to me. I could feel her breath on my cheek as she spoke. "Jackson never wanted to deal with him, but I thought he might work with you. I was right." She hooked a finger on my jacket to keep me close. "And I got more than I bargained for. You've impressed me, and that's not easy to do."

I was still reeling from the knowledge that she'd worked with my father, but her nearness made it hard to think. I closed my eyes briefly. Before I could speak, the door at the end of the room swung open.

Jackson stood in the opening, and Zara was brash enough not to move an inch.

I wasn't.

I cleared my throat as I took a step away from his daughter. "Sire. It's a pleasure to meet you in person."

He was taller than the communication-pod image, but the blues of his eyes was just as piercing. There was a stillness in how he stood, with an air that proclaimed he was the one in charge. "How did things go with Arabella?"

"Fine," I answered steadily. "She's taken care of."

He nodded a few times. "And where is your ship?"

My insides twisted. "Still at sea, sir."

"I see. And do all your merchants have their permits?"

I was happy to give a good report there. "They will arrive by the end of the month."

He had moved opposite the desk as though this were my office and he was visiting. Someday, if he passed the company over like he said he intended to, that would be the case. It was impossible not to envision that all now. "And tell me, why am I getting reports that Queen Isla is creating an exact replica of these communication pods, with intent to distribute them in two weeks?"

My exaltation withered. I looked at Zara to see if she knew. From her shocked expression, she didn't. "I have no idea," I managed.

"You didn't tell her then?"

"Of course not," I said. Jackson had been working at this for a long time, but Queen Isla had resources he couldn't, allies already forged, merchant paths already established, and loyal followers. If she beat us to distribution, our product would never go anywhere. "I would never do anything like that."

But Jackson was looking at me as if I'd done this to him, and that I'd done so maliciously. "Where is yours, then?"

I dug it out of my pack. "It's taken a fair share of water, but

I never showed it to the queen." It made a hollow sound as I set it on the desk. He eyed it.

"I gave you two. Where is the other?"

I flinched. *Emme.* I treaded carefully. "Aboard the *Royal Rose*."

"Then call it. You can use mine."

I didn't move. I didn't care for Jackson to see how I'd left things there. If he knew I didn't have command of my ship, then he would question my authority over any of the seas, and I would lose my value to him.

Plus, there was the slight chance that Emme had been the one to share the information with the queen, and if I connected to that device and the queen's face showed up . . . it didn't bear thinking.

Jackson watched me like he could read all my thoughts. "You won't connect with it, because you don't have relations with the *Royal Rose* anymore, right?"

He knew.

But Zara didn't. "What do you mean? He's the captain."

Jackson's smile was twisted. "Do you wish to tell her? Or were you planning to woo my daughter in an effort to gain prestige in my company?"

I chose my words carefully. "My relations with the *Royal Rose* are strained, but they can be fixed."

"Most crews wouldn't want their captain back after he tried to burn down their ship," Jackson countered. I only did that to get away unscathed, but the defense sounded weak. And Jackson wasn't done. "I knew Arabella never went to Kwoli, but you were so determined to launch our company now, despite all the risks involved, that you refused to consider that we needed to bide our time."

My jaw clenched. He'd sent me on a fool's errand.

"This partnership cannot work unless we trust each other," I said.

Jackson's chuckle was dry. "I agree. And you are a wild card. You are erratic and impulsive, and you've burned down relationships that this company needed—effectively burning down your usefulness to me."

My ears were ringing as he spoke.

"I have the connections," I insisted. "You still need me to spread your designs across the seas."

"My design is worthless!" he snapped. Zara and I both flinched. "You made sure of that! My communication pod cannot become anything now that the queen has a hand on it, and my patrons are already leaving to align themselves with her." He thrust his finger at me. "You have destroyed me."

Zara went still as stone. That was her design, her masterpiece, and it was worthless now. When I met her eye, it was cold.

"I'm sorry," I whispered.

"Don't." Her word clipped short.

"We are going to be fine," Jackson said, softer now. "We have other technology. But you," his eyes bore through me, "will have no part in the future of this company."

"I didn't share that information with the queen." I scrambled. I'd done them no harm. "It wasn't me."

"But it was through you, through your inability to keep loyal relationships, your inability to see past your desire for power, and to be aware of what is going on around you." Jackson took my communication pod, so reclaiming the connection I had to them. It didn't matter, I had broken that too. "When I look at you, I see someone who will ruin my company, not someone worthy of inheriting it. I want you out of my house."

I turned to see if Zara would intervene on my behalf, but she was already walking out of the room. I hurried to follow her. "I didn't mean for this to happen," I protested. "I never wanted to hurt you."

"Lying to someone is always intending to hurt them." She

stopped at the front door to open it before looking at me. Her eyes were red.

"I didn't mean to," I repeated, pleading. "And I'm sorry. I can still help this company."

Her voice was detached. "It's too late. Get out."

Jackson was behind me now, making sure the only direction I went was away. As they pushed me out the door, I cried out, "Where will I go?"

"Return to your father's company," Jackson replied. "For you are no different than him."

That hurt worst of all, and he shut the door in my face to let me sit in that bitter pain.

I'd ruined it. I'd lost it all.

I was nothing.

I had been so close to having everything, and it all got ripped away from me in an instant, leaving me feeling empty inside. With what little energy remained, I tipped my head back and took in the sight of the night sky.

The emerald stars glowed, but now I knew the truth. It wasn't for me.

42
ARABELLA

The chains were buckled tight enough around my wrist that any movement was met with excruciating pain. It meant I slept in a sitting position, every single night. Soon the pain in my wrists didn't bother me as much as the hunger in my belly. I was given a glass of water and slab of dry meat each morning, and that was it.

The pain. The hunger. The loneliness. It was, as if instead of killing me, the queen hoped I'd curl up and die on my own.

I wasn't as easy to break as that. And the quiet allowed me time to think. To *plan*.

My scheming was interrupted by a grating sound down the hall. I was the only prisoner in these cells, yet they brought six guards each morning to feed me, and by the grind of keys, there were four locked doors between me and freedom. My best chance for escape was that window of time in the morning where they came with food.

But it wasn't morning now. The slit of a window showed a brilliant orange sky as night was seeping over the land.

Why were they here now?

The obvious answer was that they were here to kill me. The queen had been silent about my judgment so far, with no word as to when she would release me. Now the verdict would come.

The thought of death terrified me. It unraveled the darkest parts of me and threatened to crumble them apart. But I would never fold into the despair of looming death. I'd expected it time and time again.

I needed a plan.

It was only a single pair of footsteps this time as the fourth lock was undone. If I was ever going to escape, this was my best chance.

Then the figure appeared, right at the edge of the bars.

Queen Isla, dressed down today in riding pants and a collared vest with her hair in a simple twist. The only jewelry she wore was the faded wedding band as if she needed to prove to her country that she had the late king's approval. If he could come back from the grave, I was certain he would not give it.

"I wouldn't expect a queen to come to the prisons," I said coldly.

"I wouldn't expect to find Arabella the Ruthless inside one, yet you seem to frequent them these days." There was a coolness to her tone, though, that said she didn't come here to fight.

She wants something then. Good.

I eyed her, waiting to see what it was. She noted this and gave a tiny smile. "You were a hired hand for my husband. Now you will be mine."

I threw one foot over the other where I sat, pretending to mull it over. "What good does that do for me?"

She arched a brow. "It keeps you alive."

"It makes me a slave," I corrected. "You're not offering me my life back; you're offering servitude."

"I'm offering glory. And that's all you want. You will be feared again. You will be revered. You'll be the shadow in the night that people tell stories to their children about, telling them to be careful so Arabella the Terror doesn't get to them."

I could get used to that nickname.

"I am new to the throne," Isla went on, "and there are those who seek to undermine me. You will be my hand throughout Julinbor to keep such people in check."

It wasn't the sea. I wasn't getting my home back. But perhaps it was a life after all.

"Can I move about as I wish?"

"To an extent. You'll need to be fully available whenever I call upon you."

"Is there pay?"

"A modest one."

"Living quarters?"

"Near the castle." She put up a hand before I could ask another question. "You were feared on the seas. Take my offer, and you'll be feared on the land. Do you want it, or not? Because I have other pirates I can ask."

I snorted. "None would do the job half as well as me."

Because of Emme's oathbinding, I could never return to sea without her knowing. But I could make myself quite comfortable on land if I had to.

I'd escaped death again. "I accept," I told her. "I am at your bidding."

"Oathbind yourself," she ordered.

I hesitated, before grinding my teeth together. She'd never trust me any other way, and I'd never get out of here on my own. So be it. "I, Arabella Katrina Salinda, oathbind myself as your hired hand."

"And that you'll never bring harm to me," the queen added.

I might not have agreed to it before, if I'd known that, but it was too late now. I'd find another way to undo this. "And that I won't harm you."

The burn on my skin was immediate, but it didn't hurt. It felt more like freedom.

"Good." The relief was clear in Isla's voice. She pulled out a key from her pocket. "Then you are released from here—to me. And I've got jobs planned already."

The cell opened, and she freed my wrists. I stood and rubbed them. I could run or strangle her and free myself from the oathbinding. But the binding stung like it knew my thoughts, and Isla's eyes were sharp, and her hand was on the dagger at her waist. So I didn't do any of those things. Arabella the Terror. That was who I was now. I bowed my head. "As you wish, Your Majesty."

43

EMME

The bristly halyards were rough in my hands as I checked for fraying while Arn penned a letter at my side. Then another letter. Then another. The floor was scattered with crumpled letters, some of them bearing a single sentence that Arn had decided wasn't good enough, and others an entire page that he'd signed before throwing away, running his hand through his hair and starting again.

Soon the floor of the cabin was coated thick enough that I could hardly see the floorboards, and Arn was no closer to finishing this letter than when he'd started two hours ago.

When he groaned, I stood to rub his shoulders. "How about: hello, I'm alive, and I'd love to meet with you?"

I thought that sounded fine, but Arn shook his head. "It's not good enough."

I pulled a chair to sit at his side. "Your dad is about to find out his son is alive. That's more than good enough—it'll be the happiest day in his life."

Arn tapped the quill against the paper. "I wouldn't count on that," he said sourly. He dropped the quill to crumple the paper.

"You hadn't written anything on that yet," I said with a laugh.

"Whatever I would have written, it would have been rubbish."

His exhaustion was clear from every syllable and from the weary draw of his shoulders—and reasonably so. We'd said our goodbyes to Emric and Raven a few weeks ago and had spent sunup to sundown fixing the ship by building a new mast from scratch. We were almost done, but still stranded until we got our sails up. If it wasn't for Raven's crew of children, making runs to land for supplies, our ship wouldn't have made it.

"Take care of my crew. They are yours now."

"I'm honored to watch over them," I told her. "They will be safe with the Royal Rose."

She and Emric had crossed to the Commander, *but not before I thought of one last thing. "The emerald stars."*

She stopped. "What of them?"

"You thought they were for me," I reminded her. "I think they are for you. A daughter returning home to rule her kingdom and to forge a new peace over the lands. The prodigal child? It was never talking about me. It was always you."

Her gaze was thoughtful, then she smiled. "Maybe so. But the children that I'm leaving behind? You're getting the real treasure there." She moved away from them like every step hurt, until she was on deck beside Jakob and Emric. She raised a hand. "Until we meet again."

It took some adjustment for everyone to acclimate to the young one's needs, but we were making it work. Arn was setting up lessons for the children and conjoining our two crews, which involved a series of tests to determine their current knowledge level. Until lessons started, everyone's focus was on fixing the ship.

And if that wasn't enough, we were planning a wedding.

Then, to top it off, Arn wanted to make amends with his father. Last his father heard, Arn had drowned with the king's navy. Now he would find out that his son was alive and had become a pirate and had purposefully let him believe he had been lost. It was a delicate letter, but likely Arn could send any of the notes scattered on the floor and make his father happy.

Still, I wanted to be compassionate, so I resolved to sit there and support him until he found the right words. And besides, I'd been restlessly waiting for news of my own parent and had none, so I'd gladly take the distraction of his.

Another letter had arrived this week—one bearing a shell as a seal. Coral had been true to her request and written a letter asking for the support of our captain in her claim as ruler under the seas. The letter was tucked away in the wood-paneled cupboards as it awaited the captain's approval—a position that remained unfilled. I could only imagine how often Arn thought of that, even now as he wrote this letter to his father.

I placed a hand over his arm. "Would tea help?"

"I'll reward myself with it later, once I finish the letter." He had shucked off his jacket and was in a midnight black shirt with rolled sleeves. I didn't see Arn in dark colors often, but it made the pale color of his hair stand out and brought attention to his bright eyes.

He saw the way I was looking and grinned. "What?"

"Just excited to be your wife."

The door to the cabin opened, and Clarice entered. The shaved side of her head had grown long enough that she now kept it in twisted little knots while the other side was still as untamed as my own. She'd taken to teaching the children how to wield a sword, and despite her rough exterior, she was a favorite of theirs. It was obvious from how she interacted with them that she had a soft spot for the little ones too.

The young ones were behind her, as was the rest of our crew, as Clarice spoke. "We are holding a meeting."

"For what?" I asked.

Her gaze darted to Arn. "Did you not tell her?"

He stood. "I suggested last night that we vote on a new captain today," he explained.

Frankly, I was surprised reclaiming the *Royal Rose* wasn't his first task aboard, but I'd taken it as a sign of growth that he was more concerned with fixing things with the ship and crew than taking it over. But the crew couldn't go without a captain forever.

"As first mate, you're in line for it," I told Clarice, testing out what competition Arn would have for the role.

She scrunched her nose. "Too much politics with that. You'd have to make sure people like you, agree with you, do your bidding, and don't revolt. I wasn't made to keep people happy. Besides, I thought—"

"Let's go out and see what everyone else thinks," Arn interrupted as he ushered me out of the cabin and into the misty evening.

The clouds hung low, dampening the air with a warm heat that brought promises of spring. Before long we'd be seeing longer days and brighter colors, perfectly symbolizing the new life ahead of us.

Arn wound up to the helm. Even though we'd been anchored down the past few weeks, it was still a familiar sight to see him behind the wheel. "Crew," he announced, "it's about time the *Royal Rose* had a captain again. Tonight, we will vote for one, then celebrate."

The children were gathered together at the prow, with their ship roped to ours. Tess was near them, fluttering between joining their fold and keeping back as one of us. As the children became more integrated in our crew, I suspected she'd be less reluctant to form friendships among them. Those hardened edges would come undone with time.

She caught me looking and gave me a small smile. That was progress.

"To be a captain is no small thing." Arn's voice rang out.

"You must be brave enough to put yourself first in line if we ever come to battle, yet selfless enough to put yourself last among the crew. You must be wise, caring, and strong."

The crew was quiet, waiting for Arn to nominate himself as an option and to start the vote. None of the others stepped forward, even though Arn gave pause for it.

When no one spoke, Arn did. "I nominate Emme as captain."

All heads swung to look at me, and I wasn't sure I was hearing right.

Arn held a hand for me to join him at the helm. "Over the past few months, Emme has been fighting for this crew with selfless abandon, giving everything she has—including oathbinding herself, meeting before the queen, and sailing with Az Eloians—to guarantee your safety. She has always put others first and would serve you well as a leader."

Tears came to my eyes. "But it's your ship," I whispered.

"She's as much yours as mine," he replied softly. "And I'll happily spend the rest of my life caring for you both."

He faced the crew. By Clarice's smile, she'd known this was coming.

Arn raised a hand. "What will it be, then? Who do you name as captain?"

Clarice's strong voice of the First cheered. "Emme!"

Others followed. First the four from our original crew, then the new recruits, then the children. I even heard Tess's voice in there. "Emme. We vote for Emme."

When the last voice had died down, they waited for me to speak. I feared no words would come, but thankfully, I managed to say something. "I love this ship, and I love this crew." I looked over them all through glassy tears. "It would be an honor to serve as captain."

I cut my gaze to Arn. "If you hadn't dragged me out from the confinements of the Banished Gentlemen tavern half a year ago, I would have missed out on so much."

"Aren't you glad that after asking so many times, I finally let you come along?" His grin was lopsided.

I laughed. I should have said yes to the first time he asked. Everything I was now, it was because of him. And that's how I knew I couldn't do this without him. "I hope to be a good captain," I told the crew. "But I can only do that job with this man at my side. For the first time, I suggest the *Royal Rose* is captained by two, by Arn and me, so we can share the weight of the job equally."

Now it was my turn to surprise him. He looked at me, stunned, as I grinned. This was always his dream. He loved the ship more than I could, and he loved being her captain. Together, we could do great things here, and I wouldn't want it without him. To be the one to finally hand him the helm back—it was an honor. And it was something he deserved.

I faced the crew. "I know many of you have never seen Arn as captain." Only four remaining members knew him by that title, and many here had only known him a few days. "But you can take my word for his character. Arn Mangelo is every bit a captain, someone who fights hard for his crew, learns from his mistakes, and gives his life—and his hand—to protecting us. If you'll have him, I vote we captain together."

The reply was quick to come from the four who had sailed with us from the beginning, and I knew how much their approval meant to Arn. At their cheer, he brightened. His eyes were glossy by the time the rest of the crew had joined. "Yes," they said one after another. "We will have him."

Arn came to my side. "It would be the finest honor to captain alongside Emme. Thank you for the second chance."

They finished their cheers, then Bo was pouring the ale, and the celebration was starting. Someone started playing a flute, dancing began, and dinner was served. I waited to join them, first running a hand over the wheel—my wheel—and marveling at the beauty of it all. Arn stood silently at my side, letting me take it all in.

The evening reminded me of that night so long ago, when we sat around telling ghost stories, watching the stars fall, and listening to the mermaids sing. It'd been the first time I'd had a taste of what a family on deck could be like, and now I saw it even clearer. Now it was my life. My family.

A sea captain. I was captain of the *Royal Rose*.

The name felt odd in my head, as if I were trying to take someone else's place, but it had a pleasant ring to it. For so long I'd searched for my place, and now I'd found it. I didn't have Ontario's deep pockets. I didn't have Arn's confidence. But I would fight with everything in me for this ship.

I took a firm hold of the wheel, felt the wind against my face, and closed my eyes. I breathed it all in. "This is perfect."

"Almost," Arn said. He'd snuck a hat behind his back and placed it on my head. "Now it's perfect."

I peered up at the edges of the hat. It fit right, as if it belonged there all along. "How do I look?"

Arn's gaze held more than a simple look ought to, and it captivated me. "Like a captain." His breath was warm in the moment before he kissed my lips. "My captain."

ACKNOWLEDGMENTS

It's hard to believe the idea that once began as desperate pirates, organized in sticky notes across the dining room wall, with poorly made maps and only a sliver of plot, is now a whole trilogy and that it's done. I'm not certain I'm ready to leave the high seas behind, but it'll be a delight to share this with readers and see it live on through them.

There were so many people who helped make this possible, but I first want to thank the team at Enclave Publishing and Oasis Family Media. You took a chance on an author no one knew and patiently helped mold the series into something better than I could have done alone. It would only be half of the tale it is without you, and I am forever grateful you welcomed me into the fold. From Christmas cards to phone calls to constant encouragement, you've created a publishing house that I'm proud to be a part of.

A huge thanks to all of my editors, who took a chaotic manuscript and molded it into something coherent. I'm always blown away by your knowledge and am blessed to have someone help me through writing these books! Steve and Lisa Laube, Sarah Grimm, and Megan Gerig, you are all wonderful. Thank you so much. Cover design blew me away, and that's all thanks to Emilie Haney!

To my incredible social media guru, Trissina, I have leaned on your wisdom time and time again as you help me navigate not only promoting my book, but also standing as a Christian in a world where it isn't always easy to do so. Thank you for all that you do for us authors!

Jonathan, you supported me when I reignited my love for writing books years ago and dove all in headfirst. From the late writing sessions to the hours of research, this went from a hobby I did in the corner of our living room to a career that has reached many lives, and you stood by my side through it all. I'm lucky to have someone like you. I couldn't do it alone.

Thank you to all of my friends on social media who turned writing from something I did alone into something I can share with others all across the world! Your undying love for stories fuels my passion, and none of this would be possible without you.

Biggest thank you to God, who has given me the ability to write and the means to do so. May the stories I tell bring you glory.

ABOUT THE AUTHOR

Victoria McCombs is the author of The Storyteller's Series and The Royal Rose Chronicles, with hopefully many more to come. She survives on hazelnut coffee, 20-minute naps, and a healthy fear of her deadlines, all while raising three wildlings with her husband in Omaha, Nebraska.

BEWARE THE WATERS.

THE DANGEROUS DEEP BRINGS RUIN TO ALL.

 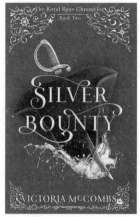 

THE ROYAL ROSE CHRONICLES

Oathbound

Silver Bounty

Savage Bred

Available Now!

www.enclavepublishing.com